UNTIL TOMORROW COMES

BEAUTY IN LIES BOOK ONE

ADELAIDE FORREST

Copyright © 2021 by Adelaide Forrest

All rights reserved.

No part of this book may be reproduced in any form or by any electronic or mechanical means, including information storage and retrieval systems, without written permission from the author, except for the use of brief quotations in a book review.

Cover Design by Adelaide Forrest

Proofreading by Light Hand Proofreading

❊ Created with Vellum

ABOUT THE AUTHOR

Adelaide lives in her tiny house with her husband and two rambunctious kids. When she's not chasing all three of them and her dog around the house, she spends all her free time writing and adding to the hoard of plots stored on her bookshelf and hard-drive.

She always wanted to write, and did from the time she was ten and wrote her first full-length fantasy novel. The subject matter has changed over the years, but that passion for writing never went away.

She has a background in Psychology and working with horses, but Adelaide began her publishing journey in February 2020 and never looked back.

For more information, please visit Adelaide's website or subscribe to her newsletter.

CONTENT & TRIGGER WARNINGS

Beauty in Lies is a DARK mafia romance series dealing with topics that some readers may find offensive or triggering. Readers of Adelaide Forrest's Bellandi Crime Syndicate series should note that this series is much darker.

Please keep in mind the following list WILL contain specifics about the ENTIRE series and may spoil certain plot elements. Please avoid the next page if you don't wish to know specifics.

The following scenarios are all present in the Beauty in Lies series. This list may be added to over time.

- Situations involving dubious, questionable, or nonconsent
- 13 Year Age gap, with both characters being of legal age at the time a physical relationship forms.
- Forced Pregnancy
- Branding
- Forced Marriage under threat of death & violence
- VERY graphic violence, torture, and murder
- Drug use, attempted date rape, and dubious situations while under the influence
- Kidnapping/Captive Scenarios

SOUNDTRACK

Until Tomorrow Comes Playlist
https://open.spotify.com/playlist/
3tszVNZDP4oH9Z6JpcWsoV?si=VwqyL-
7dQTynZo9_OJV0DQ

"Snake Charmer" – Jiovanni Daniel
"Jekyll & Hide" – Bishop Briggs
"Run Baby Run" – 2WEI
"Devil's Gonna Come" – Raphael Lake
"Cold Blooded" – UNSECRET
"Hunt You Down" – The Hit House
"The Time of Our Lives" – The Venice Connection
"Love It" – UNSECRET
"Can't Help Falling In Love with You" – Tommee Profitt
"Sentenced to Death" – Colossal Trailer Music
"Paint It, Black" – Ciara
"Wicked Game" Ursine Vulpine
"Stimulated" – UNSECRET
"Walk" – Saint Chaos
"Causing Love" – RAIGN

"Born for This" – Manafest
"Talk To Me" – Apocalyptica, Lzzy Hale
"Die Trying" – New Medicine
"I'm So Close I can Taste It" – Graffiti Ghosts
"Champions" – Kurt Hugo Schneider
"Hate You" – Jim Yosef
"Pray" – Egzod
"Nightmare" – Besomorph
"Tonight is the Night I Die" – Palaye Royale
"Feeling Great" – Sdms
"Silence" – Cemre Emin
"The Heresy" – Mushroomhead
"Chemicals" – The Glitch Mob
"Appetite" – Casey Edwards
"Dancing with the Devil" – Kitty Antix
"Prisoner" – Raphael Lake
"Omens" – UNSECRET
"Wolf Totem" – The HU
"The Devil You Know" – Blues Saraceno
"Darkness Below" – Red Moth
"Shine" – Matt Beilis
"Kiss the Devil" – Bel Heir
"Make Me Believe" – The EverLove
"LOVELOST" – Margo
"Blinding Lights" – The Weeknd
"Losing You" – UNSECRET
"The rainy road" – Rahul
"Baby, I'm jealous" – Bebe Rexha
"Man's World" – MARINA
"Revolution Bones" – Paolo Buonvino
"Riverbound" – Comaduster
"The Devil is a Gentleman" – Merci Raines
"Devil's At Your Door" – SWARM

"Odds Are" – The FifthGuys
"Origin" – Besomorph
"Dark in my Imagination" – Of Verona
"Vanguard" – Jo Blakenburg
"We Are the Darkness" – Rok Nardin
"Alpha" – Little Destroyer
"Devil in Disguise" – EMM
"Get My Way" – Vosai
"Killer" – Valerie Broussard
"Murky" – Saint Mesa
"Sweet Dreams" – Dexter
"Every Breath You Take" – Chase Holfelder
"Coma" – Ash Graves

PART I

UNTIL MEMORY FADES

If you've already read the prologue novella, Until Memory Fades, then you can skip directly to Until Tomorrow Comes. If not, the prologue is included for your convenience and is necessary to understand the relationship between Rafael and Isa.

1

RAFAEL

Sixteen months ago.

The greatest shock didn't come from walking up to a building stained with blood and tears, but from the cold and stark weather as snow drifted over the frozen ground.

Why did anyone insist on living in a place where the air hurt their face? And where the fuck was the sun?

The warehouse loomed in front of us as we left the rich, comforting warmth of the Ferrari. The massive structure might have blended in with the other abandoned commercial properties in the area, had it not been surrounded by an eerie feeling of death. Even in a graveyard for buildings, nothing could disguise the ghosts that lurked around Bellandi's famed warehouse. I didn't know that I believed in spirits, despite my mother's belief in the afterlife, but even I felt all the tortured souls who clung to this place where they had drawn their final breaths.

It certainly didn't help that they'd probably choked on their own blood as they fought for air.

An ordinary person might have wondered how Matteo

conducted his wet work in such an obvious location without fear of repercussions, too lost in their grand illusions of being safe in their first world country, where crime couldn't happen to them and bad things only happened to strangers in the night.

Most people were naïve enough to believe the police could ever truly be a threat to men like us.

Then again, most people were fucking idiots.

At my side, Calix ran a hand through his hair, looking just as aggravated as I imagined he had to feel. While fighting in Matteo Bellandi's war was a necessary duty born out of allegiance, nothing could stop the impatience that came with knowing only a ticking clock stood between him and the girl he'd pledged to marry walking down the aisle to another man.

His rumpled suit was a stark contrast to the smooth lines of mine. In other circumstances, I might have reprimanded him to remember that people were always watching us and judging any imperfections they found. It was unnecessary to give them any more ammunition to work with.

After a long flight—even in the comfort of my jet—and knowing that he was mere hours away from his Thalia? I mostly couldn't fault him for it.

"You could have at least changed before we got off the plane," I argued, quirking a brow up when he groaned at me in response. "Need I remind you, Matteo Bellandi is my ally. He needs to be *yours*. You will be far more directly affected by his friendship than I will, given the proximity of Philadelphia to Chicago. Ibiza is an entire world away."

He scoffed in response. One of the few men who dared to show such impudence in my presence. But Calix had come to Ibiza when he wasn't yet a man, his family banished from the city they called home in a violent uprising by the other families that had once been friends. He quickly became the closest thing I had to a brother.

"Right, because you don't have world domination on the brain," he said, falling into place behind me. I touched my hands to the front doors of the warehouse, probably taking my life in my hand as I grasped the knob and turned it. The heavy steel door heaved open with a groan, and I stepped into the vast, open space of the main warehouse.

"Doesn't look like they're here, after all," Calix grunted, glancing around the room. I pressed a finger to my lips before pointing down to the trail of blood splatter that led to the back hallway. Pulling my cell phone from my back pocket, I dialed Matteo's number one more time, hoping to alert him to our presence before it led to a bloody standoff.

The line connected as he finally answered my calls. "You're as bad as one of Simon's one-night stands today. Won't take a fucking hint. What do you want?" Matteo grumbled into the phone. The sound of a man's pained whimpers filled the background noise.

It seemed we hadn't arrived too late to enjoy the fun.

"Well, I suppose if I'm not wanted, I can take my men back to Ibiza," I drawled.

"You're early," Matteo returned. As if I didn't know that.

"Lorenzo indicated things were progressing faster than expected, and you might need assistance sooner. I live to please. Now, where are you hiding in your blood-soaked warehouse? I suppose we could play a game of hide and seek, so long as Ryker promises not to throw a hatchet at me when I win."

"Freezer at the back," Matteo grunted, disconnecting the call.

"You're no fun," I chuckled, glancing to Calix, who studied me with a demented smile.

"Wonderful. Like Chicago in February isn't cold enough, now we have to go inside a fucking freezer," Calix grumbled as I made my way for the hall at the back. With the worn edges covered in rust, the freezer door didn't look capable of functioning. But sure enough, Matteo stood outside the door with one of his men, waiting.

My eyes met Matteo's first, his gaze as hardened as mine. "It's good to see you, Rafael," he said. The man at his side widened his eyes, staring at me in shock for a moment before he snapped his face back into an expressionless mask. Not yet broken. If the mask needed practice, then his training hadn't been as thorough as what Matteo and I had lived.

"You mean it's good to know you have reinforcements," I said, my voice lacking all inflection. Matteo was perhaps one of the closest things I had to a friend, but that didn't mean we were warm and fuzzy. We had a mutual understanding. We stayed out of one another's way and only offered support or opinions when necessary.

He hadn't called and invited me to his wedding by any means. Though I had heard about it through the grapevine and been shocked. In our lives, women were a weakness.

I couldn't imagine any single woman ever being worth risking my life for.

"Mostly that. Just make sure your men behave while they're in my city," Matteo ordered, but there was no animosity to his tone. Our rules were fairly similar, though he was slightly more strict on protecting women. I didn't allow human trafficking in my organization, but I didn't protect people who weren't my concern either.

"They know the drill," I returned, making my way to the freezer door.

"Ryker's inside with his latest toy. You know how he feels about being interrupted." Matteo laughed. Calix took a step back, avoiding the doorway as I wrenched the door open and stepped into the freezer. The sound of something cutting through the air filled the space, the slight and nearly imperceptible whisper of Ryker's hatchet as it traveled through the space between us. I lifted my hand, catching it by the handle before it could sink into my shoulder. The wooden handle I held in my palm was stained with blood that had soaked into the porous surface over years of use, but fresh blood coated it where Ryker had gripped it to throw it at me.

Ryker grinned at me, his face twisting maniacally as my face split into a matching smile. "You missed," I said.

"One of these days," he said, wiping his hands on a rag and glaring at the blood caked beneath his fingernails. Calix and Matteo strolled into the room, sensing the foolish game, that would only stop when one of us was dead, had ended. Men like Ryker and I needed a bit of senseless violence in our lives.

It had been nearly a week since I'd watched the life bleed from someone's eyes. Considering there were only two ways to make a man like me feel alive, fucking and killing, I desperately needed a fix.

How fortuitous for me that a lovely bloodied meatsack sat in a chair, waiting for Ryker to go back to his torture session. "Who is he?" I asked, stripping off my suit jacket. Folding it neatly, I handed it to Matteo's man lurking in the doorway. "If it crumples, so will you," I warned him. He swallowed, nodding and pushing the freezer door closed to lock the other five of us within it.

"Perhaps you would be liked more here if you didn't threaten the men," Simon barked from the corner. He always kept his distance from me. There again, he'd never been a fan of mine.

"I'm uncertain what gave you the impression I want people to like me," I said back, stretching my lips over my teeth in the bastardization of a smile. He scowled at me, rolling his eyes to the ceiling in a move I'd killed men for in the past. Matteo glared at his bodyguard, one harsh look making the other man straighten his posture and disguise his hatred.

Men took it so personally when you fucked their sister.

"He was one of our dealers until about a month ago. Then he just up and disappeared for a few days," Matteo answered. "Didn't hear a word from him, and we figured he was dead. He said he was visiting his sister, but we've had eyes on her. He was never there, so I'd like to know where he's really been."

"I bet he wishes he was with her now," I chuckled, trailing my eyes over Ryker's handiwork. Missing fingernails, entire sections of skin missing from his chest and stomach. "Are you close with your sister?" I asked him, grabbing his forehead and shoving his face until he stared up into my eyes. Touching Ryker's hatchet to his cheek, I let the sharp blade pierce the skin ever so slightly to punctuate my words.

"No," he wheezed, the tiny glance to his left the only sign that the words were a lie.

"Hmm," I said, playing along for the moment. "What about your wife?" I asked, grabbing his left hand and snapping the ring finger back until it cracked and he yelled out in pain.

"She has nothing to do with this," he rasped.

"I'm not a Bellandi, boy. She's about to have everything to do with this if you don't start singing," I said, smiling at him as I slid the wedding band off his finger and tossed it into the air. "Maybe I'll even wear your wedding ring while I fuck her. I always wondered what it was like to be married," I teased. I was many things—a criminal and a murderer among them—but a rapist I was not. He didn't need to know his wife would beg for more if I paid her a visit.

They always did.

He swallowed, glancing to Matteo to see if the other man would interfere with my threat. He wouldn't, because Matteo knew that there were certain lines I wouldn't cross. I clung to my humanity by a shred, and I wouldn't sacrifice the rest of my soul to the devil by forcing myself on a woman who didn't want me. Not when I never lacked for a willing bed companion. No woman was worth that.

"He said he'd rape her and kill her if I didn't do it," he whispered, glancing to Matteo. "I'm sorry, Boss. I didn't—"

"Do what, Jake?"

"There's a bomb in the cash bag. He has the detonator. He's supposed to monitor Sandro after he picks it up and detonate it when he goes to collect from *Indulgence*. Sandro parks the car close enough to do decent damage to the back, and the hope is he'll take out Lino and Enzo in the process," Jake admitted, hanging his head. "That's all I know. Just, please, get my wife out of town before Murphy comes for her." The name Murphy made anger flood my veins. He was a man who wanted nothing more than to take Matteo's city from him and turn it into a trafficking hub.

"He should leave her to die for your betrayal. If you had come to him in the first place, that's when he could have offered to protect her," I snapped, stepping out of the man's space. There was nothing I detested more than a traitor who turned his back on the organization that gave him a home and put food on his table, when others might have condemned him.

"I'll see that she and your sister get a ticket out of Chicago. That's the best I can do, given the circumstances," Matteo said. He nodded to Ryker, who held out his hand for his hatchet, waiting for me to hand it over so he could deal the killing blow.

I smiled at him instead, swinging the hatchet into Jake's forehead so it lodged directly between his eyes. Blood trickled down the sides of the blade, running over his lips until his head slumped forward and the handle propped him up slightly when it hit his chest. Ryker pouted as Calix chuckled, shaking his head as if it was childish that Ryker and I fought for the right to kill people.

Turning for the door, I tugged it open and accepted my jacket from the man who foisted it on me anxiously. Patting his cheek briefly to thank him for keeping it pristine, I shrugged it on and made my way for the front of the warehouse. "Where are you going?" Matteo asked.

"I think I'll pay my friend Enzo a visit!" I called back as Calix hurried to keep up with me.

The fucking icy wind of winter greeted me the moment we stepped outside.

Why couldn't war come in July?

2

RAFAEL

It wasn't the first time I'd been to *Indulgence,* though it had still been under Matteo's father's management then. After his father's untimely demise, Matteo renovated and brought the club into the modern era with clean and modern lines that reminded me of my own clubs in Ibiza.

Only the best of timeless elegance for our houses of endless sin.

A man I'd never met before headed us off before we could make our way up the winding steps to the offices, stepping into our path with his arms crossed over his chest. "We're here to see Lorenzo Vescovi," I said, knowing from our conversations that the name would aggravate Enzo to no end.

"He's busy," the man said shortly. "What can I do for you gentlemen?" He glanced toward Calix and the two silent bodyguards at our backs, and I smirked at the reinforcement of my earlier statement. In our business, appearances mattered. One either needed to be a stone-cold man in a suit who tolerated no shit, or a meathead with tattoos covering all visible skin, if he wanted to intimidate the locals.

Sometimes both.

"Enzo will want to see us. This is Calix Regas, and I am Rafael Ibarra," I said, watching as recognition settled over the man's features. He nodded dutifully, turning on his heel and guiding us up the steps and past the VIP area. Up another flight of stairs, and we came to the offices on the top level of the converted warehouse that housed Matteo's favorite nightclub.

The door of the first office stood ajar, and our guide lurked in the open door. "Yeah?" a male voice asked from within. Having had enough phone conversations with Enzo to coordinate our assistance, there was no doubt in my mind that he was the voice's owner.

"Rafael Ibarra and Calix Regas are here—" His voice cut off as Calix and I shouldered our way into the office. Santiago and Nikolaus lurked in the hallway behind us, standing guard without getting in the way. They'd make themselves known at the first sign of trouble, but they relaxed in the moments where we were as safe as possible with allies.

"The polite thing to do is wait for me to invite you in," Enzo said, a grin teasing his mouth. His gaze moved to Calix and he nodded his greeting, reminding me that the two men had met several times when I sent Calix to represent me in business dealings, when I couldn't be bothered to come stateside. A dark smile played at my lips when his attention came back to me, and he blinked at the shock of mismatched eyes that often drew attention to my face and worked to camouflage the devil that lurked within.

"Enzo," I greeted, holding out a hand for him to shake.

He grasped my hand, returning the gesture with a polite smile. "Can I get you anything?"

"What about me?" Calix grinned, moving to the whiskey on Enzo's desk and helping himself to a drink. "Fuck, I forgot what a bitch that flight is."

"You're early," Enzo said, smiling at Calix indulgently.

"Ah well, you know how it goes. My timeline has moved up. I need Matteo's war to finish so he can help me with mine," Calix said, not showing the slightest bit of remorse as he shrugged off potential loss of life. He'd become a man watching me act ruthlessly in my father's name, until the day came when I ended his tyranny and became ruthless because I wanted to be. Death was simply part of life.

He'd worked and trained every day since his banishment, and when the time came, Calix would take back what was his.

All of it.

"They set a date?" Enzo asked.

Calix nodded grimly, his nostrils flaring as he sipped the whiskey and set the glass down with a sharp thud.

I nodded, glancing at Calix. "We have less time than we expected."

"Your father will still lend his support for both of our wars? What does he expect in return?" Enzo asked as he sat. I grinned at him, exchanging a knowing glance with Calix.

"Matteo did not tell you? My father is dead. I am the Ibarra legacy now." I dared him to ask the question that hovered at the forefront of his mind.

"Was he…sick?" he asked as I studied him.

"Did Matteo ever tell you the story of how my mother died?" I asked instead of answering. I strolled around the office and eyed the names on the wall where Enzo coordinated his security team. "My father belonged in the Spanish Inquisition. He was, for lack of a better word, insane with his beliefs. His marriage to my mother was arranged, but he hated her because he thought her light eyes and heterochromia traits of her 'witchcraft.'" I scoffed. "So naturally, he had her burned at the stake once she stopped being useful, and he determined her to be barren when she never gave him another child after me."

"Christ," Enzo muttered, scrubbing a palm over his face. I'd seen and done plenty of evil in my life, but nothing would ever top watching my mother burn alive.

"I was seven at the time. I never forgot the sounds of her screams. I sleep much better now that my dreams are filled with his instead." Calix chuckled at my words, tipping his lips up comically in a move that was quite unlike my usually somber companion.

To be fair, he'd done his fair share of drinking on the plane after we departed Spain. The whiskey in his hand only exacerbated the situation, and I watched as he gave Enzo jazz fingers, his mouth making a whooshing sound to indicate I'd burned my father alive.

An eye for an eye.

"How many men have you brought?" Enzo asked, changing the conversation as he moved around the desk to study the names alongside me. He spun suddenly to glare at the doorway when a man appeared in it, his lungs heaving with exertion, gripping the liquor cabinet harshly.

"She's gone," the man gasped. Enzo's body stilled suddenly, his face turning white while his eyes narrowed with rage.

"What the fuck do you mean she's gone? You were supposed to be watching her!" he yelled, getting in the other man's face. The man wisely swallowed nervously, and I wondered just how far Enzo's anger would take him in retaliation for whoever he'd lost.

"I swear, I must have looked away for a few seconds. I've looked everywhere, Enzo. She's not here."

"Is Rebel here?" Enzo asked, looking around the man in the doorway frantically. When he stared back at him blankly, Enzo barked, "The dog!"

"No. The dog is gone too," he admitted, backing away slowly.

"Who is missing?" I asked, glancing back and forth between the men. My fingers twitched at my sides, eager to taste the violence that vibrated through the air. Monsters sensed blood on the horizon, and I was one of the worst nightmares I knew.

"My woman," Enzo answered. "Murphy targeted her, so she's been under Bellandi protection. It would be safe to say she's not happy about it." He shoved the man out of the way, making for the stairs. "I'll deal with you later," he warned as he shouldered past. "Call Matteo!" he yelled as Calix and I followed him out of the office.

"Call Matteo and tell him I've gone with Enzo," I ordered, leaving Calix at the club and striding after Enzo as he made his way for the front doors. The cold air assaulted my face as we barreled through them and into the freezing wind, heading for an SUV parked at the front of the lot. He didn't bat an eye when I climbed into the passenger seat alongside him, too focused on finding his woman before someone else did.

Santiago hurtled himself into the backseat just before Enzo hit the gas and pulled out of the lot.

Judging by the fury on his face, his woman would be lucky if he didn't tan her ass for what she'd done.

*E*nzo pulled into the parking lot at a boxing gym, shoving his door open and racing inside without care for what I might do in the meantime. I watched him fling open the front doors in his desperation to find her as I slowly climbed out of the SUV to look around.

My gaze came to a halt across the road, my entire world narrowing down to the sight of the woman who walked down the sidewalk with her friend on the other side.

As pretty as she was, there was nothing about her that should have demanded my attention. Nothing that should have captivated me so much that I froze solidly in place and studied her, but something did all the same. She couldn't have been over eighteen, fresh faced and smiling up at her much taller friend with the innocent smile of a child who'd lived a guarded and safe life. My eyes never left her, even as I sensed Enzo approaching; only his firm touch on my shoulder drawing me out of my stunned stare for just a moment before she captivated me once more when she turned toward us.

Her deep chocolate hair shone with notes of cherry undertones in the faint sunlight that emerged from behind the clouds, seeming to settle on her alone. Her skin was a bronzed olive, contrasting her sage eyes so vividly as she stared at me from across the street.

The coloring of the bottom corner of her left eye was different somehow, darker than the rest, though it was impossible to get a good look from so far away. I held her gaze without shame as she studied me, squinting to see me past the sun glare that must have interfered with her vision. It didn't seem to stop her from sensing the predator lurking across the road, from wondering what kind of monster lurked in the shadows and watched a young girl he couldn't touch.

I'd never touch a child.

It wasn't desire that settled over me so much as an instinctive knowledge that one day, when she was older, she'd be a force to be reckoned with.

One day, when she was older, she'd be mine.

3

ISA

"What the fuck, Mom! She was out just as late as I was!" Odina yelled downstairs. Groaning, I dropped my forehead against the window and waited for Chloe's beat up old Toyota to show up in front of the house. I'd run out barefoot if it meant I didn't have to deal with Odina's crap for once.

Just once, it would be nice to go out and forget I had a twin sister who drove me up the wall.

"Language!" Mom snapped, and I could just imagine the finger she waved in Odina's face. My sister was a far braver woman than me for daring to swear at her in the first place. "We both know Isabel only went to that party to get your drunk ass home safe. You are grounded. That's the end of it."

"That's so fucking stupid. I'm sixteen! All my friends go to parties without their parents breathing down their necks. It's part of being a teenager!" Odina argued back.

"Your sister has made it through her teen years just fine so far without making poor decisions," Mom said, and I winced, knowing just how unhelpful the words were when speaking to Odina. There'd been a time when we were close, when the thought of not having her as my best friend felt like an agony that would tear me in two.

But something had changed between us as children. As she spiraled into her pit of rebellion and destructive behavior, I'd done everything I could to protect her and mitigate the damage she caused. Which of course only made her hate me more.

"Of course! The fucking golden girl can do no wrong. Selfless, *perfect* Isa," Odina snarled, her footsteps thudding through the house as she made her way into the backyard. She'd climb up into the treehouse we'd called our haven as children, look for the cigarettes she kept stashed there, then rage at me when she discovered I'd taken them again.

I watched through the window as she hurried up the ladder, her mouth running a mile a minute as she cursed Mom and me to Hell and back for the control we tried to exert over her life. I didn't understand why she couldn't comprehend that it came from a place of love.

All I wanted was the best for her, and I wouldn't watch her throw her life away for something that might not even matter to her in a few more years.

"Your sister has a devil inside her," my grandmother said, scaring the bejesus out of me when she popped up in my bedroom behind me. For an eighty-year-old woman, she had the uncanny ability to sneak up on anyone and everyone. "I don't know what she expected. Hanging around graveyards as much as she does."

"Nohkomach." *Grandmother.* I sighed, pressing a hand to my chest over my racing heart. "You don't even believe in the devil," I scolded, grabbing my purse off the desk in the room I shared with Odina.

Grandmother scoffed, turning her face to the window behind me to watch Odina throw the crates she usually sat on around in the treehouse. "That girl just might make me."

Unable to stop the chuckle that rose in my throat, my chest shook with it. If Odina hated Mother and me, she was downright terrified of our grandmother, and rightfully so. The woman was a menace. One stern look from her and I felt my soul quake in fear. "Are you going to the Center?" she asked, referring to the Menominee Community Center where I spent most of my free time. Grandmother was a staple there, teaching what she knew of our language to my generation, and my parents' before mine.

"Not today," I said with a small smile. "I'm going to lunch with Chloe."

"Ah," she said, her smile brittle. It wasn't quite disappointed, not when she knew I spent far more time at the Center than any teenage girl would normally. "You'll be back tomorrow?" Our heritage was the most important thing to my grandmother: the continuation of our legacy, something that disappeared bit by bit with every day that passed. "You're my only hope, Isa," she said.

I stepped toward her, reaching up to touch a hand to her cheek. "I could never forget who I am and where we come from, Nohkomach," I murmured, glancing back at the window when Chloe honked her horn from the driveway. "I'll see you in a couple of hours," I said with a smile, and I made my way for the door.

My grandmother's eyes felt heavy on my back as I left, but I refused to turn and look back at her. Her stare was ominous. If I'd learned anything in my life, it was that nothing good came from the omens in my grandmother's eyes.

I'd decided long ago that I didn't want to know when

something bad came for me. A death I didn't see coming would be the ultimate mercy.

I'd never have to know true fear again.

iiis:

Chloe parked her car in the lot down the road after hunting for a parking space for nearly twenty minutes. Sometimes, Chicago traffic made me grateful that I didn't have a car of my own. Anywhere I couldn't get by walking, I had Mom or Chloe drive me, so it just seemed easier.

Not to mention less expensive, and since I worked a part-time job as it was and barely had any money to spare? I felt nothing but grateful for the missing expense. Shoving open the passenger side door to a squeak of protest, I climbed out of the car and pulled my thin canvas jacket tight over my chest to cover the bulky cream cable-knit sweater I wore underneath. Even the combination of the two didn't replace the warmth of a true winter coat, but Odina had borrowed mine the week before.

By borrowed, I meant set it on fire in her last tantrum.

"You need a new jacket," Chloe said with a frown, slamming her driver's side door and jabbing the button on the remote to lock the finicky thing.

"You need a new car," I said, sticking my tongue out at her when she glared in response.

"The difference is one costs $100, the other costs thousands, Isa. It's okay to spend your money on yourself sometimes, you know? It doesn't always need to go to helping your parents with your grandmother's medical bills," she said, her voice softening at the end. "They'll make it work. They always do."

"It's just a coat." I shrugged. "I'm used to the cold, and I have plenty of warm sweaters." Even as the words left my mouth, I took off down the sidewalk at a determined pace, ready to hide inside the warmth of the restaurant. The icy wind whipped through the fibers of the sweater, my jeans not doing anything to protect my legs from the bitter cold that settled in my bones and turned my skin red within moments.

Why did I live somewhere that the air hurt my face?

It probably had something to do with my grandmother's ancestral connections to the land Chicago had been built on. So many Native American Nations had once called the land home, and while many had left the city in favor of reservations or more rural skies, there were still a vast number of us living within the city. Modernizing and paving our own way forward.

I just wished we could do it somewhere warmer.

"What are they going to do when you go away to college?" Chloe asked, hinting at the issue that approached far too quickly for my tastes. I was already scouting schools, choosing between programs and having to make the choice between a school close to home and one farther away.

I knew what the obedient daughter should do, but I also had to wonder who I would be if I wasn't so focused on everyone *else*. If I had the time and distance to be who I wanted, *who* exactly would I be?

My not having the first clue depressed me more than it should.

Chloe nudged my shoulder with hers playfully, trying to draw me out of my sudden melancholy. "The good news is that Odina will be out the door as soon as she graduates. Your parents won't have to deal with her shit, so they can focus entirely on your grandmother."

"I'm not so sure that's good news. Odina may be a handful, but she's still their daughter. She just... needs guidance," I sighed. Chloe and Odina were not fans of one another. In fact, they were more likely to tear each other's hair out than have a conversation.

"She fucked your boyfriend, Isa. When she got caught, she said she felt sorry for the guy because nobody should have to be frozen out by the ice princess."

"To be fair, he wasn't much of a boyfriend if he couldn't tell the difference between Odina and me," I said with a laugh.

"You're identical twins. If you two stood in a room in the same clothes, I'd never know who was who, and I've known you both since we were six."

"Is your nose broken? Odina smells like pot, booze, and cigarettes more often than not. I've never even had a glass of wine." Chloe laughed at the ridiculous polarizing nature of the two of us as we turned the corner. A few steps passed in companionable silence, my gaze drawn to the boxing gym across the street. *Fists of Fury* had always caught my eye when we came to our favorite diner, the tiny Filipino woman who ran it inspiring the part of me that could never come to the surface. Kickboxing lessons weren't something I could afford, and I hardly had the need for them when I didn't believe in violence.

But something about the way she owned her body and turned it into a tool appealed to me on a dark level, wanting the ability to protect myself from harm. Women who looked like me went missing every day, and the rape statistics for Native American women were horrifying.

One in three.

The odds weren't in my favor to walk through the rest of

my life unscathed, even if I wasn't as limited in access to justice as those who lived on a reservation.

A man stepped from the passenger side of an SUV in the parking lot, unfolding his long suit-clad legs to stand behind the door until he closed it and stepped around. My eyes trailed up over the way his body moved as he buttoned his suit jacket, the glare of the sun in my eyes shielding his face from view as he stepped forward to the sidewalk on the other side of the street.

I waited for him to emerge from the shadows, willing back the rare sunshine so I might see the face of the man who captivated me. He remained faceless, an enigma that I couldn't quite grasp as darkness clung to him like a second skin.

As I watched, his gaze felt heavy on mine, regardless of the fact that I couldn't see it. I felt it, and I knew, without a doubt, that he could see me. Unfairness settled over me, his eyes an assessing stare. I could almost feel the tendrils of darkness enshrouding him, reaching across the street to wrap me in his endless night.

Another man stepped up to him, resting a hand on his shoulder in the fuzzy peripheral of the sun glare. The weight of the man's stare left me for a moment, and I drew in a ragged breath, the first sign that he'd stolen the breath from my lungs.

The weight settled back on me once more, only Chloe's voice at my side turning my attention away finally. She nudged me, taking my hand in hers and pulling me away and toward the diner. I turned my head and watched over my shoulder, waiting for the moment when I might see the man I could never know.

The one who had danger written all over every sinful line in his body.

My vision turned white as we made our way into the little diner. The owner, Damek, greeted us, and Chloe spoke in hushed tones at my side as my ears rang. The pounding of my heart in my chest echoed through my body and made it feel impossible to catch my breath. "What's wrong with her?" Damek asked. His firm hand came down on my shoulder, sending me tilting backward as the force brought me back to reality. He took one look at my eyes, his brow furrowing in concern. "Her pupils are dilated. What's she on?" he asked Chloe.

"Nothing!" she protested, shaking her head. "You know Isa better than that."

"She looks like she's seen a ghost. Sit her down. I'll grab some malinovka. She always loves it," he murmured, patting my head affectionately. He walked to the kitchen, leaving Chloe to drag me over to a booth as far from the windows as she could manage. I flopped down into the booth, grateful that I didn't need to support my weight anymore. My entire world had flipped upside down, with only a glance from a man I couldn't even see.

All the more reason to stay away from men like that.

"What the fuck was that?" Chloe asked, scrubbing her hands over her face as Damek slid two glasses with the Czech raspberry soda we loved so much in front of us.

"You okay, Isa girl?" he asked, staring down at me.

I sipped my soda, nodding my reassurance as the carbonation grounded me and reminded me of who I was.

Just Isa.

Nothing special, and the idea that a man who wore a suit and rode in a luxury SUV like that would be interested in an almost seventeen-year-old girl with no makeup on and her hair in two braids was comical.

"It was like you were *gone*," Chloe said. "You didn't even

hear me calling your name."

"I'm sorry," I said with a deep exhale. "I don't know what happened. I've never—"

"Wanted to run across a busy street and jump a man at first glance? Yeah, I'm aware," she laughed. "I couldn't even get a good look at him."

"Me either. The sun blinded me every time I tried, and trust me, I fucking tried," I hissed, sucking back more soda while Chloe opened her menu. She smirked at me, knowing I didn't drop swear words often. I couldn't get in the habit of it when it was likely to get me smacked with a shoe if my grandmother heard me.

"It's for the best," Chloe said. "There was something seriously wrong with him. Who stares across the street at a woman like that? Fucking creeps do, that's who."

I bit my bottom lip, knowing that in any other circumstance I probably would have agreed. But creepy felt like too mild a word for the man I hadn't seen, and the thought that he might do the same thing with other girls made me want to stab someone with a fork.

It was ridiculous, because he would never be mine.

I glanced out the window wistfully, staring at the space he'd stood before and the now empty parking spot where the SUV had been, as a man stepped into Donak's diner and smiled tightly before taking a seat a few tables away.

"What are you getting?" I asked Chloe, trying to turn my attention away from the man I'd never see again.

He was far too dangerous for anyone to get involved with. A girl like me would burn with desire from a single look, let alone if he actually touched me.

Responsible girls didn't get involved with phantoms from the shadows.

And I was nothing, if not responsible.

4

RAFAEL

The girl's friend nudged her, hissing something in her ear, and they turned and made their way into the restaurant behind them. "Come on. She isn't here," Enzo said, making his way to the SUV. I couldn't take my eyes off her as she looked over her shoulder to watch me while her friend dragged her into the illusion of safety the restaurant offered them.

Did she understand the danger she was in? Or was she too young and innocent to comprehend that she'd stumbled into the path of a nightmare?

"Rafe!" Enzo barked, demanding I get in gear. Only the knowledge that his woman was missing prevented me from ripping out his throat. I suddenly had an inkling of understanding for what that might be like.

I turned to Santiago, nodding to him and gesturing across the street. "Follow her. I want her name," I growled. Santiago looked like he might argue, given his place was to protect me at all times, but one stern glare telling him I meant business sent him scurrying across the street to do as I'd ordered.

"You can't touch her, Rafe," Enzo warned. "Matteo won't tolerate it, and we both know she's young. Too young for the way you looked at her."

I was silent as I climbed into the passenger side of the SUV, staring at the restaurant until it faded from view when Enzo pulled out of the lot and made his way back toward *Indulgence*. The sharp ring of my phone filled the silence that echoed between us, and I answered with disinterest. "Yeah? Got it." I ended the call and looked at Enzo, relaying the information from Calix. "They found your Sadie. A block away from *Indulgence* in a coffee shop eating a scone. They have eyes on her, but Matteo told Calix you'd want to deal with her yourself." He sighed in what I had to guess was relief that she was alive and well, even if he might kill her himself for the worry she'd caused.

He turned his attention back to me once he knew she wasn't in any real danger, likely suspecting that the same couldn't be said for my *princesa*. "Please tell me you understand that you can't take that girl, Rafe," Enzo murmured. My jaw tensed as I prepared for the fight I suspected was coming. I was no pedophile, but nothing would stop me from taking what was mine when she came of age.

"Do you often tell one another not to claim your women? Why is it you think I will tolerate your interference?" I asked, violence ringing in my blood as I turned to face him, silently warning him that he should back off if he knew what was good for him.

"It's different. She's too young."

"I'll discuss it with Matteo, and we'll work out an arrangement. I've no interest in rape, Enzo. Particularly raping a girl who has not yet become a woman. But we monsters can be patient, can we not?" I asked, raising an eyebrow and daring him to deny the truth. Matteo waited twelve years to make Ivory his once more. Ryker stalked Calla for four years before he plucked her from her mundane life. Lino waited close to a lifetime.

Good things came to those who planned.

"Isa," I said finally, after my phone dinged with a text. "Her friend calls her Isa."

S trolling through the Bellandi estate, I ignored the sputtering man at my back in favor of making a beeline to Matteo's office. I cared little for the woman and children playing in the yard, that I could see through the windows. There would be time for Matteo to introduce me to his family later.

All that I cared for in that moment was the pulsing need to establish my rules for Isabel Adamik in the sixteen months that would pass before I could claim her as mine in a permanent fashion. "You can't just barge in there. He's on the phone!" the man protested at my spine. I smirked at him over my shoulder, taking the doorknob in hand and turning it. Matteo's furious eyes met mine as he glanced up from his desk, heaving out a sigh of frustration before he nodded to the man over my shoulder with a resigned expression on his face.

"I'll call you back," Matteo grunted, ending the call with the press of a button as I moved into the room. Unbuttoning my suit jacket, I took the seat opposite him at the desk and made myself comfortable as the man at my back closed the door behind him and left us in privacy. "Enzo mentioned you'd developed a disinterest in knocking," Matteo drawled, his lips curving up despite his desire to seem irritated.

"To knock is to ask permission," I said, glancing down at

my nails thoughtfully. I'd missed a spot of blood under the edge of my thumb when I'd washed my hands clean of the punishment I'd dealt Enzo's man, for his failure of letting Sadie escape.

An old-fashioned beating seemed so rudimentary considering my own methods, but I'd never complain about the ability to act on the violence that simmered in my blood.

"And the great Rafael Ibarra asks permission of no one, not even his lifelong friends, apparently," Matteo noted, raising a brow at me. Enzo had undoubtedly warned Matteo of my interest in the *almost* seventeen-year-old girl who'd consumed my every thought since I'd seen her the day before.

Punishing Enzo's man had been the only thing to offer me even a moment of respite from her haunting face in my head.

"I've done nothing," I said, matching his eyebrow raise as we stared one another down.

"Yet," he added, daring me to contradict him.

"I won't touch her until she's eighteen," I answered, shrugging my shoulders as if it was inconsequential to me, when the thought of waiting so long felt like an agonizing torment to rival the worst of my methods.

Matteo sighed, leaning back in his chair as he studied me. "How intent are you on this?"

"How intent were you on Ivory when she stumbled back into your path?" I returned, clenching my fingers around the arms of my chair. His gaze fell to the tense movement, studying it as he considered his next words carefully. Matteo Bellandi needed my men for his war. Without them, he would have a much more difficult time triumphing over the allies Tiernan Murphy had amassed, simply because they wanted to keep selling people as bodies to fuck, and that couldn't continue under Matteo's reign.

He sighed, hanging his head. "You won't touch her until she's graduated from high school," he said, laying down the first of his terms. His jaw tensed with the knowledge that his wife would likely refuse to tolerate his concession, but there was nothing he could do without being a hypocrite.

He hadn't done much better in his pursuit of Ivory, and that had worked out well for him.

Eventually.

I nodded, considering the words with a purse to my lips. While I didn't like the demand, it was one I'd contemplated myself. Her May birthday wouldn't be too far off from graduation as it stood, and it seemed like a small sacrifice, considering everything I would put her through when I stole her away from everything she knew.

"I'll be leaving men in Chicago to keep an eye on her," I returned. "Will that be a problem?"

"Not as long as their sole purpose is to keep an eye on your girl, but I don't want her harmed. Until the time comes and you take her to Ibiza, she is to live a happy and peaceful life." I nodded my agreement, because the entire purpose of her security was to keep her safe and untouched by the sins of my world.

Or the greedy hands of teenage boys who might think to take what was mine.

"What are your intentions for her when you take her? Will you release her when you've had your way?" he asked, wringing his hands thoughtfully. Everything I knew about Matteo told me he would never allow me to take Isa if she was to be anything but a permanent fixture in my life.

"She'll be my wife," I answered, knowing the answer would placate him. I hadn't made the decision prior to speaking the words aloud, but something in them felt like the truest words I'd ever spoken.

"And you'll treat her well?" Matteo asked. I bit my bottom lip as I considered my answer. I couldn't say that I would ever treat a woman *well*. I was too much of a ruthless bastard for that, but understanding crossed Matteo's face. "You won't abuse her?"

"No. I won't abuse her, though I imagine there may be times when my definition of that word differs from hers," I chuckled.

Matteo glanced at his wife through the window where she played with his children. "Yes, I imagine there will be. I suspect you and I may have different definitions as well."

I nodded as I glanced out the window, the sudden desire for a child of my own overtaking me as I watched his entire world giggle outside.

I suspected he was right.

5

RAFAEL

Two days later

I stepped out of the car, glancing toward Lino and Georgio where they hid from the cold in the front of the SUV. Three men stepped off the private jet I'd sent back to Spain for the purpose of transporting one *very* specific family to Chicago. The three brothers made their way down the steps, bowing their heads respectfully as they approached me. I stretched out a hand to greet the eldest first, one of my most trusted men whom I'd left behind to help Alejandro, my second-in-command, manage my day-to-day operations in my absence. With his calm demeanor, Joaquin was easy to overlook: a shadow as he moved through the Ibiza streets at night, quietly ridding my territory of any who dared to deal without my permission.

There was nothing that happened on my island without my knowledge.

The middle brother, Gabriel, worked in technology mostly, helping to develop the top-notch surveillance that gave me eyes even where my men couldn't go. Both would help to monitor Isa, but both would need to remain out of sight and out of mind.

The youngest brother was the one who I desperately needed in Chicago. At just sixteen years of age, Hugo had already proven himself a valuable part of my business. Infiltrating the youth of Ibiza without raising suspicions, he kept his eyes peeled for boys he thought would be appropriate to join my ranks.

Not because we sought to take advantage of the vulnerable, but because we gave them a place to belong when they lacked one in their lives. Some might argue they were better off on their own rather than in the clutches of a Spanish crime syndicate, but I took care of men loyal to me.

Gabriel shook my hand with a cheerful smile, the tech-inclined man far too friendly for my liking. If he'd been only a little younger, he might have been a more appropriate friend for my Isa, more easily blended into the culture of an American high school.

Hugo reached out a hand, a serious frown on his face as he studied me. I knew the boy who sought to rise in my ranks as his brothers had wasn't interested in babysitting a teenage girl that he couldn't touch.

Turning my attention back to Gabriel, I finally spoke. "I want video surveillance in the common areas of the home, nothing in the bedrooms or bathrooms," I clarified. Not only did I not want to cross the line into perversion with her, but I wanted nothing to do with the sister, who Santiago had confirmed was a troublemaker. "Audio surveillance in her bedroom, nothing in the bathrooms."

"You've got it, Boss," Gabriel agreed.

"Trackers in her parents' cars and her friend's vehicle. Audio surveillance there as well, to be safe. Hack the security system at the Center where she spends her time and in the school. Anywhere you find she spends a fair amount of time, I want access." He nodded his head in agreement. I turned to Joaquin, staring him down. "When I say no one touches a hair on her head, I mean no one. If you value yours remaining on your shoulders, she will not be harmed in the slightest."

"You've got it. She'll be perfectly safe with all of us watching her," Joaquin agreed.

"What am I doing going to High School?" Hugo asked, earning a sharp reprimand from Joaquin when he smacked him in the back of the head.

"Respect, boy. You know better,"

"Sorry, El Diablo," Hugo murmured, nodding his head.

I smirked, shaking my head as the nickname poured from his mouth without thought. While it was undoubtedly what they called me on the streets, it wasn't often someone dared to say it to my face. Joaquin pinched his brow between his thumb and pointer finger, heaving out a sigh like his brother was an insufferable twat that just wouldn't learn. "You are here to befriend Isa," I said simply.

"Befriend her? Why?" he asked. Even Gabriel shook his head as his brother dared to let his curiosity get the better of him. But I found I couldn't fault him exactly. The only times I ever put surveillance on a person was when I suspected they'd betrayed me. What could a teenage American girl do to betray a man like me?

"Have you ever seen something and known it was yours the moment you laid eyes on it?" I asked him, leaning toward him to stare intently at his dark eyes. His nostrils flared, betraying his nervousness. He shook his head, and I suspected it was true. With his brothers being very trusted members of my family, Hugo would have wanted for nothing. "Isa is mine," I said. "When she's old enough, that will become official. Your job is to befriend her and monitor her in a way that your brothers can't do. I want you to be her confidante. I want to know every *thought* that runs through her pretty little head. I want to know what boys she has a crush on, so I can *crush* them."

"What do I do if she wants to go on a date?" Hugo asked, staring at me with wide eyes. My reputation as a man who didn't care about the pussy that walked in and out of my life preceded me.

"Tú lo manejas," I warned. "She will not go on a date, because you will make sure of it. Fail me in this, and I'll cut off your cock and make you eat it, Hugo." He swallowed down the lump in his throat, nodding his head in understanding finally. "She is to remain just as untouched as the day I laid eyes on her. You have the support of the Bellandis after I return to Ibiza. That combined with your brothers should be sufficient to dissuade some high school boys from touching what is mine, should it not?"

"Yes, Rafael," Hugo agreed.

"Good," I said, turning to get back in the SUV and escape the blasted cold weather. One of Matteo's men waited in a second SUV, prepared to give them a ride to the house they would call their own for the sixteen months they called Chicago home.

Life would be better once we were all back where we belonged on my island.

With Isa at my side.

6

ISA

*A*s someone who prided myself on never getting into trouble and always doing what people expected of me, getting called to the Principal's office wasn't something that I ever imagined would happen. It was entirely possible that it somehow had to do with Odina, but they usually called my parents for that. As much as it might feel like it sometimes, I wasn't her mother.

I thanked fate for that every day.

"Hi, Isa," The principal's assistant said when I walked into the front office. "Go ahead. He's waiting for you."

I swallowed, murmuring a soft, "Thank you," as I wrung my hands in front of me anxiously and chewed the corner of my mouth. Moving through the office, I knocked on the wall next to the open door, stepping in when the Principal's eyes met mine and he smiled kindly.

"Isa," he said, standing from his seat behind the desk. A boy I'd never seen before stood from the chair facing the desk, spinning to face me. With olive skin and dark hair, he smiled at me. "This is Hugo Cortes. He's our new foreign exchange student. Here all the way from Ibiza."

"Hey," the boy said.

"Hi," I said, giving an awkward wave as I looked back to Principal Davis.

"I'd appreciate it if you could show Hugo around the school. He's a very advanced student, according to his transcripts, and the two of you have the same course schedule. Would you mind?" Principal Davis asked. I heaved a sigh of relief, finally understanding that I'd been called to the office to play student host. Without the threat of detention hanging over my head, I could finally breathe.

"Of course," I said, a tiny laugh escaping as I fought back the hysteria at how ridiculous I'd become. So focused on being the dutiful daughter to prevent my parents from further stress, I'd never stopped to consider just how much the thought of being in trouble bothered me. "Do you have your locker number? We can drop off your stuff and then we'll probably have time to make it to History."

"Locker 193," he said, handing me a slip of paper with his information and schedule on it.

"Right next to mine," I said, smiling up at him despite the weird feeling that settled in my stomach. That locker had already been claimed for the year. Shrugging off the lengths they went to in order to make sure he felt at home in Chicago, I turned for the door and gave Principal Davis one last wave before we stepped through and made our way out of the front office.

Our lockers were on the second level, so I headed for the stairs while I thought of a way to break the silence. "So, Ibiza, huh?" I said lamely, wincing at the terrible attempt to fill the void in conversation. It wasn't that I was typically antisocial, I just didn't bother with people most of the time, since I always had my head buried in a book or was working.

There was a difference; I'd swear it until I died.

"Yeah. It's a crazy place to live, but I love it," he laughed. "You get used to it, you know?"

"I can't imagine that," I said. "But it sounds amazing. I've always wanted to go to Europe."

He nudged my hip with his as we walked. "You'll get there one day."

"Yeah, I don't know about that, but a girl can dream, right?" We made it to our lockers, and I went through the motions of showing him how to get it unlocked since they were finicky on a good day. The school just didn't have the budget for replacing them, even though they were old enough that my Mom had used the same ones when she'd been in school.

"What about you?" he asked as he deposited his backpack in the locker and dug out the history book from the stack within. "Born in Chicago?"

"Yeah. Born and raised. I've never left the city, actually."

"Well, that's just sad," Hugo laughed, wincing when he realized how harsh it sounded. I chuckled in response, knowing the truth in the words. I couldn't even say I'd visited other parts of Illinois. Travel, even of the limited variety, required money and time I just didn't have.

"It is," I agreed, slamming the door closed on the metal locker. It clanged as I pushed harder, finally latching closed. Hugo watched the process, repeating it on his with a disbelieving chuckle.

"Those needed to be replaced like twenty years ago."

"So if you love Ibiza so much, what brings you—" I cut off as a hand came down on my jean-clad ass in a harsh slap. I spun with a scathing retort ready, all too familiar with the offending hand and wondering what I could do to get my point across. Shock consumed me when the sound of the lockers rattling hit my ears before I could even finish turning around. "What the hell, Wayne?" I asked as my eyes finally caught on to what stared me right in the face. Hugo had Wayne pinned to the lockers with a forearm pressed against the front of his throat.

"That," he paused, his handsome boy face twisting into a snarl, "was fucking rude."

"Relax, Bro," Wayne laughed. "Call off your watchdog, Isa," he said, raising his hands as if he was an innocent and hadn't been smacking my ass every day for nearly a year. "It was an honest mistake. I thought you were the easy sister."

Hugo furrowed his brow at me in question, but something seemed...off about the movement. I tilted my head to the side. "I have a twin," I explained after I got over my shock at the display of violence. "But Wayne didn't mistake me for Odina. *Nobody* confuses us."

"Might have something to do with the fact that Odina spends more time on her knees than her feet," Wayne said with a cruel smirk.

"And?" I asked. "If she's a whore, so are you." I shrugged, far too used to the judgmental comments Odina got for her actions. She was no angel, and she made stupid choices frequently, but I also wouldn't see her condemned for things the guys got away with.

"I'll be a whore for you, baby," Wayne returned. I rolled my eyes to the ceiling.

"Let him go. He's not worth getting suspended over," I said to Hugo, grabbing his arm and pulling him away from the pathetic jerk who would hump anything that moved.

"Some advice, kid? You're wasting your breath with this one. She's the ice princess out of the two, and she will never let you stick it in. If you want a good lay? Give Odina a call.

They look *exactly* the same, so you don't even have to close your eyes to pretend you're fucking this one."

"If it's so easy to pretend the sister is her, then why don't you go bother Odina?" Hugo asked, tossing him a wink as I tugged him down towards AP History. Guiding him to the classroom, I again wondered about our shared schedule. I'd never seen a foreign exchange student in my Advanced Placement classes. Talk about throwing him into the deep end on his first day.

"Don't worry about Wayne," I said, instead of fretting about it. "He's just ridiculous."

"He doesn't get to touch you without permission. That's not cool," Hugo scoffed. He looked down at me, twisting his lips thoughtfully. "No boyfriend?"

"No," I said, hoping to all that was holy that we weren't going there. I didn't have an interest in dating after the last douche canoe of an ex.

"Good. Keep it that way, because guys just aren't worth the time, honestly," he said, slinging an arm over my shoulder in a very friendly gesture. "And now you've got someone to look out for you and keep the assholes away."

We walked into the history room just before the bell rang, and I couldn't shake the feeling that he meant that literally.

Wayne came to school with a broken wrist and black eye the next day.

I didn't ask, and he didn't smack my ass.

7

RAFAEL

One day later

A handful of pages scattered the desk in front of me in the office of the Chicago home we'd rented to accommodate us during our stay. A life reduced to a dozen pages, my notes were strewn all over the information in front of me.

Isa deserved a life of luxury, not tutoring students who most often were forced into studying with her. Not babysitting the brats of wealthy families in the area who didn't pay her anywhere near enough money to walk home with baby food in her hair. She most certainly shouldn't have had to give most of the money she earned to her grandmother's medical expenses.

All of that would change very soon.

My hands gripped the edge of the desk as I stared at the miscellaneous pages in front of me as I thought over my plan. Something was missing. The key to Isa's personality hovered at the edge like something I couldn't grasp. The workaholic tendencies seemed illogical, given her age and station in life. Where many of the teens in her neighborhood were much like Odina, finding thrills wherever they could, Isa had never so much as taken a step off the path her parents had laid out for her.

The question was *why?*

Nothing on paper gave any reason for it, and her behavior when she was alone didn't appear to change, either. I'd listened to her in her room at night, the silence deafening.

She rarely listened to music. She didn't touch herself at night when nobody was watching.

Nothing.

It was as if she was already dead. Like the moment eyes stopped watching her, she ceased to exist.

It made her dangerous. It made her unpredictable, and things I couldn't predict, I couldn't control. If I didn't understand her, I wouldn't know how much of a fight to expect when I took her after her graduation.

Would she scream and rage? Would she bleed me to save herself? Or would she take it all with the quiet acceptance that she seemed to move through the motions of her life with?

My cell phone vibrated on the desk, rattling over the papers as it moved closer to me. "Yeah?" I asked, hitting the button to answer the call. It stayed on the table while I turned on the speakerphone, and Alejandro's voice filled the space.

"Are you still staring at them?" he asked, referring to the collection of pictures that accompanied the materials Joaquin had gathered for me. An empty smile, hollow, as if she didn't even realize that her life was nothing more than a series of duties and responsibilities that should never have been hers. Next to the blinding beam of her sister's overly bright, intoxicated smile, it only seemed even more fragile.

The two girls standing side by side were almost exact replicas of one another if you took away the different tastes in clothing, but something lurked in Isa's eyes that wasn't there in Odina's gaze. I couldn't explain it, and the knowledge that, even after my infiltrating every part of her life, she still maintained her secrets drove me to the point of desperation.

"No," I grunted instead of answering with the truth of the maelstrom inside of me. I needed to keep my distance from Isa until she was mine, lest I drive myself mad with the need to understand her secrets.

"Liar," Alejandro chuckled. "She's pretty, in a sad sort of way," he said, echoing my own thoughts.

"But why is she so sad?" I asked him, sinking my teeth into my bottom lip. Music pounded in the living room as my men enjoyed the slew of women and booze that welcomed them to Chicago, but I had no interest in any of it. Much like my Isa, I rarely indulged in alcohol.

And the women weren't her, with her haunted eyes and the sectoral heterochromia that called to me on a level I couldn't understand. Never in my life had I met someone with multi-colored eyes besides myself and my mother, and finding it in the woman who captivated me from a distance?

The odds must have been impossible.

"There's nothing in the files?" he asked, his voice contemplative.

"Nada," I agreed. "When she was young, she fell into the river and nearly drowned. It explains her fear of water, yes, but not this."

He chuckled. "Maybe she just needs you to bring her to life."

I scoffed in return to his sappy sentiment that neither of us believed. The reality of my life and the way Isa would have little choice in our relationship meant that I'd be far more likely to drive her further into herself. I *needed* to know what lines she wouldn't tolerate me crossing. "Que te folle un pez," I spat with a chuckle. *I hope you get fucked by a fish.*

His laughter faded as he quieted. "If she really is as fragile as she sounds, have you considered going about it in a way that's not so traumatic?" he asked.

"Like what?"

"If she loved you, finding out you're *El Diablo* may not seem so world ending. Women will forgive a man many things for the sake of love."

"I think that's mostly regarding looking at another woman too long. Not murdering *chupamedias* who get in my way, and stalking her." I rolled my eyes to the ceiling, flopping back in my desk chair in exasperation.

"I still think it would be less traumatic than kidnapping her off the streets and taking her to a place she doesn't know," Alejandro mused.

"You're drunk," I said, ending the phone call with the stab of my finger against the button.

But his words struck home; the reality of what I would undertake to make Isa's insertion into my life as seamless as possible settling over me.

But I didn't have the first clue how to get her to fall in love with me. I spent more time pushing women out of my bed than I did trying to pull them closer.

I had sixteen months to figure it out, and somehow I knew that when I finally peeled back all the layers to understand what lurked beneath the surface in Isa, it would all be worth it.

I'd set her free.

8

ISA

Three days later

I tossed back the rest of the bottle of water left in Mom's car, shoving open the door and making my way across the street. Cars covered it, and I'd been lucky to find a spot where I didn't have to walk a mile just to get to the house and drag Odina's drunk ass back when she stumbled in the heels I knew she'd probably stashed in the backyard before sneaking out.

It was beyond my comprehension why I continued to cover for her when she didn't care about getting caught. I could only argue that she was my sister, and sisters were meant to look after one another. Even when one insisted on being a complete pain in the ass.

Kids from school stood around the yard mingling, with some making out on the grass. Wayne's party was supposed to be the "party of the year" according to the people I knew who had been invited. It was safe to say Wayne hadn't invited me. He hadn't so much as spoken to me since his fight with Hugo on Monday.

That was just fine with me.

I made my way inside as nausea churned in my gut. I did not have time to be sick, and if I threw up on Wayne's carpet, I'd make Odina clean it up.

Ugh.

The front door was wide open as I stepped through it, the pounding of music blasting over cheap speakers assaulting me as soon as I walked in. Glancing around the room for a glimpse of Odina, I cursed the fact that we'd been born on the shorter side. At 5'4", finding her in a sea of people taller than us proved impossible. Shoving my way through the party, I searched every person I passed.

"Have you seen Odina?" I asked a girl I knew sometimes hung out with her. She shook her head and pursed her lips in disgust, shrugging off my need to find my sister as just typical party-pooper Isa. With a sigh, I made my way to the dining room, where I finally spotted her sitting on the table with another one of her friends standing between her spread legs. They were clothed, thankfully, though it wouldn't have been the first time I walked in on her having sex. Both girls were giving flirty glances to one of the football players who watched Odina grab a handful of Megan's ass and squeeze.

He reached down, adjusting the erection that pressed against the front of his pants while I fought down the bile creeping up my throat.

Gross.

I moved over to them, tapping Megan on the shoulder. She smirked, eyeing me before walking away. "Can't beat twins," she said, shrugging playfully as she waved to Ben, the football player who moved closer.

"Fuck yeah! I always wanted to fuck both the twins," Ben said, stepping up to my space.

"Keep dreaming," I said with a saccharine smile. "From

what I've heard, you don't have nearly enough dick for one girl, let alone two."

Odina snorted, spraying beer all over him as she burst into laughter. "Isa brought her claws tonight, I see," she murmured. Reaching up a hand, she stroked the hair back from my face in a rare moment of affection. I might have thought she was putting on a show for Ben, but her brow furrowed when she found the sweat slicking my face. "Are you feeling alright? You're burning up."

"I'm fine," I said, closing my eyes briefly as dizziness made me stumble slightly. "Let's go. I just want to go home."

"Aw, we can't leave just yet!" she protested, grabbing my hand and trying to drag me to the dance floor as I tripped over my own two feet. "You just got here. Come dance with me, Isabel."

"We have to get you home before Mom and Dad notice we've been gone," I argued, pulling back on her hand to tug her to the door. My grip slipped, sending me stumbling back into the table. Liquor bottles rattled around on the surface behind me as I steadied myself, looking up into Odina's face as she came closer. The furrow to her brow was gone, lost to an arrogant grin that widened as I watched, and replicas of my sister appeared in my peripheral vision.

"You're like a fish at night. I knew you'd drink that water," Odina said with a cruel smirk. "I am *so* sick of being the bad sister. I think, deep down, you want to be just like me. You're just too afraid to let yourself. I want my twin back from the goodie-goodie who took her away from me." Odina pouted, taking a sip from her red solo cup as I swayed on my feet.

"What the fuck did you do?" I hissed, reaching to grab the dining room table to support my weight as my legs turned to jelly beneath me.

"Relax," she groaned, rolling her eyes. "It's just something to take the edge off. Losing your virginity hurts like a bitch. You'll thank me in the morning. I wish someone had roofied me my first time."

"You fucking—" I paused, swallowing around my tongue as the words didn't want to form, and I clenched my eyes closed to shut out the spinning room. "Roofied me."

"*Technically,* I did," a male said, stepping up behind me and wrapping his arms around my waist. I shoved him off, falling forward, and it was only his grip that stopped me from crashing to the floor. "Easy, baby."

"Off," I protested, turning to face Wayne when he didn't take his hands off my waist. He used his grip to guide me to the dance floor, his hips swaying side to side as he moved to the beat of the music that made my brain pound against my skull with every pulse.

A vaguely familiar voice protested, calling my name from the haze that I couldn't quite grasp. "Let's get you home," Hugo said as his face filled my vision out of nowhere, but my weight sagged, my body feeling a hundred pounds heavier as the drugs hit my system and I lost all sense of who I was.

Of who I'd be when I woke up in the morning.

"Isa doesn't want to go home. Do you, baby? We're having fun dancing," Wayne said. The side of my face hit his shirt, breathing in the scent of sweat and teenage boy that I never wanted to smell again.

"Shit, what the fuck did you give her?" Hugo asked as his hands touched my face and he pried my eyes open to look at him. As my eyes drifted closed once again, I heard nothing else as a few moments passed. Only the soft sway of my body as Wayne moved us to the music lulled me to sleep.

"I didn't give her anything she didn't take all on her own. She's a big girl. Isa can make her own choices."

Hugo laughed, the sound far more menacing than anything I'd ever heard as his voice filled my ears. "Man, you have no fucking clue the shitstorm you just unleashed on yourself. Bad fucking move."

Vaguely aware of moving, of being spun around and my legs being shuffled forward by force, I flinched back when my sneakers touched the base of the bottom stair and hands wrapped around my thigh to guide me up the step. "Not such a prude now, is she?" someone asked with a dark chuckle that made the hair raise up on my arms.

Someone murmured something in warning, but everything went silent as my vision went dark around the edges.

Until my body wasn't mine anymore.

9

RAFAEL

The phone vibrating on the coffee table shouldn't have startled me. Given it was midnight on a Friday, Bellandi business was at its peak hour. But even so, I answered the phone with the instincts of a panther, jumping to my feet with my keys in my hand the second I saw Joaquin's name fill my screen.

"What?" I barked.

"We have a problem," Joaquin said. "She went after her sister to a party. From what I've seen, that's not abnormal for her."

"Get to the fucking point," I ordered, pulling open my front door and making my way out to the Ferrari waiting for me.

"Hugo said she's on something. Some punk is trying to take her upstairs, and he's having trouble intervening in a way that doesn't raise suspicions, since Isa isn't asking for help. Does he risk his cover?" Joaquin asked, as I started the Ferrari and peeled out of the driveway.

"Give me the fucking address. Now," I growled, throwing

the car into gear as I punched the address into the GPS and swerved through traffic.

God fucking help any cop who tried to pull me over.

Isa:

High school parties were nothing like in the movies. There was no massive house owned by some rich kid whose parents were gone for the weekend. Nothing valuable to be destroyed that would end up in the kid getting caught.

Just a shitty house in a shitty neighborhood with no parental supervision on the entire block. I stalked past the teens lingering in the yard, storming through the open front door. The smell of booze and weed was too familiar to me as it invaded my senses, my eyes scanning the room to catch a glimpse of Hugo. Isa was far too short for me to find quickly, and I didn't have the time or the patience to struggle to find her, knowing she was at risk. He stood on the stairs, blocking the *coño* who tried to guide Isa up them. The boy had his arms wrapped around Isa's waist, with her slumped in his grip and looking barely conscious.

So unlike the girl who didn't take any risks, and my blood instantly boiled with the possibilities. From what Joaquin had said, she hadn't been inside long enough to get drunk off her ass, even if she had been so inclined. "You're not taking her upstairs. She's going home," Hugo said, crossing his arms over his chest. His eyes connected with mine over the boy's shoulder, and he puff up his chest, knowing that he had all the support he'd need in whatever happened.

"Yeah, and who's going to stop me? You aren't her fucking boyfriend, so why do you care?" the kid asked Hugo, posturing like he wasn't a pathetic excuse for a wanna-be man.

I stepped up behind him slowly, keeping my steps as quiet as I could. Hugo didn't move a muscle, didn't speak to give me away. I waited, willing back the need to kill. Certain that taking the life of a minor would be a new low for me.

Even if he was a dirtbag, until I knew the truth of whether he'd drugged Isa, he'd live to see another day.

Time slowed as he took another step forward, fully prepared to confront Hugo on the stairs with a nearly unconscious girl in his arms.

I leaned in, my breath hovering above his head as I said the words meant to startle him. "Me."

He spun, stumbling over the step when he faltered back at the rage he saw in my eyes. Isa wasn't so fortunate, tripping over the legs that couldn't support her weight when he dropped her to catch his own balance with his unbroken wrist instead of hers. I caught her with my left hand, curling her into my chest to keep her from hitting the floor.

"Who the fuck are you?" the kid asked, reaching out a hand to wrap his grip around Isa's forearm. Glancing down at his sausage fingers touching her delicate fawn skin, I tried to push down the rage I felt when the tips of his fingers indented her flesh.

"How old are you?" I asked him, tilting my head to the side. I took his hand in my grip, twisting it backward as I pried it from Isa's arm. Keeping her clutched against my chest, I watched his face twist in pain and felt nothing but satisfaction.

"Eighteen, man. Fuck, let go," he begged. Hugo whistled behind him, echoing the sentiments that rang in my head. Eighteen was not a minor.

Eighteen was a man. In my country, legal to drink and gamble. Legal to fuck. *Legal.*

Releasing his hand, the same fingers that had twisted his shot forward. His pulse beat against my palm as I wrapped it around his scrawny neck. The room went silent as everybody froze and moved out of the way. I lifted Isa off her feet with my arm wrapped around her, guiding her barely aware body toward the wall as I pushed him back.

His head connected with a resounding thud.

It still wasn't enough.

"What—" I paused. "Did. You. Give. Her?" He fumbled for purchase, grabbing my hands and dragging short nails down my skin while he gasped for breath.

"Can't breathe," he wheezed.

"Answer the fucking question," I ordered, adjusting Isa at my side.

"Roofies, man." I released his throat slightly to let him continue talking, clenching my teeth while I waited for my answers. "Odina gave them to me, I swear. She opened her Mom's car so I could slip them in the water bottle when I picked her up earlier."

I turned my head to Hugo, giving him a look. He nodded before I spoke, but I still confirmed *exactly* what I wanted in the meantime. "Find the fucking cunt." He darted into the crowd, undoubtedly ready to do exactly what I demanded.

"I don't think Isa believes in violence," I mused thoughtfully, turning my attention to stare down at her. She tilted her head up at me as I spoke, the shock of her eyes meeting mine for the first time reverberating through me like a claim that I would *never* escape.

I'd thought myself the captor in our relationship, but I suspected she'd own me just as thoroughly as I possessed her.

When her eyes rolled back and she faded back out a bit more, I turned my attention to the boy who swallowed against my palm. "Fuck, Isa" he laughed. "I thought you were a prude! You just like older men, huh, baby?"

I narrowed my eyes on him, clenching my fingers tighter so he gasped. "Are you always so *estúpido*?"

"Man, you ain't gonna do shit to me! There's an entire room of witnesses," he laughed on a wheeze. I nodded, releasing him as I leaned into his space.

"That may be so, but they have to go home at some point. Don't they? And who will protect you when I return?" I asked, watching as his face paled and he realized the severity of the situation. Normally, I wouldn't be bothered with killing a man if I couldn't do it in the moment.

For the first time, it was personal. I wouldn't tolerate another man being the one to watch the life bleed from his eyes as he fought for his last breaths. I'd be the only one to have that right.

Hugo stepped up to my right with Odina at his side, cursing and spitting at him as he dragged her to my view. The moment I turned my gaze to her, she silenced, staring up into my face in shock. She recovered quickly, smiling in a way she must have thought was seductive. Her eyes met mine, and it sent a shock of revulsion through me. They weren't Isa's, but they were close enough to be a mockery of everything I saw in her.

"Well, you could have just told me a handsome man demanded my time," she purred. In a move I'd practiced far too many times to count, I ran my eyes up over her body and to her face, and gave her an uninterested look that conveyed just how unimpressed I was. She glanced to her sister, rolling her eyes the moment she realized she was tucked safely in my arms. "Why do the fun ones always like the innocent virgins?" she asked, stepping closer to me. Her hand touched my thigh, moving toward my fly as she spoke. "Let me show you who the fun sister is."

I caught her hand, flinging it away from me before she could touch what wasn't hers. "How fun could a pale imitation be?" I asked, my voice cruel. She flinched, and I knew the words struck home. Whatever issues she had, they stemmed from some seriously misguided jealousy over the sister who only wanted to do right by her.

"Then what the fuck did you summon me for?"

"I know about the roofies in the water," I said simply. "I will make one thing very clear. If your shit *ever* touches Isa again, I will be the one to make sure you get your shit together. I promise you will *not* like my methods."

"Yeah. Okay, hotshot," she laughed. "That's an awful lot of trouble to go to for a bitch who won't even fuck you," she said, nodding to her sister.

"*If* you ever endanger her intentionally again, I will make you disappear," I threatened, meaning every word. "You will not be in Isa's life to put her at risk." Hugo touched my shoulder, nodding down to Isa where she stared up at me with wide eyes. I sighed, wishing I could dedicate more time to making sure Odina truly understood the consequences of her actions in the future. "Deal with her," I said instead, sweeping an arm beneath Isa's legs to lift her up and cradle her against my chest. "She's not to breathe a word of this. I don't give a shit what you have to do." Tucking Isa's head into my shoulder, I strode out of the house as the crowd of teens parted to let me pass.

I'd known the moment I saw her that she'd be trouble for me. I just didn't realize I'd be threatening to kill two self-centered twats so soon.

Joaquin emerged from the shadows, hauling open the

passenger door of my Ferrari and then disappearing once again after he gave me a nod. He knew that both his brothers would suffer for what they'd nearly allowed to happen to Isa, but he wisely refrained from commenting.

As I set her body in the seat and buckled her up, she lifted a tired arm to cradle my face in her palm. "Phantom," she whispered softly, the breathy note to her voice making the void in my chest clench.

If I'd had a heart, it would have beat for her.

I drew her hands off my face with a clearing of my throat, forcing distance between us to prevent her from crossing any lines in her intoxicated state. Dropping into the driver's seat, I started the ignition and drove more carefully than I might have without her in the car with me. She watched me cautiously, and not for the first time I wondered what she saw when she looked at me. Even in her only half-awareness, I couldn't help but be conflicted about what I wanted her to see.

Did she see *El Diablo?* Or did she somehow see a man that I wasn't even sure still lived inside me?

She blinked those uniquely stunning eyes, reminding me of just how wrong it had felt to have her sister's locked on me. "You were m-mean," she whispered, fighting for each word.

"I was mean?" I glanced back to the road in shock, having been so distracted by her that I'd forgotten I was driving. *Never* in my life had I been so unaware of my surroundings.

"To my sister," she slurred. "Shouldn't have said she was imitation."

"I hardly think me being mean matters when the bitch drugged you," I said, watching as her head settled further into the seat. She didn't answer, sleeping the rest of the way as I drove to the home Joaquin had rented for him and his brothers.

When we finally made it, I lifted her into my arms and brought her into the house after Gabriel opened the door. "She needs a bed," I said, even if I detested the idea of her sleeping in any bed but mine. At least Hugo knew I would slaughter him if he so much as looked at her wrong.

I'd only just settled her in the bed and pulled the covers over her when Hugo and Joaquin got home with her mother's car and theirs. Hugo came into the room as I sat on the edge of the bed and ran my knuckles over her cheek. After slipping her shoes off her feet, I reached beneath her and pulled the phone free from her back pocket, touching the button to bring up the lock screen. "Passcode?" I asked.

"6948," Hugo said immediately. Punching in the numbers, I rattled off a text to her mother saying that she'd crashed at Chloe's house after she had boyfriend problems, and that she didn't want her mother to worry.

"The sister?" I asked, setting the phone on the nightstand once that was done.

"Dealt with. She promised she wouldn't say anything about your threats, too," Hugo said.

"And what did you offer her for that bit of damage control?" I asked, glancing up at him. He hesitated, glancing to the window as he scrubbed the back of his head and then looked down at Isa. "What?"

"Nothing," he said. "She said she'd keep the secret, as long as I promised whatever we were planning would hurt Isa in the end."

"La hostia," Joaquin cursed. *Holy shit.*

"Something made Odina hate Isa so much that she would drug her and want her hurt," I said, standing from the bed with one last rueful glance at Isa. "I want to know what," I growled as I strode from the house.

I knew, without a doubt, that I couldn't see her again until she was mine. Until her vague memory of me faded and she wouldn't recognize me when we met.

10

ISA

My head throbbed as I forced my eyes open, squeezing them shut the moment the light trickling in through the window assaulted my vision. "Ugh," I groaned, touching a hand to my forehead. I finally sat myself up, wincing from the pounding in my skull and glancing around the room.

I didn't know where I was.

Plain white walls stared back at me, not a single decoration or poster so much as touching them. The bedding was nice, softer than what I had at home, but gave away nothing with the simple grey color. A single dresser was on the opposite end of the room, clothes piled on the top as if the owner hadn't had time to put them away.

Touching my chest in a panic, I confirmed that all my clothes were still on. Nothing felt sore or violated. Heaving out a breath, I fought to search through my fuzzy memories of the night before.

The water, and my sister helping *drug* me, stood out amongst a sea of blurry shapes and faces I couldn't quite grasp.

A phantom in the night, tendrils of darkness threatening to wrap me in their embrace.

I swung my legs out of the bed, standing and looking around the floor for my shoes. I found them tucked neatly against the wall, standing and stumbling over my feet as vertigo crashed over me and threatened to send me to the floor.

A sharp knock came at the door, and I spun with a shocked gasp as Hugo opened it slowly. The unmistakable sense of relief struck me in the chest at the sight of him. I didn't know him well enough to be relieved to see him, but the familiarity of him was a comfort in the sea of unrecognizable surroundings that threatened to swallow me whole. "You're awake. We were starting to worry."

"We?" I asked.

"My brothers and I," he said. "How are you feeling?"

"Like you saved me from being raped." I sighed, hanging my head between my hands. Hugo ducked out of the room, coming back with a *sealed* bottle of water and a fresh bottle of aspirin.

I smiled my thanks as the seal cracked on the water when I twisted the cap off. Pressing in the cap on the aspirin as I twisted, I pulled the cotton from the bottle and shook out two. I downed the pills with a hard swallow of water.

"Don't worry about it. I don't like guys who take advantage of vulnerable girls," he said, reaching out to pat my hand as tears stung my eyes. I would never be able to thank him enough for intervening.

The thought of what might have happened to me if he hadn't been there was one nightmare I never wanted to think about again.

"Want me to take you home? My brother can take his car so we get your Mom's car home, too."

"Thank you. That would be amazing. My family must be freaking out. I always get Odina and I home before they wake up."

"Ah," he said with a sheepish grin. "I had you unlock your cell last night." He gestured to the phone on the nightstand. "I texted her that you were okay and with Chloe."

"Thank you," I said, furrowing my brow as I read my text message to my mom. She'd replied with a thank you early this morning, saying she was off to work, but we'd talk when she got home. At least I wouldn't have to deal with the questions about why a boy brought me home if I was supposed to be with Chloe. Dad would be at work too, and my grandmother would already be at the community center.

"Come on," Hugo said, nodding to the living room. "You can meet my brothers officially. Joaquin helped me get you here last night."

I followed slowly as I thought about the blank face in my memory, almost dreading the moment I saw my phantom in the flesh. How could a real person ever compare to the fictional one I'd made up in my drugged state?

"This is Gabriel," Hugo said, pointing to a man in his mid-twenties. "And this is Joaquin. They came to stay with me while we're away from our parents so I wouldn't be all on my own in the windy city," he said with a mocking tease.

My eyes landed on Joaquin's cold brown stare, feeling none of the spark I'd assumed would be there, given the hazy memory I had of him and the way he'd made me feel the night before. Disappointment struck with the realization that it must have been the drugs in my system that made me imagine my reaction, and that he couldn't have been the same man who watched me across the street earlier in the week.

That it was nothing but a coincidence, my mind playing

tricks on me and creating connections where there were none.

"You mentioned," I said with a brittle smile as I turned to his brother. "Thank you, for helping me last night. I don't know what I would have done if—"

"No more trying to help your sister," Joaquin said with a sharp reprimand. "She wants to fuck up her own life? That's on her, but don't let her drag you down with her."

I sighed, nodding as the reality of it settled over me and knowing he was right. I'd spent far too many years trying to make up for Odina's selfishness and pull her back from the brink. I'd wasted my childhood being determined to make up for a single mistake that hadn't even been entirely mine.

The time had come to give up on saving someone who didn't want to be saved.

It should have felt like a part of my soul tearing in two. Isn't that what they said about twins? Instead, it felt like a breath of relief to not have to worry about her anymore.

To be fair, Joaquin's gaze on me proved to be a distraction from the things I didn't *want* to feel. It would come later: the feeling of grief I'd never let myself have. For the bond that had ended when Odina and I were too young to understand the consequences of a simple accident.

I didn't understand why I felt nothing but disappointment meeting the man who'd helped me get out of a really bad situation. But the feeling was there nonetheless.

I missed a man who didn't exist.

How could you miss someone who didn't even have a face in your memory?

11

RAFAEL

The brothers came home after dropping Isa off at her house. The closed curtains likely served as a stern reminder of what waited for them when they stepped inside. Still, like dutiful soldiers, they didn't blubber or beg as they moved in and closed the door behind them.

A week.

Less than a week they'd been responsible for watching my *princesa*, and they'd allowed her to be drugged by her bitch of a sister and nearly raped. To be fair, none of us could have expected the depth of her sister's hatred for her, but that didn't mean Isa ever should have been at that party to begin with.

I'd take care of that, after I took care of the first of the Cortes brothers.

Hugo dropped to his knees in front of me, hanging his head as he waited for his punishment. "I should put a bullet in your head for what you let happen," I snarled, standing from the chair I'd occupied while they brought Isa home. "But Isa has already grown to trust you. I can't just replace you with another friend." I strode around him, moving to his brothers, who bowed their heads respectfully and waited for my verdict. "Very clever of you to introduce Isa to your brothers, offering them the same protection. She would question them disappearing so suddenly. I can't have that. Can I?" I asked, turning a glare back to Hugo. I'd underestimated the boy's cunning, and he raised his head to meet my eyes and showed me just what I knew I'd see.

The move had been very deliberate. He would either be an excellent ally, or eventually there would come a day when he tried to reach too high, and I put him down like a dog in the dirt.

"She doesn't need to see them with no shirt, however," I said, stripping off my suit jacket. The fireplace in the corner burned with the branding iron as I rolled my sleeves up. Both Gabriel and Joaquin swallowed, but stripped the shirts off over their heads. They'd bear the mark of their failure for the rest of their lives. Such was the way of the Ibarras. Grabbing the brand from the fireplace, I held it up and inspected the straight tally mark that would mark their chests.

Moving to Joaquin first, I held his eyes as I pressed the white hot metal to his flesh next to the sole mark that already occupied his chest. Skin sizzled, popping beneath it as he gritted his teeth and clenched his eyes closed. I knew better than most the feeling of your flesh melting.

My father had been fond of reminding me of my failures.

When I drew back and placed the brand in the fire once more, Gabriel gagged around the smell of burned flesh that filled the room. Hugo watched with horror-filled eyes as I took the brand to his other brother.

One failure. One mark.

Hugo was fortunate to get away without one, simply

because I couldn't have her see it and match it to mine later on.

"I'll owe you your mark in sixteen months," I said to Hugo as I pressed the brand to Gabriel's skin. Hugo swallowed but nodded, accepting the fate for what it was.

Inevitable.

The anticipation of the event would be even worse than if I'd just gotten it over with. Hanging over his head for over a year. His brothers had a more merciful punishment. "If you fail me again, I will kill your entire family and wipe your legacy from the Earth," I told Joaquin, stepping back and unrolling my sleeves. As I slipped my jacket back over my shoulders and buttoned it up, the three men observed me. "I do not care that your mother is alive and breathing. I will slaughter *all* of them. There isn't a line I won't cross for Isa. Remember that, and you'll earn your places back with me when you return. Understood?"

They nodded solemnly, and with that part of my day out of the way, I slipped out the front door without another word.

When I slipped inside two weeks later, every light was on in Wayne's home, as if he truly thought it could keep the devil away. He sat on the couch, a knife in his hand, while his parents slept soundly upstairs. The drugs on the coffee table showed just how far his fear had driven him in the weeks I'd left him to look over his shoulder in fear.

Watching and waiting for the phantom that would come and put him out of his misery.

He was barely aware, high off the dirty heroine he'd

injected into his own body in his desperation to escape into a high. I leaned over him, slapping his cheek until his eyes rolled open. Terror filled them, even through the haze that must have been so similar to what Isa had felt, that night he'd tried to touch what was mine.

"Where are your witnesses now?" I asked, watching as he prepared to yell for his parents. But I'd already ensured they'd sleep through the night, courtesy of roofies from the same dealer that had supplied the ones used on Isa. "They won't help you."

"What the fuck," he asked, his words trailing off. "I'll call the police."

"Go ahead," I said. "You'll be dead before they can get here, and I don't have to do a thing to make that happen. You killed yourself, you see?" I asked, tapping the empty syringe on the coffee table. "An overdose. Heroin laced with fentanyl. I'm told it's quite common when you buy the cheap shit."

"What?" he whispered, eyeing his trusty stash like it had betrayed him. Perching on the edge of the coffee table, I watched as he fumbled around to find his phone. But I'd watched and waited just long enough for the drugs to have already taken effect, making his movements uncoordinated and sloppy.

When I'd found his phone on the floor, I kicked it under the edge of the couch so he would never find it in time. I watched his movements fade altogether, his eyes drifting closed. "You never should have touched Isa," I said finally as I waited for his heart to stop altogether. When his chest no longer rose and fell, I took his wrist in my hand and checked for a pulse I already knew wouldn't be there.

My only regret was that I couldn't make him bleed. That he hadn't screamed in agony as he died.

But Isa could never know my role in his death, and an overdose was so easily explained in a teenage boy.

Emerging from the house, I hurried to my car, unseen. I pulled the Ferrari from where I'd parked a few houses down, turning toward the Bellandi estate. The time had come to tell Matteo exactly what my plans for Isa entailed.

Her photo sat on the passenger seat next to me, and I picked it up and sighed.

All that was left was to wait.

PART II

UNTIL TOMORROW COMES

Rafael

I came for war. I left with an obsession.

With one look, Isa captivated me. She consumed me, drawing me into her world without ever knowing the dangers of mine.

I intend to make her mine, no matter what lies I need to tell to manipulate her into falling in love with El Diablo. It should be simple enough, but secrets lurk in the depths of her multicolored eyes, and I'll do anything to understand what broke her before I had the chance.

Because she's mine to break.

Isa

Rafael Ibarra tore through my life like a raging inferno.

Consuming every part of me he touches, he promises to show me passion and the real Ibiza. Though our tryst can never be anything but temporary, I never want to leave the man who makes me wish things were different. But there's a nightmare hiding within his multicolored gaze, a phantom rattling at the cages who wants to devour me, to take me and claim me as his.

He's temptation, pushing me toward sin with his wicked touch. But the sins of the flesh are different from the sins of the mind, and as much as I hate his secrets...

I will never tell him my own.

1
ISA

Whirlwind adventures weren't for planners. They weren't for the meticulous list-makers who couldn't function without order in their lives.

They weren't for girls like me.

"Where the hell did I put my packing list?!" I groaned, looking around the room in search of the worn slip of paper I'd abused over the past week. Moving to the desk in the corner with the stack of books about Spain I'd borrowed from the library, I shoved them to the edge frantically.

"Language, nōhsehsaeh," my grandmother warned, poking her head into the room. The lines on her face were lighter than I could remember them ever being. The circles under her eyes had faded after she'd been selected for a medical grant and had the bypass heart surgery she needed.

"Sorry," I said with a wince, finally finding the paper with my notes all over it. The edges were torn from all the nights I'd spent agonizing, ensuring that I wouldn't forget anything I needed for my trip to Ibiza. "What if I forget something?"

"I am sure Hugo will make sure you have everything you need," she reassured me, stepping in and wrapping her arms around me. "He wouldn't allow you to visit his country without making sure you're prepared. He cares for you," she said, pressing her lips to the top of my head.

"It's not like that," I explained, and my grandmother nodded her head in response. My family adored Hugo and had practically adopted him as we grew closer after Odina's betrayal left a void in my heart. But my grandmother was the only one who didn't think we'd end up together.

"It is good that it's not. Hugo still plans to stay in Ibiza when your trip is over, yes?" she asked. I nodded, trying not to think about the loss of one of my best friends. *Both* of them really, since Chloe would go off to college in Philadelphia while I stayed in Chicago to be close to my family. "It will be strange, not having him to look out for you."

"I can look after myself," I reassured her, stepping out from her arms as I looked over the packing list one last time and tried to heave my suitcase closed. My breath caught in my chest as I turned to face her, remembering how weak she'd been after the surgery a few months prior. I couldn't shake the thought that something bad was coming for us, and *nothing* could be worse than losing my grandmother. "Are you sure you'll be alright while I'm gone?"

She scoffed. "I don't need my granddaughter to babysit me. I'll survive the twelve days without you, my darling girl." She sat on the edge of my bed, patting the mattress for me to join her. I did, willing to give my grandmother anything. She sighed. "Promise me you'll have fun. A girl should live a little on vacation. Real life will wait until you get back. Try not to worry so much."

"I'll try," I said, even knowing it was probably a lie. I'd explore with Hugo and Chloe at my side. I'd enjoy my time with my friends while I had it, but I didn't know the first thing about actually living.

My eyes caught on Odina's empty bed and the lack of mess on what had once been her side of the room. "You're not your sister," Grandmother said, reaching up to touch my cheek. "You can let go a little without being lost." I nodded, even if I doubted the words. There'd been a time when Odina and I were exactly the same, before the accident changed everything.

Before she hated me enough to ruin her life just to make me miserable.

"Okay," I said, instead of arguing. The same demons that haunted Odina plagued me. The same nightmares called to me from the depths. I just believed that I had a family that loved me to keep me from succumbing to their temptations, where Odina had lost that.

My grandmother stood from the bed, leaving me to grab my suitcase and lug it down the stairs. My parents greeted me, wrapping me in their arms the second my foot touched the first story. The knowledge of my trip and the suddenness of it couldn't have come at a worse time.

I'd never told them about our entries when Hugo encouraged Chloe and me to apply for the contest, because the odds of us winning had been so slim with the number of applicants. The Appreciation Program was only in its second year since being created, offering American students who made their Spanish friends feel at home the chance to explore the city of their birth in Spain.

When they'd notified Chloe and I they'd selected us, there'd been nothing but shock. A shock that had come the day after graduation and the day after Odina turned her back on us for the last time. In the week since, I hadn't seen her or heard from her once.

My life was far more peaceful without her in it, and that only made my guilt worse.

"Promise me you'll call us when you land," Dad said, hugging my head to his chest. They'd set me up with an International Calling plan despite the expense, needing that ability to contact me in case of an emergency.

"I promise," I said with a tight smile to prevent his shirt fabric getting caught in my mouth. His face was too thin as I pulled back, too affected by the absence of his other daughter to eat a decent meal. I had to hope that my being gone would help.

He wouldn't have to look at Odina's face every time he looked at me.

Mom held out her arms for me to step into her embrace, her face tight with the threat of tears. "You have your Euros?" she asked.

"Yes, I have Euros and the debit card and traveler's checks from the program. I'll be fine, Mom," I said with a grimace. She nodded, wiping the tears away from her eyes.

"My baby girl," she whispered, stepping back and cupping my cheek in her hand. "You stay away from trouble, you hear me? A place like that is bound to be filled with it."

"We live in Chicago," I laughed. "It isn't exactly a Mormon community."

"I've looked at pictures on that internet," she said with a frown. "It's one big party. One with very few clothes. Did you know there are beaches where people don't wear bathing suits!" She shivered back her revulsion, looking at me in warning. "Don't you dare."

"Mom," I groaned, rolling my eyes as my grandmother chuckled in the background.

"How else is she supposed to land herself an affair with a handsome Spanish stud to show her the ways of passion?" she asked, nudging my side playfully.

She loved to rile my mother up, even as my Dad groaned, "Mom."

"What? Sex is a spiritual act. She should know what she wants from a man if she's ever going to settle down and teach her husband one day," my grandmother inserted with an innocent smile.

My mom's Catholic upbringing begged to differ. "Can we not?" I groaned. "My sex life, or lack of one, is none of anybody's business."

Mom swallowed but nodded, looking at me with expectations in her eyes. The good daughter didn't have sex with boys at school or men she met in Spain. The good daughter didn't drink or do drugs or dance in no clothing.

The weight of those restrictions came down on me, pushing me further into the place where I knew I had to belong.

Because the good daughter was the only one she had left.

I was mostly silent in the backseat while Chloe sat up front with her mom, who chewed her bottom lip so hard I wondered if there would be anything left when we came home. No parent wanted to see their barely legal daughter go to Europe without adult supervision.

Glancing out the window as we drove, I tried to quell the nerves in my stomach. I'd never left Chicago. What business did I have going to Ibiza? I didn't even know who I was without my responsibilities to my family to dictate my every action.

I steeled my spine, sitting up straighter as I exhaled. My grandmother was right. The trip was my one opportunity to forget about who I had to be at home. It was the only chance I'd have before immersing myself in the college experience and my studies, I'd be a fool not to take it.

I didn't know what that meant for me. If I'd lose my virginity to a Spanish stranger, drink for the first time, or go to a nude beach and try to let go of the insecurity that I was unattractive. Boys were never interested in me. Not the way they were Odina.

Every time I thought maybe, just maybe, one would ask me on a date, it never came. Given that the last boy who'd seemed to want to touch me had overdosed on heroin two weeks after, I wondered if I was cursed. Maybe I'd finally find out.

Chloe's mom dropped us at the airport, sharing an excited hug with her daughter before she confirmed we had everything out of the van and went back to get in the vehicle.

Hugo and his brothers were already waiting at the curb with their bags. Hugo looked at my suitcase like he wanted to carry it for me, but his own bags limited that ability. He sighed when I pulled the handle up and wheeled it toward the machines to print our tickets. Flipping him off only made the twisted bastard laugh.

"Are you two going to bicker the entire flight to Spain?" Chloe asked as she gave me a saccharine smile and stepped up to a kiosk to print her ticket.

"Probably," Gabriel said with a bright smile.

I stuck my tongue out at the middle Cortes brother, ignoring the scowl Joaquin gave him and the sharp elbow to his side. I didn't understand the eldest of the three in any way. His demeanor was always off, like his brothers were foolish for not treating me as if I was made of glass and required kid gloves.

The one time I'd suggested spending my birthday money on a kickboxing lesson, he'd practically bugged his eyes out of his head. Girls like me didn't need to worry about things like that, according to him.

Whatever the fuck that meant.

"Hush," I said as I stepped up to the next available kiosk to print my own ticket.

"Sweet! I got upgraded to first class!" Chloe said with a bright grin. My heart dropped into my throat, realizing I'd probably not get to sit with her on the plane. The moment I logged into my reservation, the same words stared back at me.

"I did too," I whispered, glancing over at Hugo when he held up his own First-Class ticket. "That's so weird," I said.

"Nah." Hugo shrugged it off as his brothers printed their tickets. "It happens a lot. It's hard to fill up first class since it's a lot more expensive for what is basically just more leg room. So they randomly upgrade people if they get last-minute economy bookings when the flight is full. No use having empty seats," he explained. "That's why I booked our flights together. Just to be safe."

"Makes sense to me!" Chloe sang as she followed Hugo while he led the way through the airport.

I shoved down my feeling of foreboding as my tentative excitement built. I hadn't really let myself look forward to the trip, always believing something would go wrong at the last minute. My ticket would go missing. I'd get held up at security. I'd miss the flight for any number of reasons.

Although we had a long journey ahead of us, with a stop in Lisbon before landing in Madrid and getting a connecting flight to Ibiza, for the first time in what felt like forever, I was excited to see what was coming my way.

I just hoped I wouldn't regret it.

2

RAFAEL

My shoes tapped against the tile as I made my way through my home. Most of the men kept their distance from the main house even on a good day, but knowing that only hours stood between me and *mi princesa* being in my arms meant they most definitely were as far away as the island would afford them.

Regina stood in the kitchen, chopping garlic to cook something for Alejandro that night. My greatest regret in going to meet Isa was that I wouldn't get to eat it.

I hated being away from her cooking.

"*Mi hijo*, why must you pace so much?" she asked, casting a wrinkled smile my way. She'd been my mother's best friend once upon a time, the only reason I tolerated her overly familiar greetings. She was the closest thing I had to family.

Regina had even taken my mother's place in my father's bed after he burned her alive. Not that she'd had much choice in that matter. Miguel Ibarra wasn't known for his kindness to women.

"Where's Alejandro?" I snapped, snatching a bite of

peach off her cutting board while she tutted at me and waved her knife in my face. Another day, I might have laughed at the audacity of the woman.

"If he's smart? Hiding," she said, wrinkling her forehead while she turned her face back down to the peaches. Glancing at the watch on my wrist, I frowned. Isa's flight was due to arrive in a matter of hours, and she would make her way to Ibiza Town shortly after.

I very much needed to be in the city before then, so I could ensure all my plans went off without issue. I detested depending on other people to move the pieces into place. Nothing set me on edge more than the lack of control I felt knowing that if the hotel manager failed to give Isa the invitation to the party at my hotel, she wouldn't come.

I'd kill the fool and then have to come up with an alternative plan.

"I know you are eager to see your Isa," Regina said with a smile as she wiped her hands on her apron and took mine in hers. The stickiness of the peaches touched my skin, making me frown in consternation. "But she will love you. How could she not with a face like this?" she asked, tapping the end of my nose. I scowled at her as I moved to the sink to wash the peach juice off my skin.

"I imagine it would be easy not to when he scowls all the time," Alejandro, my second in command, said as he stepped into the kitchen with his arms crossed over his chest.

"Where have you been?" I growled, my voice holding every bit of the warning that had sent the rest of my men running to the other buildings in the compound to keep busy. "I'm due to leave in less than an hour."

"Rafael, you will be gone for a week. We will survive with you off the island for a few days," Alejandro said, raising a brow at my impatience.

I scoffed. "I have complete faith in your ability to keep my home from burning down. I am more concerned with how your conversation with Pavel went." He pursed his lips in thought. The hesitation did not bode well for my desires to delay the bastard's requests for a meeting. "Regina could make a nice supper out of your tongue if you aren't inclined to use it," I warned him.

He sighed, finally opening his mouth to tell me what I needed to know. "He does not want to wait. We knew he would be impatient. His livelihood is at stake."

"More like his life," I returned. "I do not care what you have to do to make him understand, but I will have nothing to do with Pavel until I have Isa safe on my island. He *will* wait until I deem it an appropriate time to discuss his removal as Pakhan."

"I'm fairly certain talking about his removal won't help him lean toward patience," Alejandro said with a shake of the head.

"So remind him he has sons. He doesn't need five of them, but I could kill one for every opportunity he takes to annoy me," I said, making my way to the windows to overlook the pool area. The Mediterranean Sea shimmered with azure waters down below where the compound I called home sprawled into the hillside of my private island, *El Infierno*.

A simple walk down a wooden path would take me to the beach that I knew Isa would love when she finally came to the island and got over her fear of the water.

"Mi hijo, you cannot threaten a man's lineage because you are impatient. Off with you!" Regina said, shooing me toward the front door. My bag already waited for me in the car, loaded by the house staff.

"Verify the arrangements with everyone one last time,

please?" I asked her. She rolled her eyes but nodded her head in agreement. She would do as I asked, because she knew better than most what the consequences might be should I be disappointed. I may not murder my mother's best friend, but I had no such loyalty toward random business owners who didn't do as *El Diablo* commanded.

"I'm going!" I protested, making my way down to the path that would take me to the marina.

When I'd hurried down the steps, there was no doubt in my mind, as I watched my men load my neon orange McLaren onto my yacht, that Isa would need time to adjust to her new life.

She'd have ten days.

Tossing my keys to the valet driver, I climbed out of the McLaren and made my way toward him. "Not a scratch," I warned. He nodded his understanding, eyeing my car like the masterpiece it was. I had several vehicles in my garage, but the McLaren was my favorite for the moment.

Moon was a massive white structure and looked commercial in the front, but the interior was pure luxury, and no hotel in Ibiza Town could compete with the views from the pool area. It would be the perfect place to seduce Isa and start our lives together, second only to my home.

Sadly, that wasn't an option. Convincing Isa to go up to a hotel room with a strange man would be tricky enough. Taking her home with me would prove impossible.

As I made my way into the hotel lobby, the reception desk shone with the brilliance of blue stone mosaics artfully placed along the front. "What can I do for you, Sir?" the woman behind the desk asked, her lips moving before she even glanced up from her computer. The moment she did, her eyes widened, and she dropped her mouth open. "Señor Ibarra," she said, reaching out a hand to probe the manager standing next to her.

He grinned, bringing up the reservations on his computer. "Señor Ibarra, I have you for ten nights in the Penthouse Suite. Is that correct?" he asked.

I nodded in response. "I trust the couple didn't give you any trouble with switching to the private villa?"

"Not at all. They were shocked, understandably, but thrilled to have a space to themselves in such a way. Thank you for your generosity. We would have accommodated your request either way, of course," he said.

"Of course," I agreed. The man wasn't stupid enough to think that anyone in Ibiza could deny me what I wanted without risking his head.

He handed me the key card for my suite. "Your bags will be delivered shortly."

"The arrangements for the party are in order, I presume?"

"Invites have been sent to the hotel, along with very specific instructions, as requested," he confirmed. I nodded without another word, turning and making my way to the elevator that would take me to the Penthouse Suite on the top floor of the hotel.

A woman followed me in, sliding her body in front of me to press the button for her floor with a smile. I pulled my phone from my pocket, ignoring her presence entirely as I scrolled through my text messages to pass the time. The woman stepped off with a huff, clearly unaccustomed to being dismissed so readily. I'd gotten that reaction often over the past sixteen months.

But none of them could elicit even a modicum of interest from me. It was a reaction I never could have expected, something I would have mocked my men for before laying eyes on my princesa.

Stepping out of the elevator on the top floor, I strode across the hall to the only door. The Penthouse I would spend my week in occupied the entire level, and a quick swipe of the key card turned the light green so I could step into the room.

I pushed the door open, making my way past the entry table and into the kitchen of the suite. Through the living room, I passed the chess set resting on the coffee table as requested and moved to the sliders and opened them.

Stepping out onto a terrace, one of two on the level with our suite, in addition to the private rooftop terrace we had to ourselves, I looked out over the water as my phone dinged with the alert of a new message.

I swallowed as I read the memo from Joaquin. It was just one simple word. Nothing that should have changed my life, but it did.

Landed.

Isa was in Ibiza.

3

ISA

The sun hit my face in a crash of warmth the moment we stepped out of the airport, lugging our bags behind us. If Chicago hadn't been warm before we'd left, I might have collapsed into a puddle with the joy I felt in that moment.

The air didn't sting my face, and I didn't have to suffer through the cold weather without a jacket.

There was only sunshine and blue sky as I tipped my head up to search for clouds. Not a single one lingered on the horizon, nothing to taunt me with the promise of dreary weather lurking around the corner. The breeze was practically nonexistent, but it smelled like saltwater.

I'd never understood what people meant by that scent. Having never been near the ocean before, I wouldn't have thought I'd understand it so instinctively. But there was no doubt in my mind that was what it was.

"How does it smell like the ocean and pine trees all at the same time?" Chloe asked. I realized she was right when I drew in another deep lungful of island air.

"The beauty of Ibiza," Hugo said with a grin. "When we

get away from the airport, you'll smell the almond flowers too. It's just...Ibiza," he said, exhaling a huge breath as he closed his eyes and tipped his head up to the sun above. "It's good to be home."

"I can't imagine whatever possessed you to come to Chicago. If this is what it's like all the time, then I never want to leave," I joked, stepping out of the way when a large crowd of travelers came out of the airport behind us.

"You could always stay," Hugo said with a shrug, but his eyes turned sad as he tilted his face away from mine. The reminder that the end of the trip meant the end of seeing him every day plagued me.

"Where are your parents?" I asked to change the conversation.

"Oh, they aren't coming," he said, rubbing the back of his neck the way he did whenever I said something that made him uncomfortable. "They're really traditional. People aren't allowed to visit our house, so the program booked us a couple of hotel rooms in Ibiza Town for the week instead."

"They what?" I furrowed my brow at him, opening my mouth to say something when Joaquin interrupted.

"Trust me, it's better this way. You don't want to meet them unless you absolutely have to," he said, stepping toward one of the two black SUVs waiting at the curb. I followed him, only halting when Hugo caught my arm in his grip and pulled me toward the second vehicle.

"We aren't going together?"

He shook his head, a note of sadness in his face as he studied me. "Joaquin and Gabriel are going home."

"Oh," Chloe said. The smile dropped off her face while she watched them load their bags into the back and turn to us. The moment was awkward at best. I wouldn't say that I'd gotten close to either of Hugo's brothers, as they kept their distance from us most of the time, but still the knowledge that I may never see them again was like a prick to my heart.

A foreshadowing of the pain that would come when I lost Hugo.

Gabriel stepped forward, wrapping his arms around me and pulling me into a hug as tears stung my eyes. "Get into some trouble while you're here, yeah?" he asked, resting his chin on top of my head.

"Yeah," I said with a sniffle, drawing back to look at Joaquin.

He surprised me when he sighed, stepping forward and hugging me in the same way his brother had. He stared down at me when he pulled back, wiping a tear off my cheek. "Head high, *mi reina*. It will be over before you know it."

He stepped back, keeping his eyes on mine while he and Gabriel climbed into the back of the SUV without another word. It pulled off, and I looked over to Hugo to find him studying me intently.

"That bastard didn't even say goodbye!" Chloe protested as Hugo sprung into motion suddenly. He grabbed our bags, loading them into the other vehicle while I watched Joaquin and Gabriel drive away.

Until they faded to nothing but a memory.

B y the time the car service dropped us off at the hotel, I was ready to collapse into a puddle on the closest bed.

Chloe had other ideas as she practically danced her way into the boutique hotel with her suitcase swaying behind her as she walked. Hugo stepped up to the concierge, speaking Spanish with the man behind the desk while he checked us in.

"Señorita," a man from behind the desk said as he stepped around. He reached back over, grabbing two postcard-sized sheets off his desk. He held them out to Chloe and me, and I took the thick cardstock in my hand. The champagne invitation sparkled in the light with gold paint that dripped down it so luxuriously I touched it with a finger to see if it was still wet.

It felt like liquid sin, as my fingers slid over the glossy surface.

"Our sister hotel is hosting an exclusive party tonight. I'm certain the guests would love to see you there," he said. I turned my eyes up to his, meeting his brown stare as I tried to hand the invite back to him.

"I wouldn't even know what to wear to something like this," I laughed.

"It's by the pool!" Chloe said, shoving her invite in my face as if I couldn't read the words on my own.

Meet me in the moonlight.

Was it normal for an invitation to seem so personal?

"A bikini and some kind of coverup is the typical dress code," the man agreed.

"I don't own a—"

"I brought you one. Thank you!" Chloe chimed as Hugo stepped forward and took another invitation from the man who scowled at him. He said nothing, as it was simply decided that he'd be attending any party along with us. That they seemed more inclined to invite women didn't bode well, but there was no diminishing Chloe's high.

"I've heard of this hotel," she squealed as Hugo led us to the elevators at the side of the lobby. "It's *the* hotel in Ibiza. I can't believe we got invites."

"I just want to take a nap," I protested. It wasn't that I didn't want to enjoy my time in Ibiza. I absolutely wanted nothing more than to step outside my comfort zone and experience what life could be like if I let myself enjoy it.

Just not right that second and not jumping into the deep end with a moonlit pool party.

"You've got plenty of time," Hugo said with a chuckle as he wrapped an arm around my shoulders and gave me an odd look. "In typical Ibiza fashion, the party doesn't start until midnight."

"I'm usually in bed by then," I snapped, shrugging off his shoulder. "What's up with you? What's with the faces?" I asked, jabbing him in the side with an aggressive finger.

"He's probably just wondering how we can convince you to lose your v-card tonight," Chloe said as the elevator doors closed us into the tight space.

"I'm really not," Hugo groaned. "Please don't make me think about her sex life."

"I don't have a sex life," I said, rolling my eyes as Chloe's face filled my vision.

"That changes tonight," she said. "We're in fucking Ibiza, Isa. Going to a party full of wealthy men who probably know *how* to fuck. Don't be the virgin when you go off to college. Please," she begged.

I bit my lip, wondering what was so wrong with being a virgin. Watching my friends have their hearts walked all over throughout school by boy after boy, I had to think I was the lucky one. It wasn't like I was waiting because I believed my one true love would come to sweep me off my feet.

It just hadn't happened.

It was hard to be interested in high school boys when I dreamt of phantom hands reaching out from the inky darkness to wrap me in a suffocating embrace. It was hard to want a boy to hold my hand at the movie theater when I woke up in a sweat after dreaming of hands on my throat.

How could a man ever compare to a phantom who didn't exist?

"Fine," I groaned as we stepped out of the elevator and made our way down the hall. I wouldn't give it up to just any man. He couldn't touch me in the way I wanted, not if I wanted to remember who I was supposed to be, but I didn't want someone to make love to me, either.

My life was a juxtaposition of reality and desire, and of using one to beat back the other daily. Phantom shadows stood everywhere, calling me to the dark. Pulling me from the depths of memories better left in my past.

As Chloe pushed open the door to our room, I moved into the space and dropped my suitcase by one of the beds. *"Estoy enfermo,"* I joked, likely butchering the pronunciation and looking away from Hugo as he smirked at me.

"You're not sick," he laughed. "We won't let you stay in the hotel room tonight, *entiende*?"

"*Claro*," I sighed, refusing to look back at him. I wished I knew more than just the basic Spanish he'd taught me, and would have loved nothing more than to curse him out in his first language.

Hugo said his goodbyes, going to the room next to ours to get some sleep before the party. I knew it wasn't worth the effort to fight. I stared out the window, looking at the center of Ibiza Town in the distance while my face burned with the heat of the sun.

Then I turned and went to take my nap, hoping it would rejuvenate me enough that the dark side of desire stopped calling to me.

4

RAFAEL

Making my way through the lobby to the pool area at the back of the hotel, I admired the dim lighting and orchid glow to the water, courtesy of the underwater lights I'd arranged on Isa's behalf, in her favorite color. Lounges remained on one side of the pool, but the rest of the deck had been cleared for mingling or dancing. People already enjoyed the festivities, either swimming in the warm water of the pool, making their way down to the private beach, or dancing away to the steady and seductive beat of the approved list of music I'd given to the manager for the night's event.

I loved Ibiza's techno as much as the next person, but Isa required something more subtle for her first foray into the world of sin and desire.

The closed guest list meant that, while there were enough people around to make her feel comfortable, it wasn't overwhelming. We wouldn't be trapped in a crush of bodies when I convinced her to dance with me. We'd be able to move to the cabanas on the beach if she wanted to talk without the music serving as a distraction. I had arranged everything to absolute perfection while the poolside bar served drinks faster than normal. The threat of displeasing me served as a wonderful enticement for good service, but I didn't care about the service any of the other partygoers received.

Only one woman mattered to me.

Feminine nails trailed over my shoulders, threatening to leave pink marks on my skin as I jolted away from the invading touch. "Hello, handsome," the woman purred, staring up into my face as she gave me her brightest smile.

"I'm with someone," I said, turning on my heel to scour the party for Isa. I'd have recognized her anywhere after spending far too many months looking at her photos, but there was no sign of my unique beauty anywhere.

I suddenly wished I hadn't left my phone in my room, wanting nothing more than to check for updates from Hugo. It didn't matter that he hadn't messaged me to say they were on their way a mere ten minutes prior. I needed to see her.

If I had to suffer through her absence for much longer, I might climb out of my skin.

Or skin somebody alive. The latter was preferable.

Making my way to the pool, I stepped down into the shallow water and made my way to one of the lounges in the shallow edges. Water slid over my skin as I laid out my body in a way that would give me a perfect view of the entrance.

Time ticked by in an unending cycle while I waited, watching as a handful of women filtered into the pool area with bright smiles. More than one set of eyes landed on me, naïve to the monster lurking in their midst, but my single-minded focus on the entryway squashed anything that might have developed into an unfortunate and deceptive situation I would have difficulty pulling Isa back from.

The manager's eyes met mine as he walked past, a subtle

and secretive smile curving his lips up. Everyone wanted to know the woman who captivated El Diablo. Everyone wanted to be part of the rise of a queen.

Only a few chosen individuals could know of her existence until I got her home to *El Infierno*.

Even if I hadn't been watching, I'd have known the minute she walked into the pool area. Her presence sucked all the oxygen from the air, demanding attention in the way that only Isa could.

The pictures I'd seen of her through the years hadn't done her justice. Nothing could compare to her in the flesh after the months that had separated us.

I waited for her to turn her head away from her friend Chloe. Watched her walk in her wedges as if she wasn't sure how to navigate in them, but still managed it with a delicate grace many couldn't hope to achieve. A tropical printed dress covered her bathing suit, vaguely sheer enough to hint at the curves underneath. I focused on the line of cleavage the cover-up revealed down the center of her torso, dipping low enough to show the string that connected the two sides of her bikini together. Rope wove between the fabric on either side, connecting it over her tight stomach and then flowing down to her feet to cover her legs except for the slit that rode up to reveal her thigh.

I turned my attention to Hugo to glare for a moment, meeting his eyes as they widened. He had the grace to look sheepish as he shrugged. I moved my gaze back to Isa, swallowing down my rage that he'd allowed her to leave the hotel in that dress.

Had she been with me, it would have been fine. She'd have me to keep the wolves at bay, but knowing that other men had seen her before I could prevent them from molesting her with their greedy stares?

It set my blood to flame.

She glanced over at Hugo, following his gaze to the pool. The same shock I'd felt years ago vibrated through me the moment her eyes hit mine. The moment those stunning multi-colored eyes connected with mine, the music stopped. Everything ceased to exist but the way her breath caught and she parted her lips only slightly.

Her right canine snagged her lip, nearly biting it in a move that spoke to just how little Isa wanted to commit to anything.

She lived a life of half-measures, even when expressing her desire for me.

I'd fucking fix that.

5
ISA

"Oh fuck," I whispered, my lips burning with the words. There wasn't an expletive in the world that could begin to describe how screwed I was the moment his eyes touched mine.

Something shifted within me, forbidden desires rising to the surface despite my attempts to shove them down deep where they belonged.

"What?" Chloe asked, moving at my side. I felt the moment she saw him. Her body went rigid; her breathing turned shallow as she studied the panther watching me.

Anyone else, and I would have said I was mistaken. That his eyes could only be on my stunning friend, who wore her sexuality like only a woman who felt free could truly do. But somehow, there was no doubting where those mismatched eyes landed.

I felt them on my skin. Felt them in my soul.

I turned away from him, making my way to the bar while Chloe raced to keep up with me, laughing. "What are you doing? You need to get your ass in that pool."

"No, I need a damn drink. That's what I need."

"You don't drink," Hugo said as he stepped up beside me at the bar.

"I do now," I snapped at him, spinning forward when the other man's eyes met mine once again in my view behind Hugo. A sinful smirk graced his face as his lips tipped up.

"And what exactly are you drinking?" Hugo asked, nodding his head to the bartender.

Groaning, I dropped my head on the bar. "I don't know. What do I start with?"

"Wine," Hugo laughed. "Maybe I won't end up holding your hair back while you puke this way." He turned to the bartender, catching his attention and ordering. *"Un vino tinto."* My eyes tracked the bartender's movements, watching as he poured the liquid from the bottle and into the glass.

Even watching the process, anxiety hit me the moment he placed the glass in front of me. Without a seal on the bottle, the memory of being drugged felt closer than ever. I swallowed back the panic attack that hovered at the horizons, threatening to blur my vision, and lifted the glass to my mouth. Forcing down a hard swallow of the liquid, I found it easier to breathe as soon as the first gulp went down despite the bitter flavor.

It was irrational to see drugs in all fluids everywhere I went, but after my sister had played a part in my near date rape, I found it almost impossible not to suspect everyone of such a thing.

"What are you doing?" Chloe asked, taking the wineglass from my hand and setting it on the bar top. "What happened to living?"

"I'm living. I'm drinking and enjoying the music," I argued.

"You're *hiding*. Let him show you exactly what it is to live,

Isa," she said, biting her bottom lip as she looked over her shoulder at him.

"I am not hiding," I whispered, rolling my eyes up to stare at the moon in the sky overhead. "I'm being practical. I wouldn't know what to do with a man like *that*."

"Honey, nobody knows what to do with a man like that. That doesn't mean you can't lay back and let him take you to heaven," she giggled. Hugo groaned his frustration at our side, drawing a laugh from even me despite my anxiety. "You can't stay a virgin forever."

"Who the hell said I would want to?" I took another sip of my wine, fortifying my decision with every swallow of the bitter cherry flavor. I hated it instinctively but couldn't stop drinking. Not when I had a feeling my life was about to be turned upside down. "I just think someone a little less..." I paused, chewing the corner of my lip as I thought of the right word, "intense would be a good start."

"You don't want to lose your virginity like me with someone who fumbles around and doesn't know what he's doing. You want the mystical unicorn who looks like he could make your vagina implode with a *look* and make you one of those rare lucky as fuck women to orgasm when you lose your virginity. Just go talk to him," she urged, her smile turning reassuring as she studied the panic in my face.

"I can't," I told her, shaking my head. Her eyes filled with disappointment, and I hated knowing that my friend worried so much about the seriousness of my life. Chloe was one of the few people I'd ever told about the accident and how it had unraveled Odina, even though we were too young to understand what it would mean one day.

"I don't think you'll have much choice," she blurted, her tone changing to a sharp excitement. Grabbing my head, she spun me to face the pool. The man stood from the lounge he'd laid on in a graceful unfolding of limbs. He stepped off the lounge ledge and into the shallow end of the pool, making his way up the steps slowly.

His eyes held mine as he moved, and Hugo and Chloe had to use their hands at my shoulders to turn my body to face him as he slowly made his way through the water. Water dripped down his broad shoulders, over the rippling muscles of his torso, and my breath caught as I watched it trail over his olive skin. He smirked when my eyes traveled back up to his face, his gaze knowing as he studied me intently.

His concentration never left my face, something so unnerving about the single-minded focus as he prowled toward me like a predator in the night. With his impossibly beautiful face and striking eyes, he looked like something from another world.

From somewhere meant to tempt women to their deaths.

One of the attendants handed him a towel as he emerged from the pool, but he never even glanced at her as he took it and held it at his side.

"I should have worn a potato sack," I whispered to Chloe. She burst into laughter at my side, stepping away as his long gait closed the distance between us. The faintest hint of stubble covered his face, his dark hair dry and parted to the side in a half-styled, tumbled in bed kind of look. As his face filled my vision, he leaned further into my bubble than was comfortable.

Towering over me, with a thumb and forefinger he caught me beneath the chin and lifted my face up, so he could stare down at me with the same intensity he had when he'd been on the other side of the pool.

One blue eye, one green, those eyes narrowed on me like a panther narrowing in on its dinner.

I knew he'd eat me alive, but I hadn't expected the weird déjà vu I felt when he reached up his other hand and touched the soft skin just under the brown part in my left eye and caressed it with an odd tenderness. His touch burned me as he crowded me, crossing all the acceptable boundaries that should have existed between two people who'd never spoken a word to one another. His minty breath wafted over my face as he loosed a sigh, dropping his forehead against mine and closing his eyes while he sank his teeth into his lush bottom lip.

I stared up at him for a moment, turning my gaze over to where Chloe watched with her mouth parted in shock. She waved a hand at herself, seeming to encourage the crossing of all the boundaries I should've had.

But there was nothing about him that made me want to push him away. None of the revulsion I expected to feel that someone would invade my space. Just an odd sense of belonging as I turned my face back to his to find his eyes open and watching me. He pulled his forehead away from mine, tilting his head as he watched me.

I spun back for the bar quickly, grasping my wine in my hand and taking a massive swallow. Chloe elbowed me in the side when he didn't walk away, giggling at me as I tossed back the rest of my wine. "*Otro?*" the bartender asked, moving to refill my glass as I nodded. I sucked back more wine with none of the hesitation I'd felt before, knowing he clearly had no intention of taking the hint and leaving me alone, despite my best efforts to ignore him.

"*He estado pensando en ti,*" he said at my back. The rough, raspy sound of his voice curled around the words, making them his and claiming them in a way that I would never find again. Even if someone said the same words, they'd never be like him.

He left me with no choice but to turn and face him, and I swallowed back my nerves before doing just that. As I pressed my spine into the bar to keep as much distance between us, he eyed the gap as if it was an affront to everything he knew.

"Lo siento. No hablo Español," I said with a sheepish smile.

"I've been thinking about you," he murmured, the accent of his voice in English somehow just as attractive as when he'd spoken Spanish. I bit my bottom lip as he stepped closer, reaching down to take my hand in his. He ran calloused fingers over my palm, staring down at it as if he needed to memorize all the lines.

"That's very sweet," I said with an uncomfortable laugh. "Is it normal to be so forward in Ibiza?" I asked, pulling my hand back from his grip. He released it reluctantly.

"Yes," Hugo laughed, inserting himself into the conversation and giving a warning look to the stranger who seemed intent on invading my space. "Spanish men are not known for subtlety."

"Have some more liquid courage," Chloe urged me, slipping my wine into my hand. I brought it to my lips, already feeling the effects. The stranger moved next to me, tapping his fingers on the bar once before the bartender raced to serve him. Chloe elbowed me in the side, making wide eyes at the service he commanded.

"Un chupito de whisky," he said, watching as his drink was poured. He left it on the bar, turning his attention back to me and staring down at me.

Unnerving me with every second that passed.

"What are you so afraid of, *mi princesa*?" he asked, his eyes gleaming as his lips tipped up into a brilliant smile.

I huffed a quiet laugh, my own lips forming a hesitant smile to match his as an odd moment of intimacy passed between us. With his multicolored gaze bearing down on my own, it was impossible to deny that it felt like he saw me. That he saw everything that longed to break free from my carefully crafted persona of obedience and responsibility. "You," I whispered. The admission echoed between us as my friends stilled at my side.

He tilted his head, something dark passing behind his eyes. Reaching down to take my hand in his, he tugged me away from the bar and toward the area where other people danced. *"Baila conmigo a la luz de la luna,"* he said, his deep voice raising the hair on my arms as those sinful lips formed Spanish words so smoothly I nearly melted into a puddle at his feet.

"I don't understand," I said with an awkward smile, shaking my head as Chloe inserted herself and pried my wine glass from my hand while he guided me away.

My friends were traitors.

"Dance with me in the moonlight," he translated, pulling harder until I stumbled into his arms.

"I don't know how to dance like this," I admitted, glancing to the side at the women who rolled their hips and bodies to the smooth Spanish beat that pulsed through the air.

"I'll teach you, *mi princesa*," he said, dropping his voice low. His hands touched the back of my shoulders, giving me a little shake as he smiled. Rough fingertips trailed over the bare skin of my back to either side of my spine as his eyes held mine. I leaned into the touch, craving more despite myself, and he used the increase in the distance between us to move them to my hips. The pressure of his fingers guided them to the music, moving them in ways I'd have never considered possible.

My hands dug into his shoulders, clinging to him in the belief that I would fall on my face if not for his support. With a glance around, I worried what I must look like with him guiding me through the motions of dancing in a way the others did without hesitation. A few people around the space watched us in shock, only worsening the insecurity I felt. When I turned back to him, he touched his forehead to mine again. "Only me and the music," he whispered, winding my hips in a roll from side to side.

I moved as he guided, until the pressure of his fingers faded and I dared to try to move on my own. I might have looked like a monstrosity for all I knew, but he never let me feel it. Not with his skin beneath my hands, his eyes on mine, and his touch burning through me.

There was only him.

We continued to dance for a few songs, my body growing more comfortable with every song that passed, until sweat dripped down the back of my neck beneath the curtain of my hair. Tucking a strand behind my ear, he pulled away and drew me to the edge of the patio. Stairs at the edge led down to the beach, and I hesitated at the top.

Heels, even wedges, were new to me. Wearing them in sand didn't seem like a promising thought. I followed him down the steps anyway, pausing at the bottom to bend down and take them off so I didn't break my neck. He grinned, shaking his head before I could get the straps undone. He grabbed me around my thighs and lifted me off my feet to walk me to one of the daybeds set up in the sand. Squealing with nervous laughter, I stared down at him as he set me down gently.

"You're trouble," I teased, shaking my head at him.

He smiled that double edged sword of his as his face took on a dark glow that called to the worst parts of me. "Princesa, you have no idea."

My mother's warnings rang in my ears as I contemplated what she would have to say about the mystery man consuming my thoughts and tempting me to be reckless. "Does trouble have a name?"

"Rafe. What is *mi princesa's* name?" he asked, the smooth notes of his voice pulling me to smile.

"Will you call me it if I tell you?" I teased, laughing when he leaned in and touched a hand to my face.

"Would you want me to?" he returned quickly.

I bit my lip, shaking my head. I contemplated giving a fake name, anything to make it easier to walk away and never see him again when all this ended. "Isa," I said instead.

"Isa," he murmured, leaning in to run his nose up the side of mine. His lips touched mine briefly while he held my eyes, nothing but a delicate brush of his soft flesh on mine. "*Eres mia.*"

He touched his mouth to mine again, more firmly, his mouth tormenting me with a delicate tease that I couldn't get enough of. I wasn't even aware of moving closer. Of leaning into the touch and needing more, until he curled a hand beneath the curtain of my hair and held me still as he teased the seam of my lips with his tongue.

All my defenses dropped with just the feeling of his mouth on mine, his tongue inside me sparking me to life as I sucked back a ragged breath that felt like my first true one since the accident.

I was lost.

6

RAFAEL

She shivered in my arms, her lungs expanding with air as she drew me deeper into her. There was a moment of satisfaction, of *knowing* that the wait had been worth it.

That she was worth every second.

Her tongue met mine hesitantly, her hand touching the side of my neck as she pressed her lips to mine more fully. I kissed her slowly, cautiously testing the boundaries of what she may have been comfortable with. My innocent Isa faded, spurred on by my touch as she curved her body into mine as the sense of rightness filled her.

She was mine, and I was hers. Inexperienced or not, her body wouldn't allow her to hesitate in the melding of our souls. I pulled her even closer, my fingers tangling in the hair at the back of her head in my urgency to feel her. Shifting her to her back, I rolled her beneath me and leaned over her as I pulled my lips away from hers just enough to sink my teeth into her bottom lip.

The gasp she gave me resonated through me, a recognition of everything I couldn't possibly know. Isa may have been innocent, but that didn't mean her desires had to be. I kissed her for real the next time, a deep conquering of her lips that spoke to all the impatience in my body. She moaned in response, lifting to meet me halfway as I bruised her lips in my determination to possess her. Gliding my hand from around the back of her neck, my fingers softened as they trailed delicately to the front of her throat. A single line from her chin and down the soft skin until my fingers touched her sternum.

Her lungs heaved in response to me, goosebumps rising on her skin as my touch trailed over her shoulders and down to take one of her hands in each of mine.

Lacing my fingers with hers, I guided her hands away from my body and pressed them to the daybed beneath us. Her face turned shocked for a moment as I raised our hands up the bed to rest beside her head, and gave her more of my weight. Trapping her beneath me, knowing that for just that moment there was nowhere she could go, unleashed a bit of the monster within me as I smirked down at her with all the ferocity in me.

She tested the bonds of my grip on hers, pushing up while I leaned further into her. There was a moment of fear in her eyes that bled to excitement as I watched. Knowing that, beneath the obedient exterior, my princesa had a deviant side only showed me just how perfect she was for me.

My grip tightened on hers, lacing our fingers together as I watched her process what she wanted and try to reconcile it with who she believed herself to be. The darkness inside her called to me, and I wondered if she saw the nightmare staring down at her.

There was no doubt that was what I was, but I was *her* nightmare.

Whether she wanted me or not.

"*Quiero ser tu dueño*," I whispered, touching the tip of my nose to hers. Her back arched, pushing her breasts to my chest before she lifted her neck slightly to capture my lips with hers. The young woman I'd watched in Chicago never would have allowed herself to be in such a compromising position with other people around. She'd never want to risk people seeing her devoured by a stranger.

But my poor Isa was so lost to our bond and the inexplicable connection between us that those people ceased to exist. I didn't have such luxuries, given I had to force myself to control my impulses.

This wasn't one night with a stranger, but the start of our lives together.

I chuckled, touching my lips to her cheek. Her head rolled to the side, her body moving underneath me as I whispered against her skin. "*Pasa la noche conmigo.*"

"I don't understand," she said with an uneasy laugh as I pulled away to grin at her. She knew damn well what I'd said, her body going tight suddenly as she considered the words and tried to buy time before she had to make her choice. But my Isa could talk herself out of winning the lottery if given the chance, and I'd never allow such a thing.

"Spend the night with me," I answered anyway, taking away the time she'd stalled for.

"I don't think that's such a good idea," she whispered, her head shaking lightly as she frowned and her demons crept back into her gaze. I touched my lips to hers once more, trailing down to her throat to nip the flesh there while she gasped.

"Trust me, *mi princesa*. It is a *very* good idea," I murmured, watching as she bit her own lip hard enough to draw blood in her confusion. "Let me show you what it is to burn."

She swallowed, determination settling in her eyes when she finally nodded her agreement.

"Okay," she whispered. I stood from her slowly, holding out a hand to help her to the edge of the daybed. She hesitated briefly, reconsidering as her eyes met mine and she sucked back deep breaths.

The moment she placed her smaller hand in mine willingly, she sealed whatever question had remained as to her fate.

I would never let her go.

*I lifted her off the daybed, her body pliant in my arms as she gave me everything I needed to know there'd been no mistake.

Somehow, from across the street when she'd been a girl, I'd known the woman she'd grow to be would become my obsession. I wanted to devour her body, to know every inch of her physically, as I did about her life. Then I wanted to pry inside her head, to understand how she had come to be so guarded.

She stared down at me, nerves creeping back into her expression when I set her on the step to go back to the pool area. Touching my palm to the small of her back, I guided her up the steps and kept my hand on her as I hurried her through the party. Hugo and her friend danced with strangers, their eyes landing on us as we emerged from the beach.

I nodded to Hugo as Chloe gave Isa wide eyes. She mouthed something to her, a check in to ensure her friend was an entirely willing participant in going to bed with me. Isa swallowed at my side but nodded her head with a shy smile as her cheeks pinked when she looked up at me.

I turned my stare down to her, kissing her temple as we entered the lobby and made our way to the elevator that would take us to the Penthouse. Ten days to convince Isa to abandon everything she knew. Ten days to bring her to life and show her everything she never knew she needed.

I had to hope it would be enough. We stepped into the elevator as Isa looked around her surroundings, her nerves increasing as I pressed the button for the penthouse. She turned her eyes up to mine, nibbling at the corner of her mouth as her doubts crept back in. Curling her into me, I tipped her head up and licked the seam of her mouth until she parted for me and invited me inside.

I'd spend the entire time inside her if it kept her from over-analyzing our contrasting financial lives. They would be the least of her concerns.

She melted into me, her body like liquid in my arms as she let me maneuver her until her back touched the rear wall of the elevator. Firm strokes of my tongue against hers, and I took everything she gave. When the elevator doors opened, I pulled away so suddenly that she swayed with the loss of my touch and let me take her hand to guide her to the penthouse doors. I shoved them open as quickly as I could, dropping my keycard on the entryway table and guiding her through the living room of my suite to the master bedroom. The room glowed with the soft light of the moon filtering in through the massive sliding glass doors that offered stunning views of the ocean. I hated to leave her, but had to in order to rinse the sand from my feet in the bathroom. Her eyes lit as she walked over to the doors, watching the waves crash against the barely illuminated sand as she slid one of the doors open and stepped onto the private balcony.

I followed when I was able, stepping up behind her and pulling her chocolate hair over one of her shoulders to give me access to her neck. Trailing my lips over her skin and trailing them down to her shoulder, I bit the flesh there while she sucked in a breath. As soon as my teeth released her, she spun to me suddenly with her lips pursed in indecision. "If we're going to do this, then there's something you should know."

I touched the rope that held together the sides of her dress, slowly untying the knot as my hands brushed against her breasts with every movement. "What's that, *mi princesa*?"

"I've never..." She paused, swallowing as the tie released finally and the sides of fabric loosened to show more of her bikini-clad breasts. I touched the gauzy fabric on her shoulders, sliding it out on either side until it was only a second from slipping off her body. "I'm a virgin," she blurted, her eyes disappointed as she waited for the rejection she thought might come.

If she'd been anyone else, I wouldn't have had any interest in going further, so I couldn't say the fear was unwarranted. But with Isa, her virginity was far less complicated.

It meant I didn't need to hunt new victims and murder the men who'd touched what was mine.

With a secret smile, I brushed the fabric off her shoulders despite her words. The dress slipped from her body, gliding down her smooth skin like liquid torment. It puddled at her feet, leaving her in nothing but an emerald green string bikini that hugged her curves tightly. The color brought out her eyes, and there could be no denying that she'd somehow chosen to wear my favorite color. It shone in the moonlight against her fawn-like skin as I touched the first of her freckles on her chest.

I'd count them when she slept, just as I'd counted the freckles on her face when I stared at her photo over the past sixteen months.

Stepping out of her shoes, she dropped her hands to the waistband of my swim trunks and the laces that confined me, but I leaned forward and snagged her lip with my teeth. As much as Isa may put on a brave face, and as much as I needed the release after the necessity of my celibacy while I waited for her, Isa needed to know what pleasure was.

To lose her virginity to me was not a kindness, and I'd need to work to make it less painful for her. Taking her hands in mine, I placed them on my chest. They brushed the raised flesh of my marks. The seven tallies tingled under her fingers, unsurprising, given I'd never been able to tolerate being touched there in the past. As I walked backwards into the master bedroom and encouraged her to follow me with a firm grip on her waist, her gaze wandered to the marks beneath her hands.

"What are these?" she asked as I sat her on the edge of the bed next to me.

"Penitencia," I replied. "Penance. It is a family thing."

"Does it hurt?" she asked, leaning forward to brush her innocent mouth against the scars. The void inside me swelled, threatening to explode with the knowledge that she would offer such a touch so innocently. Isa didn't do physical affection easily, and the care in the movement seemed to shock even her as she pulled back.

"Not anymore," I murmured, tucking a strand of hair behind her ear and kissing her mouth.

I freed her from the confines of her cage, preparing to show her all the places she was too afraid to go on her own.

As I laid her out beneath me, leaning over her and entwining my tongue with hers in a dance designed to drive her mad with lust, I slid a hand beneath her neck and untied the knot for her bikini. The one at her spine came next, and finally the flimsy fabric entrapping her breasts and hiding my woman from me came loose. I slid it off her slowly, baring her breasts to my view for the first time. I took my weight off her, letting her settle herself in the center of the bed and get comfortable.

Isa's nerves betrayed her as she squirmed when my eyes strayed down to take her in. Her body was an hourglass, soft and ripe for the taking. My rough hands looked so filthy against her smooth and lightly freckled skin. There wasn't a tan line in sight, and I loved knowing that she was entirely unmarked when she came to me.

It would mean that every tan line, every mark, every stain on her skin came from me.

I took one of her breasts in my hand, rubbing my thumb over the peak as she stared up at me. With nothing more than the thin scrap of material between her thighs to shield her from my view, I moved slowly out of fear that I would rush her.

That I'd take her too quickly in my urgency to possess her.

Instead, I tormented her nipple with my finger, leaning in to coax her to relax with my mouth on hers. When her tense body relaxed into the mattress, I shifted my weight and moved to crawl between her legs. Touching my hands to her thighs and moving to spread them, my fingers brushed over a slightly raised portion of skin. Withdrawing from her mouth, I glanced down at her leg as I moved closer to her. The scar glowed white in the moonlight, wrapping around her thigh twice and crossing over the inner corner. I brushed my hands over it, feeling Isa's eyes on me.

Filled with the need to avenge whatever had harmed my princess, I knew from one glance to her hardening features that she would be as forthcoming about her scars as I'd been with mine.

I'd wait, and then I'd know.

Then I'd *kill* whatever was responsible for her pain.

7
ISA

I wasn't sure what I'd expected to happen the moment he saw the scar. I didn't know of a single man who could think someone with that was beautiful. A hideous reminder of my stupidity and the way it had torn my family apart.

I'd expected disgust when his eyes found mine in the dim room. What I got was fury.

He was angry on my behalf, incorrectly assuming it had been anybody's fault but my own, but the scar on my leg was pale compared to the scars on my soul. To the feeling of being surrounded by darkness as shadows came closer to swallow me whole.

He closed the distance between us once again as his fingers splayed over the scar, spreading my legs even wider to make room for his muscled hips. His length pressed against the most intimate part of me, as hard as steel as he nestled between me like he was always meant to be there. His thumb touched my bottom lip, dragging the flesh down to show my teeth before he pressed the wetness to my nipple and drew a ragged breath from me.

"Rafe," I whispered, watching his eyes darken the moment the name left my lips. He leaned in, touching his wicked tongue to my nipple in a wet tease before he drew it into his mouth and sucked.

My hands went to his hair, both pulling him closer and trying to tug him away as sensation exploded through me. Blinding pleasure I'd never felt before drove me to the point of no return as I writhed beneath him. The sudden heat between my thighs was something out of a book. Something I'd only ever read about and never dreamed to have for myself.

It couldn't be possible for real people to feel this way. To burn from the inside and wonder how I didn't catch flame.

His hand touched my other breast, pinching the nipple harshly as he worshiped my right with his tongue. The shock of pain compared to the wet pleasure of his mouth made me gasp. "Please," I begged.

He slid his hand down from my breast to the strings at the side of my bikini bottom. Loosing the tie hurriedly, he shoved the scrap of fabric out of his way and did the same on the other side, until he could pull it from between my legs. I was suddenly naked with a man I had no business being with.

My apprehension went out the window the moment his finger touched me, sliding through me and exploring me. He groaned against my breast before releasing my nipple, moving his mouth to my lips again and kissing me with a need I didn't know a man could possess. His finger tormented me, brushing against my clit before sinking lower and touching my entrance. He pulled his lips from mine, staring at my face and watching as he pressed it inside me. I bit my lip, the feeling uncomfortable but not particularly painful. Totally lost to the way his mismatched eyes watched me. To the feeling of him looking inside me and watching me unravel.

"You're so wet for me, Princesa," he groaned, applying more pressure until he worked his finger inside of me. His thumb pressed against my clit, leaving me full and burning alive with need. He pumped that treacherous finger in and out of me slowly, driving me higher and closer to the precipice of something I didn't know I'd been capable of ever reaching.

Not that I'd tried.

A second finger joined the first, pressing in and stretching me while I winced from the burn. He grinned down at me, touching his lips to the valley between my breasts and lowering himself between my thighs. His lips trailed a kiss over my stomach until he laid flat on his and stared at the core of me. I closed my legs instinctively, shaking my head. "You don't have to—"

"Hush, Isa," he reprimanded. Leaning forward to flatten his tongue against my clit and making circles around it. He groaned the moment his mouth touched me, echoing the moan that caught in my throat and made me arch my back. The heat of his mouth was blinding.

Addicting.

Somehow, I knew I'd never be the same.

Those two fingers pumped inside of me slowly, preparing me for what I had to assume would be a bigger intrusion, considering what I'd felt when he lay on top of me.

He touched a part inside of me that felt different, hooking his fingers toward my front. "Oh," I gasped, writhing my hips up toward his face instinctively. He smiled into my clit the moment I grabbed his head, lost to what he built in me. "Fuck."

Pressing harder, he moved those fingers more firmly, and I shattered beneath him. Arching my back and spasming around him, I tightened my legs around his head as I lost control of my body.

It was his. He could keep it.

At that moment, I never wanted it back.

When I'd relaxed into a heap on the bed, fighting to catch my breath, he rose to his knees and then stood. Staring down at me, his fingers finally went to the laces of his swim trunks, untying them slowly while I watched. The material parted to show more of the adonis belt at his hips; the enticing carved muscle just below his defined abs drawing my gaze as he slid the fabric down his legs.

My breath caught, staring up at him. I might have looked like a fish, my lips opening and closing with no sound coming out. My legs closed on their own, even my vagina had the damn sense to know *that* wasn't going inside me.

It curved up toward his belly button, bobbing as he climbed back into the bed and parted my legs for him to settle between again. "I don't think—"

"We'll go slow," he chuckled, kissing me briefly as he reached between us. He gripped himself, dragging his head through my lips, and I shivered in anticipation. It was so much bigger than his fingers had been.

The moment he prodded my entrance, apprehension slithered through me. "Condom," I said, touching his stomach to stop him. He studied me for a moment, lost to his own thoughts before he nodded and reached into the nightstand.

Watching as he pulled a condom out, I didn't dwell on where they'd come from. Especially not when I read the name of the hotel on the packaging.

He opened the packet with his teeth, pulling it out and

sliding it over his length while I watched in fascination. Something about the sight of him touching himself pushed me back into desire, even despite the fear that he might split me in two. Tossing the empty packet to the side, he lined himself up once again and settled his weight over mine.

Holding my gaze, he nudged my entrance and pressed in. I burned as he worked his way inside with shallow thrusts, whimpering from the pain. "Shh," he soothed me, reaching between us to touch my clit and add more pleasure to his possession.

It didn't ease the sting as he worked through my tender tissues, but it somehow combined with the pleasure. Turning it into something else entirely. He groaned as he pressed deeper, his hips finally connecting with my body to signal that he'd somehow fit inside me. He kissed me, a rough possession that contrasted with the slow way he retracted his hips and slid back inside me. Testing. Teasing.

Pushing the boundaries of what I could take. But as the sharp pain of losing my virginity faded to a hollow ache, I reached down and took his ass in my hands. My nails dug into the flesh there, driving him harder and deeper. He moaned into my mouth, giving me what I asked for. He struck the end of me, sending a jolt of pain through me.

It horrified me to like it. It appalled me to know that what I'd always suspected lived inside me was truly there.

He took me in slow, hard drives as I wrapped my legs around his waist and opened myself to him further. His hand slipped out from between us, abandoning my clit to get deeper inside me.

I felt him everywhere.

His lips left mine, one of his hands supporting him on the bed and the other wrapping around the back of my neck to hold me still while his thrusts turned punishing, and he drew a gasp from me with every single one.

It hurt, but it felt so fucking good.

I grabbed the back of his head, holding him tight to me as he fucked me. With his eyes on mine, staring straight into me, there was nothing but him.

Nothing but his eyes on mine and him moving inside me.

"Fuck," he groaned through gritted teeth. "Fucking come, Princesa," he ordered, grinding his pubic bone against me with a roll of his hips.

I did, convulsing around him as my vision went white, and his deep groans filled my ears as his thrusts turned unpredictable and wild. He fucked me like he hated me. Until his length twitched inside me while he exploded into his own climax.

I fought for breath, my lungs heaving underneath Rafe where he'd collapsed on top of me.

I stared at the ceiling as he kissed my cheek, reality intruding as I came back down from the high of two orgasms.

What in the fuck had I done?

***

Rafe rolled off me finally, standing to discard the condom. I lay there, wondering what I was supposed to do.

A one-night stand was not the way to lose my virginity. Not wanting to overstay my welcome, I waited until he emerged from the bathroom and kept my eyes on the floor as I hurried into it myself.

I cleaned myself up, washed my hands and resisted the

urge to splash cold water on my face. The last thing I needed to do was look like a raccoon when I did my walk of shame and made my way back down to the party to hope Hugo and Chloe hadn't gone back to our hotel yet.

When I opened the door, Rafe sat on the bed. He hadn't bothered to put on clothes, lounging comfortably in his space. I averted my eyes with a shy smile, looking around the floor to see if I could find my bathing suit. When I found the bottoms, I picked them up off the floor and cursed the fact that he'd untied the strings.

"Come to bed, Princesa," he said, drawing my eyes when he chuckled.

"That's not necessary. I should get back before my friends worry." I tried not to let the words sound bitter, but I already knew sleeping with him had been a mistake. He'd set the bar too high, and I feared no other man could compete.

It wasn't enough he was the most beautiful man I'd ever seen, but he had to make losing my virginity a pleasurable experience too.

"So call them," he said, handing me his cell phone off the nightstand. I'd left mine with the front desk at the hotel for safekeeping. I took the phone, staring down at it dumbly. Sleek and black, I'd never seen a phone with seamless edges. It was like something out of a science fiction movie.

"That's okay," I said, handing it back to him. It was only another reminder of just how far apart our worlds were. This had been for one night.

The night was over.

"I should go. I don't want to overstay my welcome." He sighed, standing and prowling toward me. He again reminded me of a panther, moving through the inky darkness in the room like it was his to control.

Like a phantom. A nightmare come to life.
And I never wanted to wake up.

My breath caught with the comparison of the man I remembered from my drugged dream, Rafe's touch as he cupped my cheek driving that uneasy feeling higher. "I want you to stay." His thumb grazed the skin under my left eye, a gentle caress that felt more intimate after the things he'd done to me.

"Okay," I whispered, typing out a quick text to Chloe's number and handing him the phone back.

He took my hand, soothing the frayed edges of my soul as he guided me to the bed. He pulled me into his side, letting me lean my head against his chest as a pillow, and folded me into his arms.

Something in me settled. Something about him was familiar.

Like coming home after a lifetime away.

8
ISA

Light trickled in at the edges of my vision. As I pried my eyes open and stared at the space in front of me, the luxurious champagne and gold decor staring back at me was most certainly not the purple room that had looked the same since I'd been ten.

Weight rested over my waist, and the warmth of a naked chest pressed against my spine.

I turned under the arm, rolling to my back and staring up at Rafe's handsome face in shock. In sleep, his expression was oddly peaceful. Like the lines of his face that marked him as a decadent and dangerous sin smoothed away and turned him into a man.

His chest rose and fell with the deep breaths that only sleep could bring, and he groaned as he pressed closer to me. The steel of his erection touched my thigh, making me acutely aware of the distinct soreness between my legs after the night before.

I bit my lip, slipping out of the bed and adjusting the covers, hoping he wouldn't notice me missing. It was early, and while I would have loved to sneak out before he woke up, I needed to shower if I had to make my way across Ibiza Town to the boutique hotel that would give me respite while I grieved the loss of something I'd never really had.

A toothbrush sat on the counter, still in its original packaging. I hadn't noticed it the night before in my panic to get out of the room, but the presence seemed to mock me. Rafe's toothbrush stood in the cup, already opened from its package, having been used. The dirty feeling I'd had while I thought about leaving as soon as he was done with me came rushing back, shoved to the surface with the reality that he'd planned to have company staying the night.

Letting me stay meant nothing. It didn't mean he'd thought our night together was special, as it seemed to me. He just seemed to have a propensity for letting a woman stay the night.

I stared into the mirror, studying my face and wondering if I felt any different aside from the ache inside me. I still felt like me, despite somehow feeling like my world had shifted on its axis. A man had never affected me before, and I'd never let myself have a man simply because I wanted him.

Glancing back down at the toothbrush, I tore the package open with angry movements and squirted toothpaste on like the personal offense it was. I brushed thoroughly, getting rid of the aftertaste the wine had left me with, and rinsed it before depositing it back inside the mangled package.

He could reuse it for his next one-night stand for all I cared.

Turning the shower on, I stepped under the water before it had time to get hot. The cold spray jarred me out of my pettiness, making me instantly feel guilty for acting like a scorned lover. I had no claim to him.

He'd told me no lies. Never made me any promises beyond our night together.

I knew logically I should look at the night as a blessing. I'd had a pleasant experience for my first time, and would have a great story to tell if I ever reached a point where I wanted to talk about my sex life. Instead, all I could think about was him doing the same thing that night with a new woman.

I lathered shampoo into my hair and glared at the conditioner bottle that sat on the shelf as the rainfall shower head poured down on me. I ignored the sound of the bathroom door opening, not even daring to loose the sigh that wanted to escape. Sneaking out before he woke up would have been too good to be true.

The shower door slid open as I rinsed, making me turn incredulous eyes back at him as he stepped into the shower with me. I felt the moment he came under the spray; the water bouncing off his body and dripping onto my back from a different angle before he even touched me. When his fingers combed through my hair, helping to rinse the shampoo out of the ends, I tugged out of his grip and turned to look at him with a scowl. "I'll be out of your way as soon as I'm done," I snapped.

He tilted his head in confusion, and I sighed to rid myself of my frustration when he ignored the bite to my words in favor of working the offending conditioner through my hair. "What has my princesa in a temper this morning?" he asked, his words feeling like a violation in themselves. He didn't know me well enough to talk to me about my moods.

"Nothing," I said, reaching over to grab the bottle of body wash.

He took it from my hands, setting it back on the shelf as

he turned me around to face him. Pushing me against the shower wall, he cupped the side of my neck and used his thumb to press my chin up until I met his eyes. "Tell me."

I relented with a swallow, heaving out a breath. "It's nothing. I'm being stupid," I admitted.

"Isa, tell me so I can fix it," he said more firmly.

My eyes went to the toothbrush on the counter, finally deciding that it would be foolish to feel so embarrassed about being honest with him. Soon I'd walk out of his life and never see him again, so it shouldn't matter if I left on good terms or not. "I never wanted to feel like I was just one in a revolving door of women, you know? I shouldn't have done this. It isn't me, but that's not your fault."

He followed my gaze, turning his body. I felt the moment he saw the toothbrush, the way his body relaxed as he realized what might have upset me. "Ah. The hotel supplies many items, particularly in the penthouse suite. There are two toothbrushes in each of the other two bedrooms in the suite as well, I'm sure."

"You didn't ask for them?" I asked stupidly, my brain furiously trying to connect the dots. It wasn't necessarily a confession that what we'd had was unique, but I couldn't expect that from a man I didn't know.

"No," he laughed, running his thumb over my cheek. "But I must admit, I'm surprised by how much your jealousy appeals to me. Does it drive you mad to think of another woman in your place?" he asked, reaching for the body wash and squirting some into a loofa while I scowled up at him. I suddenly felt like the brunt of a joke and found I didn't much like it. "Because I think I would murder a man for looking at you too long," he said as he leaned in and touched his lips to mine gently while he stared at me and lathered the loofa with bubbles.

The exaggeration coated my skin, feeling like an odd compliment. I *wanted* him to be jealous. I wanted him to feel territorial over me, because it meant that I was more than just a single night.

Even if it couldn't actually last, it would give me some peace to know that maybe he'd think about me after I was gone.

He turned me away from him, touching the soapy loofa to my shoulder and gliding it down my arm until every inch was covered in suds. Switching hands, he did it with the other arm, sliding it around to the front of my body.

My nipples pebbled beneath the touch as the abrasive surface scraped them, and he covered my torso in bubbles as he pressed his body to mine. His length curved along my spine, cementing his desire for me as he moved the loofa lower and nudged my feet apart slightly so he could clean me.

I blushed at the intimate act, unable to stop myself from leaning further back into him.

"How could anyone ever compare to you, Isa?" he asked, the particular use of my name helping to further soothe my frayed edges. Princesa was beautiful. It reminded me of our different worlds, but the cynical voice in my head wondered if he'd ever used it with someone else.

Isa was me. At the very least, I'd been memorable enough to remember my name.

As soon as he finished cleaning me, he made quick work of washing himself with the loofa in one hand while his other delved into my core. "Are you sore?" he murmured, his voice skating across my cheekbone as he nipped my skin playfully.

I nodded ruefully, genuinely regretful that I didn't think I could give him a second round. I'd already made the mistake of having a one-night stand. I couldn't imagine a second round would have made me feel worse about myself when I walked out of his penthouse and never saw him again. "Yes," I whispered on a gasp as he spread my lips with two fingers and nudged my clit gently. Even the tiny touch made my hips jerk back into him as he tossed the loofa to the side.

He wrapped his other arm around me, taking a nipple between his fingers and pinching lightly while he dragged his teeth over the side of my neck. "I'm sorry I was too rough," he said. His fingers prodded my entrance, testing my reaction as I jerked in his grip, before gliding back up to circle my clit with firm sweeps.

"I liked it," I answered on a breathless sigh.

"You did." He breathed against my skin, grinding himself into my spine as he raised his hand from between my thighs and touched his fingers to my mouth. They smelled like me as he pressed inside, forcing my lips to part so he could rest them on my tongue while he watched my face. Pulling them free, he slid them back to my center and went back to working me with firm circles that drove me toward madness as he turned my head toward him and leaned forward to bite my bottom lip between his teeth. "Your pretty little pussy is going to come for me," he groaned as he pulled back. "And then I want your mouth."

My eyes tracked downward, even though I couldn't actually see him. When my eyes met his again, they were filled with amusement. "I don't know how to do *that*."

"I'll teach you, Princesa." He slid a single finger inside me, using his thumb at my clit as his mouth moved to mine and devoured me. I moaned into his mouth, my hips moving of their own volition as my orgasm crashed over me from the pain that finger added to the pleasure he gave me.

My vision went white, my body going slack in his arms, and if he hadn't held me up, I might have fallen to the shower floor as my legs turned to jelly beneath me.

He waited until my eyes fluttered open to find him watching me. His face was oddly focused on mine, so much that I flushed my embarrassment. He turned me in his arms; the water spraying down on my side as I glanced down at him. With a firm hand on my shoulder, he pressed me down until I dropped to my knees. I drew in a ragged breath as I came face to face with it for the first time. Hard and angry, veins ran up the side of his length and the head was a purple color. Looking tormented and desperate. I swallowed, reaching up a hand to wrap around him, a surprised gasp slipping free when it twitched in my grip.

I slid my hand over him slowly, the water from the shower aiding the motion as I looked up at him. "Isa," he warned, touching the back of my head and tangling his hand in my hair. He pushed me in, moving cautiously, but his grip was unrelenting as I angled him down with my hand and parted my lips. His head slid inside, the unique flavor of him exploding in my mouth as he thrust forward shallowly and gave me more of him. I drew back, releasing him uncertainly as I ran my tongue over my lips. "Again," he ordered. I did, taking him to the point just before I thought I might gag and pulling back, never letting him leave the haven of my mouth as I repeated the motion at his firm urges on the back of my head. "Fuck," he groaned, drawing a moan from me that vibrated around the length of him.

I watched as he bit his lip harshly, the skin staying indented when he finally released it. Pulling at my hair, he tugged me back until he slid free and touched his thumb to my lip, dragging it to the side and staring at my mouth with fascinating fervor. That thumb trailed down to my throat as he wrapped his hand around the front and gently pressed. "You're going to take my cock in your throat now, *mi princesa*," he murmured as my eyes went wide. He released my throat, prying my hand off his cock and angling it to my mouth. The tip touched my lips while I hesitated, something dangerous slithering through his eyes while I watched.

I swallowed back the nerves I felt seeing it, opening my mouth so he could press inside. He moved in, gliding over my tongue and hitting the spot where I gagged around him. "Swallow," he ordered, pushing more firmly. I struggled to figure out *how,* shaking my head lightly and moving to pull back, but he abandoned his grip on himself to grab the back of my head again and hold me still. My eyes watered as I looked up at him, finally relaxing my throat enough to swallow around him.

He pushed deeper, making shallow thrusts that kept him locked inside my throat. My lungs heaved with the need for air, his hand pressing tighter as if he could feel himself there. Phantom shadows hovered at the edge of my vision. He watched my face, finally pulling free and letting me breathe. I sucked back air desperately, staring up at him while he watched me. Even knowing that he would deprive me of air, even knowing that the phantoms would come back, I opened for him and let him push deep. He stroked himself inside my mouth, moving my head forward and back at a furious pace while he held my gaze with determination.

When he shoved into my throat, I swallowed his intrusion as he let out a quiet groan and pulled me to his groin. Too full, I pressed my hands against his thighs in protest as he spilled himself down my throat.

My nails dug into his thighs, marking them with red

streaks until he finally let go and I pulled back until he slipped free. He cupped my chin and ran his thumb over my lip again as I caught my breath and swallowed back the sting in my throat. *"Esta boca será mi muerte,"* he groaned.

I didn't even know what the words meant, but they brought a flush to my face anyway as he helped me up from my aching knees and plundered my mouth as if he didn't care what I'd done with it.

As if it was his, and he'd do as he damn well pleased, regardless.

His white dress shirt hung down to my knees, and I glanced at the dress and bathing suit he'd folded and draped over a chair in the dining room. Wearing his clothes shouldn't have felt so intimate, not when I'd had him inside me.

Not when he'd been in my mouth.

He'd thrown open the glass door panels that folded to the side, letting the ocean breeze blow through the suite. With only gray shorts covering his bottom half and his chest bare, he moved to the suite door when the knock came and let a staff member come inside with a cart. I squirmed uncomfortably, looking up at Rafe when he moved into the room with the other man. While the staff deposited my cell phone on the table without another word and worked to unload covered dishes onto the table in front of us, Rafe's hand came down on the back of my chair. His other reached around to the front, grasping my chin and bending me back until I stared up at him. I pulled the shirt down, trying to keep my thighs covered. His gaze went to them, turning knowing as he tormented me and leaned in to press a wet kiss against my mouth.

If I hadn't known better, it would have felt like a claim.

But the staff member's eyes never even glanced our way as he pulled the covers off the plates and went back to his cart with nervous movements that clanged dishes against each other. He nodded but never dared a glance.

"Señor Ibarra," he said, moving to the door and disappearing.

As soon as he released my face, I scowled up at him. "That was cruel. I'm not even wearing underwear! He could have seen my, my—" I stuttered.

"Your pussy?" he asked, his gaze going dark even as his mouth smiled. "I would never let another man lay eyes on your pussy, Princesa."

"Then why did you let him in here with me half naked?" I whispered. Something was *wrong* in his gaze, something sinister lurking in the multicolored depths as he settled in the chair at the head of the table beside me.

"You could have been entirely naked, and he wouldn't have so much as glanced at you."

"But why?" I asked, watching as he used the utensils to place a piece of rustic toast with tomato and some kind of meat on it onto the plate in front of me.

"Because I told him not to," he said with a shrug. To be in a world where someone wouldn't even look at a person just because he was told not to? I felt like I'd walked into an episode of the twilight zone.

I swallowed as he cut off a portion of the potato omelet and dropped it on my plate. "So, Rafe Ibarra?" I asked, deciding to change the subject. A one-night stand wouldn't be an appropriate time to tell him to reevaluate the way he ordered people around, so I had to work around how heavy that felt in my gut.

"Rafael Ibarra, if you want to be technical," he said, glancing up at me with a serious look, as if waiting for a moment of recognition that didn't come.

"I'm sorry. I don't know anyone in Ibiza. Is that a name I should recognize?" I asked shyly, taking a sip of my freshly squeezed orange juice.

He shook his head with a broad smile. "No. I like that you do not know of me," he said. The words felt like the truth, not like something he said to placate me.

I refrained from asking more, deciding I would simply Google the name after we went our separate ways, but that brought another question to the forefront of my mind. "I'm a little surprised I'm still here," I admitted. "What am I still doing here?" I asked, picking up my fork and bringing a bite of the omelet to my mouth. I groaned the second the flavor exploded on my tongue, and his eyes dropped to my mouth as I chewed.

Feeling suddenly shy as his eyes darkened and he pressed his lips together while he watched me, I recognized that it felt similar to how he watched me in the shower. My fork fell to the plate with a clatter as I took another sip of water.

"How long are you in Ibiza?" he asked, picking up his fork with a smirk that made me clench my thighs together. It was so sinful, such an arrogant tip of his lips that displayed how much he enjoyed the way he affected me.

I'd have been lying if I said there wasn't something captivating about knowing he wanted me. That he looked at me and thought about my mouth or about being inside me. Under any normal circumstances, I might have doubted the thoughts swirling inside his head. I might have questioned if he could possibly want me the way I wanted him. But Rafe left no doubt. Even when he didn't speak the words, his eyes and body spoke for him.

His eyes very rarely left me, his stare probing and intense in a way I'd never experienced. If he was a businessman, I imagined it served him well as an intimidation tactic. With me, it convinced me to take my clothes off and give him things I had no right to give.

"Nine days. I fly home early on the twenty-fifth," I said, taking another bite of omelet.

"Your plans?" He didn't eat, too focused on watching me. It made me stop eating myself, feeling unnerved by the conversation for reasons I couldn't explain. It was innocent enough. Small talk, really. But something about his stare felt meaningful, like we stood at a precipice and there would be no going back.

"Some sightseeing. The beach. I'm sure my friends will drag me to some clubs," I said with a shrug.

He reached across the corner of the table, catching my chin between his fingers and leaning close as he rested his elbow on the surface. "Do you really want to spend your time in the typical tourist attractions and parties where you can't take a breath without someone bumping into you? Or do you want me to show you the real Ibiza? The Ibiza I love?"

"What, for nine days?" I asked with a laugh. "Why would you want to do that?"

There was a pause before his answer, his forehead creasing as he huffed a disbelieving breath. "I enjoy being with you. Is that so wrong?"

"You barely know me," I pointed out, ever the pessimist. He'd likely tire of my more reserved behavior and wish he'd chosen someone more adventurous to spend his time with than me.

"I'd like to remedy that," he said. I crossed my legs, leaning back from his touch while his fingers snapped together once I removed my chin. He scowled at the distance between us, leaning back in his chair. "It's your decision, Princesa," he said carefully with a soft voice. His cell vibrated on the table, and he turned a glare to it before heaving a sigh. "I need to take this. Make the right choice," he said, standing from the table and making his way out onto the balcony that wrapped around the suite as he answered and barked orders in Spanish. He pulled the glass panels closed behind him, cutting off his voice as I stared at him in shock.

Nine days with a man who tempted all the parts of me I should push back into the cage. Ten days with a man who could show me everything.

He could show me places I'd only ever dreamed of seeing, teach me things I'd never be brave enough to ask for back home.

I should have listened to the warning in my head. The nagging sense that I'd never want to leave when he finished with me.

I didn't.

9

RAFAEL

"¿Qué?" I asked, my blood boiling as Javier, one of my men working security at the hotel, spoke on the other end of the line.

"One of our guys spotted Pavel's errand boy lurking in the lobby and at the pool area. He appears to be waiting for something, presumably you, since you haven't come downstairs yet today," Javier said. "How would you like me to handle it?" he asked, rattling off the words in Spanish quickly.

"Don't. I'll handle this." I'd given explicit instructions that I was to be undisturbed during my time with *mi princesa*, and only the morning after procuring her, I had to deal with an overzealous Russian pig who needed to have been euthanized a decade prior.

"What of *mi reina*?" he asked.

"She's to remain in the penthouse," I said. "Is he still in the lobby?"

"Yes," Javier answered. Not needing to know anything more, I accepted the unfortunate reality that I'd need to spend a little time away from Isa in order to clear up the rest of our day. Ending the call, I walked back into the suite with my phone in hand. Isa hadn't moved since I'd left her, deep in thought as she considered my proposition. The sudden urge to say fuck it all and drag her to *El Infierno* kicking and screaming threatened my patience, brought to the surface by her indecision.

What was so horrible about spending nine days in paradise with me?

"I need to run downstairs to deal with some unexpected business," I said, trying to keep the bite from my tone. "Stay here until I get back." I turned, making my way for the bedroom, and she pushed her chair back suddenly to follow me. Her skin whispered in my shirt as it brushed against her bare thigh, that scar taunting me.

There was something I didn't know about my Isa, and the thought unsettled me far more than was normal. "Maybe I should go see my friends. Talk to them about your offer. I don't want them to worry," she said, toying with the end of the sleeve nervously.

"You'll stay here until I get back. I promise to be quick." I stripped my shorts off while she watched nervously, pulling trousers off a hanger and stepping into them with hurried movements. "If you still want to leave when I get back, then I'll take you home."

Her brow furrowed at the odd choice of words. Everyone knew that a hotel would never be home. She'd never know that I didn't mean her hotel. If she didn't want to spend more time with me, I wouldn't let her go.

I'd take her to *El Infierno* and never let her leave.

"I don't know that I'm comfortable being here alone," she said, glancing around the room. I sighed, understanding that she was largely put off by the luxury. Isa would have been far more comfortable in an average hotel room, not the penthouse of the finest hotel in Ibiza Town.

"I'll be back before you know it," I said, stepping into her space and cupping her cheeks in my hands. She melted beneath the touch, staring up at me like I could be her entire world.

I would be. If only she'd let me.

I leaned closer, kissing her slowly to remind her of everything she stood to walk away from if she left. My hands held her still, and I kept my lips soft as I worshiped her mouth.

It was the kind of kiss that could move mountains. The kind of kiss that changed futures. She sighed into me, her body going pliant as I stole the breath from her lungs and made it mine.

When I finally pulled back, she swayed on her feet. Reaching up a hand to touch her lips, she watched me finish dressing. "Stay here," I said firmly one last time after I'd finished dressing and made my way toward the door of the bedroom.

It killed me to leave her when all I wanted to do was hold her in my arms and show her why she was mine.

I had to settle for taking out my rage that it wasn't possible on the asshole who took me away from her.

I made my way into the elevator, jabbing the buttons with furious fingers to take me to the ground floor. Leaving Isa so soon made me wonder how I would ever tolerate being away from her again. Would it always make my skin pulse with the steady awareness that something was missing? Would the fact that *mi princesa* wasn't in my arms where she belonged make everything else in my life but her a chore I merely had to complete so I could get back to her?

The elevator doors opened after it finished its descent. I

stepped through them, scanning the lobby for the dead eyes that came with being a soul-sucking bastard loyal to a man like Pavel Kuznetsov. For the dead eyes that came with being a man like me.

A murderer. A dealer. A thief.

I found him sitting in a chair by the fireplace, flipping through a magazine absentmindedly as though he couldn't be bothered to pay attention to any of the hotel patrons going about their day in paradise. He sensed me when I stopped in the center of the lobby, his eyes looking up to meet mine. With my mask firmly in place, I gave nothing away as I nodded my head toward the doors that went to the staff areas and the kitchen at the back of the hotel.

I showed him the ultimate disrespect I could to a man in our position. I turned my back on the muscular fucker, pushing through the double doors and claiming the kitchen as my space. "¡Vete!" I ordered, keeping my voice low. Despite the clanking of pots, every eye in the kitchen turned to me, then they quickly made their way out of the kitchens.

The Russian followed, making his way through the crowd of staff escaping the confines of the kitchens. I turned to face him next to one of the stations where someone had been preparing to chop vegetables from the looks of things. He swallowed as he stepped into the empty room, his eyes meeting mine while the stony mask he wore faded in the face of a true opponent.

It was easy for men to pretend bravery when they had connections that gave them very little to fear. Pavel must not have cared for the man much to send him into my hotel against my wishes. "I believe I said I would meet with Pavel after I completed my business in Ibiza," I warned, tapping my fingers against the stainless steel work station thoughtfully.

He puffed up his chest, seeming to reinforce his pathetic attempt at being frightening at the mention of his boss's name. "Pavel is not happy to be put off so you can stick your dick in American pussy," he argued. My fury exploded into full-blown rage at the mention of Isa in such a manner. Even without her name, she was far too good to even exist in his world. "If you're so hard up for a sweet ass, I'm sure Pavel will be happy to sell you someone that suits."

Grabbing the chef's knife off the counter, I held it out and pointed it at him as I took slow, measured steps toward him. He backed up a step, snatching his own knife from next to him as my face morphed into a grin. His uncoordinated lunge for my face was easy to evade with a step to the side as I slammed my free hand down on top of his forearm at the same time I hit him in the face with the hilt of the knife.

Another jab of the knife hilt against the back of his hand loosened his grip on his weapon, and I forced his fingers flat as I shoved it away from his grip. He groaned as I pressed his fingers to lay against the surface, realizing my intent too late and trying to push me off.

With a grunt of annoyance, I stabbed through the back of his hand and into the cutting board beneath, pinning him still. He howled his pain through the kitchen, trying to bend his fingers but finding it impossible with the chef's knife protruding from his flesh.

He'd have one less to worry about soon enough.

I grabbed the knife he'd released, touching the edge of the blade against his pinky finger and pressing down slowly. There wasn't much meat to finger bones when cutting them off, only a little give before the crunch of bone severing vibrated against the knife and it hit the cutting board on the other side.

Slicing his hand open further in his fit to escape, he

screamed as blood pumped out of the hole where his finger had once been.

"The next time you so much as mention her, it will be a much larger appendage that I take from you, and I will rip it from your body slowly so you feel every tendon tear." I pulled the knife free from his hand, dropping it back to the cutting board. Blood dripped onto it, staining the wood with red drops. He yanked his hand to his chest, snatching a towel off the counter to wrap around it. "At least it will grow in the moments before the skin splits," I suggested, raising an eyebrow at him as I moved around him toward the doors. "Tell Pavel I will deal with him when I am ready and not a moment before. He does not summon me like one of his whores. Understood?"

He nodded fervently. "Yes, *El Diablo*."

I smirked. "His next man will go back as a head in a box. If you're smart, you'll make sure it's not you." I shoved through the swinging doors, glancing at my arms to make sure there was no blood on my suit before I made my way toward the elevator to return to Isa. My body hummed with the thirst for more blood.

For death.

I would need to find a method of release over the next week that didn't end in me covered in blood or fucking out my violence on Isa's body. I'd already been too rough with her when I took her virginity, and then again in the shower that morning, and I'd need to refrain for her sake, or she wouldn't be able to walk during her time in Ibiza. It would be difficult to seduce her and show her the beauty of her new home if she never left the bed.

And for obvious reasons, she couldn't know that I was almost as thirsty for blood as I was for her. Given her hesitations as soon as my hands left her body, there was more at stake than I would have liked. Especially considering my reaction to her.

I'd known I was inexplicably drawn to her. I'd known that I wanted to possess her.

But I didn't know I would crave her company and her smile as much as I did. I hadn't known that her happiness would matter to me so quickly. I would take her without it, but I preferred her to be a willing victim in my game, rather than one trapped on a private island, who could never leave.

Stepping into the elevator, I dialed Alejandro. He answered on the first ring. "I know."

"I thought I told you to fucking handle Pavel," I growled.

"I relayed your message, Rafael. I'm uncertain why you think I can control a Pakhan who is an *idiota* under the best circumstances. He has no sense of self-preservation," he explained.

The elevator doors opened, and I stepped into the hallway outside the penthouse and dropped my voice low. "I want more security brought in. I won't endanger Isa because of negligence. *Nobody* gets near her without my knowledge. You understand me, Alejandro? This is not something you wish to test me on."

"Of course, Rafael," he said, disconnecting the call to do my bidding.

Just as it should have been.

10

ISA

I lost track of time as I stood and stared at the space where Rafe had been. The suite felt strangely empty, quiet, as though it was a crime to exist in the abandoned space. It wasn't so much that it felt cold, because it was decorated lavishly.

I just didn't belong here.

I snagged my phone off the table and made my way onto the balcony. One of the cushioned chairs called my name, and I dropped into it gracelessly as I scrolled through my recent calls until I found Chloe's number.

"You bitch!" she squealed when she answered, and I pulled the phone away from my ear while I waited for the sound to disappear. "Please tell me you are no longer a virgin."

"I'm no longer a virgin," I confirmed, rolling my eyes to the bright blue sky above my head.

"How was it? Was he as good as he was beautiful?" she sighed, and I could imagine her fanning herself mockingly.

"Can we talk about that later? He had to run downstairs, but I don't think I have much time before he gets back, and I need your opinion," I said, glancing back at the doors. The last thing I wanted was for him to come back and hear my girl talk and let it go to his head.

I had a feeling his ego was already inflated enough.

"That sounds ominous."

"Not really," I said. "He's asked me to spend my vacation with him. He offered to show me the real Ibiza. Which is great in theory, but—"

"Don't you dare 'in theory' me!" she warned. "This is a once in a lifetime opportunity. If you do not spend the rest of the trip mounting that Spanish stud until you can't feel your ass, then *I* will," she laughed.

The only thing that kept the unnatural jealousy at bay was the fact that I knew she was kidding. Chloe was the only person in the world I trusted not to screw a man I'd slept with. "But what about you? We probably won't get to spend much time together. Oh, but I could ask him if you two can tag along."

"Nope. You are not asking him if you can bring your friends along to cockblock him when he seems to have a mind to keep you all to himself. I have Hugo to entertain me, and I want you to enjoy the time with him. Just forget about all the shit waiting for you back home. For once, just have fun Isa, please," she begged, and the sound of it made the uncertainty inside me cave.

I could experience something great, and when I went home, I'd go right back to being responsible and no one would be the wiser. Nobody even had to know about my adventure with Rafael Ibarra.

"You don't think that's a mistake?" I asked. "This was meant to be one night, and now it's over a week. What if I develop feelings for him? How am I supposed to cope with that?"

"Sweetie, you probably will have feelings for him on some level. Just keep it in your head that it has an expiration date, and you'll be fine, okay? Just be safe. Be smart about it. Text me if you need us to bring your things over, and call me every day so I know you're okay."

"Love you," I murmured.

"Love you too bitch," she laughed, disconnecting the call. I stood from the chair and made my way back into the main space of the suite. While his explanation of the hotel's accommodations with the toothbrush and conditioner made sense, it didn't mean that there wasn't another woman in his life. He spoke of Ibiza as if he called it home.

So what was he doing staying in a hotel room?

If I was going to stay, I needed to know with absolute certainty that he wasn't spoken for, because there was nothing I hated more than a cheater and a liar.

I made my way into the bedroom, going straight for the closet where he'd gotten the suit he wore downstairs. There were no women's clothes or anything outright suspicious, so I went to the navy suit still hanging and slid my hands inside the pockets.

Empty.

With a frown, I turned my attention to the stacks of more casual clothing folded on the shelves and pawed through them, being careful to return them to the way they'd been before my snooping.

"Looking for something, *mi princesa*?"

11

RAFAEL

She looked too perfect snooping through my things, her innocent desperation to get to know me manifesting in ways many men might have taken issue with. But there was nothing for Isa to discover inside the hotel room. I would have no secrets from her as soon as it was possible to tell her the truth of who I was.

I leaned against the doorway of the closet, wondering how long she would remain oblivious to me watching her. She rifled through my clothes, doing a decent job of keeping them tidy enough that I wouldn't have realized what she'd done if I hadn't caught her in the act. "Looking for something, *mi princesa*?" I asked, watching as her entire body jolted with the strike of terror that shook her.

Her hand went to her chest as she spun to stare at me. She swallowed past the horrified look on her face, no doubt taking in my casual stance and my calm smile as I watched her. Despite my rage of only a few moments ago, there was nothing tight in the lines of my body. Just being around Isa soothed the demons that called to me all hours of the day.

Her face morphed into a shy smile as she stepped closer

to me. She touched my stomach cautiously, gliding her hands around to my back as she pressed her body into mine and rested her head on my chest. The move was so innocent, so unexpected, that I didn't react for a moment and had no clue what to do. When she turned her stunning eyes up to me and regret leaked into her expression, I bent forward to kiss her, to reassure the insecurity I saw lingering there.

"I was just trying to find out something about you."

"What do you want to know?" I asked with a shrug, wrapping an arm around her waist and guiding her back into the comfort of the bedroom.

"Anything," she admitted. "You're an enigma. I know we don't really know each other. At all. But it feels like whenever our conversations get too personal, you try to redirect them back to me. If I'm going to spend all this time with you, I'd like to feel like I know you just a little at least. It would make me feel less like..." She paused.

"Less like what, Isa?" I asked, a growl forming in my throat as the words I'd suspected her to say came tumbling out.

"Like a whore. Like I'm sleeping with you to have a luxury vacation. That's not what this is for me at all," she said. The words hung on her tongue unspoken as she stopped herself, not giving me the words I wanted to hear. "I like being with you," she said instead.

I'd take it. For now.

"There are things you can't know about me just yet. My business is—" I paused. "Cut throat. Because of that, I have to be careful who I trust and what I tell people." I wouldn't lie to her outright, but I wouldn't hesitate to keep things from her if I felt it necessary for her safety, and for the development of our relationship to be what it needed to be.

"What is it you do exactly?" she asked with narrowed

eyes, making her way out of the bedroom and back into the living space.

"Sales and investments mostly," I said evasively. "I could tell you all the details of my life outside the specifics of my work, but I don't truly believe that's the best way to get to know someone."

I held out a hand for her as I pulled my cell phone from my pocket to make arrangements for her clothes to be delivered to the hotel, and to have a shopper purchase something for her to wear for that day at least. Our future wouldn't wait for the delivery of her luggage.

Not when I had plans for the day.

"Let me show you who I really am."

The sleek black town car navigated the streets of Ibiza Town as Isa tugged at the white sundress where it touched her thigh, deliberately trying to pull it low enough to cover her scar. I considered the clothes I'd seen her wear in all the photos and surveillance footage I'd seen of her over the years.

Never had I seen her wear anything that revealed her legs. Never had she risked people seeing the scar.

"Eres hermosa," I murmured, turning to her and resting my hand against the scar itself. "You're beautiful." She looked down at the touch, staring at the space where the white scar emerged beside either side of my hand.

"There's nothing beautiful about scars," she said, biting her lip as she looked at it.

"Do you find mine so horrible?" I watched her furrow her brow, but she shook her head and pouted her lips at me.

"I don't like to think of someone hurting you like that,

but the scars themselves? No," she admitted, though it looked like it pained her to say it.

"That is exactly how I feel about yours, and since my opinion is the only one that matters, there's no need to fuss over it," I said. She huffed a laugh at me, shaking her head adorably. She probably thought me arrogant, like no other opinion could matter after mine because I would be the best she ever had.

She didn't yet know I would be the *only* man she ever had.

The driver parked alongside the curb in front of the Portal de Ses Taules, and I opened my door. Holding out a hand, I encouraged Isa to scoot herself across the seat and get out on my side. I helped her out, watching as her expression widened and she stared up at the stone wall in front of her. Kissing the back of her hand, I kept it in mine as I tapped the top of the car and closed the door for the driver to retreat until I summoned him.

Normally, I would have driven my McLaren, but finding a parking spot in the area was difficult even for me. Isa would do enough walking that day. I could only be pleased I'd talked her into wearing the flat sandals sent by the shopper instead of her own heeled shoes. She'd appreciate it at the end of the day.

"What is this?" she asked, letting me guide her up the stone ramp to head toward the gate.

"Dalt vila," I answered. "The Old Town. The walls are from the renaissance. The city inside is stunning, and there are little shops and restaurants. It is a must for anyone spending time in Ibiza." We made our way into the entrance, Isa's hand reaching out to touch the old stone with trembling fingertips.

"It's really been here that long?" she asked, the history

buff inside her forcing her excitement to the surface much like I'd hoped.

Humming my agreement, I captured her hand in mine and dragged our fingers over the stones so they scratched her palm. She closed her eyes; her face pinching as she lost herself to the desire of me pressing into her spine. Of our hands together.

I'd use my touch to manipulate her every chance I got.

I hadn't expected the innocent virgin to be so inclined to my rougher tastes. I'd expected to spend the next few days making love to her sweetly and then slowly acclimate her to the more...

Deviant of my desires.

But that she stood there with me willingly after I'd lost my control with her repeatedly proved just how well-matched we were. She'd give me everything I wanted and beg me for more.

As long as I kept her from questioning if her desires were wrong. I suspected my Isa would battle with that, eventually.

The entryway opened up before us as we stepped through the narrower tunnel. Her face lit as she took in the whitewashed buildings and stone streets. The timing of her trip was unfortunate, but I hadn't been willing to wait any longer to bring Isa to Ibiza just to avoid the summer crowds in *Dalt Vila*. Vendors lined the streets for the summer, selling all sorts of wares and handmade items. I guided her up the road, passing vendors who smiled at her as if she was their saving grace even as they avoided me entirely.

Nobody wanted to make eye contact with the devil.

Even as my princesa turned wide eyes to them and smiled shyly when she didn't understand what they said to her, they still moved forward as if drawn by her haunted presence. Something in her called to all of us, a history that needed fixing and a mystery that needed solving.

Our fingers interlocked as I guided her forward slowly. "Wait until you see the citadel up close," I told her, squeezing her hand to draw her attention back to me. As much as I loved watching her fall in love with the island, I wanted nothing more than for her to love me for giving it to her.

I would be the center of her universe. Not Ibiza.

"The citadel?" she asked, her voice betraying her excitement. "Sorry," she winced with a laugh as she tempered her joy. I wanted to rage against the fact that she felt the need to diminish her happiness. Like she couldn't enjoy something without feeling guilty. "I'm a history geek. I'm going to college in the fall to get my Bachelor's in Anthropology."

"Why not just regular history?" I asked, prying into the parts of her mind that I couldn't know from watching her. Hugo knew her very well, but there were certain questions he didn't think to ask. His desire to know her didn't come from a unique fascination, though I knew the boy had come to care for her in his time with her.

I already knew Joaquin had questioned me far too often over the last few months as the looming deadline neared. He adored Isa primarily from a distance, as one might a younger sister he'd been separated from in a divorce. The man had never questioned my decisions prior to Isa, but something about her had wormed her way under his skin.

For that reason alone, he'd be her personal security once she knew the truth. Nobody would protect her better than a man who was brave enough to risk my wrath in an attempt to give her a chance at the best life possible.

"I find people oddly fascinating," she admitted. "I don't like them most times, so I don't want to actually have to deal with them regularly like a therapist would or something like that. But I find the study of culture and the overall human experience throughout history, and the ways we've developed, to be uniquely compelling."

I tugged her closer to me, ducking off to the side of the street to avoid other foot traffic as we stood in front of a shop window. "You hate people?"

"Well, not *all* people, but most of them, yes," she laughed sheepishly. "People are inherently selfish at the core. They'll do whatever it takes to get what they want in life, no matter who they hurt. I think that's really depressing." She laughed sheepishly, glancing down to the ground. Her cheeks turned pink when I cupped her jaw in my hand and leaned down to kiss her. She leaned into the touch, letting me fold her into my arms despite the public location.

Eyes came to us as I kissed her, but I paid them no mind when I pulled back and tucked my face into her hair to breathe in the scent of her, beneath the shampoo the hotel offered. Her products on *El Infierno* were an expensive version of the scents she seemed to prefer at home, an exotic mix of orange blossom and vanilla. The scent of them in the bottle when they'd arrived had made me desperate to smell them on her skin once more. But it would have to wait.

"I have been pleasantly surprised by you at every turn, *mi princesa*. I vastly prefer to spend my time alone," I said as I pulled back to stare at her. Wrapping a lock of long, chocolate hair around my hand, I slid it to the back of her head and gripped her there. "But that's not the case with you."

"I think that's somehow the sweetest thing anyone has ever said about me." She chuckled lightly, the sound raising the hairs on my arms. I knew in that moment, I would do *anything* to hear the sound again and kill anyone who stood in the way of it.

I chuckled as well, turning her back toward the center of the street as we made our way up toward my favorite shop — the sole reason I would tolerate the trip into Dalt Vila anytime I was in Ibiza Town. "If you like history, then you need to see the museums on the mainland in Europe. All the monuments and the ruins are remarkable."

She sighed wistfully, her body sagging with the weight of a thousand worlds as it fell upon her. "I wish, but I don't know that I'll ever make it to Europe again. This was a freak thing where I had a paid opportunity to come to Ibiza. Coming back might be difficult."

I bit my lip to stifle the urge to tell her I would take her to see anything she wanted, if only she promised to be mine. Too much, too soon, and I would scare her off. Reminding myself that Isa hardly knew me came harder with every moment that passed.

"I am sure you'll find a way. We do what we must to achieve our dreams, do we not?" I asked, staring down at her as I said the words. She'd been everything I hadn't dared to dream for, a woman to match me, who called to me in a way I hadn't thought possible. "Come," I said, changing the subject as I dragged her into the little bakery.

"Señor Ibarra!" Samuel chimed from behind the counter. "*¿Lo mismo de siempre?*" he asked with a smile. *Your usual?* Reaching into his display case, he grabbed one of the massive pastries and slid it into the paper pocket to hand it to me.

"Gracias," I returned, handing him far more Euro than was necessary for the pastry. I would overpay him until the day I died if it meant I continued to have access to my favorite treat.

"What is it?" Isa asked as I pulled her into the little alcove between Samuel's shop and the jeweler next door.

"Ensaimada," I said, pulling it free and tearing off a piece of the spiral wound pastry. My fingers were instantly covered in powdered sugar as I handled it and held it up for her to take the first bite. "It's my favorite food on the planet. *This* ensaimada specifically, though my housekeeper makes a close second."

"Of course you have a housekeeper," she scoffed, rolling her eyes at me. Unlike most other people when they dared to be so defiant with me, her attitude only excited me. I touched the pastry to her lips, watching the powdered sugar stain them white briefly before she parted for me and let me rest the pastry on her tongue. In the moments before she closed her mouth and moaned, I was filled with the sudden desire to see my cum on her pretty pink tongue before she swallowed me down.

She chewed slowly, savoring the bite as I pulled a piece off for myself and ate it. The light, fluffy sweetness of the pastry exploded over my tongue like a cloud. "That's delicious," Isa said, swallowing finally.

"I'll feed it to you every day," I said, holding up another bite as she laughed and nipped my finger. We stood close to one another, finishing it in a comfortable silence. I loved that Isa spoke when she had something to say, but she didn't feel the need to fill every void in conversation with small talk.

Her level of comfort with the quiet, watching and listening to the people of Ibiza as they made their way up and down the streets, spoke to her as a person. She watched everyone. Listened to everything around her.

When the pastry was gone, I pulled the wipe out from the pocket where Samuel always stored it, using it to clean my fingers. Then I leaned in and licked the spare powdered sugar off Isa's lips, kissing her sweetly. "*This* is how you get to know someone, Princesa," I assured her, my lips brushing against hers as she nodded her agreement.

"Your way is better," she said with a breathy sigh, making me smile into her mouth as I molded my lips to hers. We fit together so flawlessly, it was a wonder I'd spent my entire life without her lips on mine and her body contoured to me. Never in my life had I felt such completion as I did with her in my arms, or the compulsion to kiss a woman.

Inhaling her scent, with the taste of ensaimada between us, I found my forever.

12

ISA

Rafe's hand warmed my spine through the gauzy fabric of my sundress as he guided me down the street.

My feet hurt. The consequence of hours of walking through the streets of Dalt Vila. Exploring the citadel had been everything I'd dreamed it could be as my hands touched stones that had seen centuries of history.

Entire generations of people had touched those walls, the essence of their souls captured in the porous rock. It made me want to contribute my spirit to the collection, to be a part of something bigger than me for once.

But all good things came to an end, and Rafael guided me away from the citadel when the sun started to set and the growl of my stomach echoed through the space. We made our way back down the paths to the lower part of the walled-in city, and Rafe guided me over to the edge. Leaning over the wall, I looked down at the cliff side where the blue water darkened as the sun went down. His lips touched the side of my neck as I bit my lip, suppressing the urge to moan.

Despite my exhaustion, my body came to life with even the slightest touch from him.

"Thank you for today. It was..." I paused, spinning to look up at his breathtaking face. It scared me to realize that I'd rather spend all my remaining time in Ibiza looking at him than looking at the ocean or watching the sunset. "Everything," I finished with a tiny shake of my head as emotion formed a lump in my throat.

He rested a single hand on my waist, the other cupping my cheek as he surrounded me. Was it so normal for men to be *this* physically affectionate? It seemed like he was always touching me, always claiming my body as his through a caress or staring into my soul through his remarkable eyes.

"You deserve everything," Rafe murmured, touching his lips to mine in the soft sweep of a caress. The hand at my waist slid down, grasping me around the back of the thigh and lifting while I squealed into his mouth. He deposited me on top of the edge of the wall, where I clung to him desperately as fear settled over me, and I pulled my lips from his.

I looked over the edge, panicking when I saw the water below me and the distance I would fall.

"I want to get down." I pushed closer to his body, trying to find a way down as he spread my legs and slid between them quickly. The terror was so strong that I never even noticed the people walking by and staring at the inappropriate position.

"I won't ever let you fall, *mi princesa*," he said, holding me firmly. "Fear can bring you to life." I shook my head, glancing back at the water once more as my lungs heaved with the rising panic attack.

I couldn't.

Anything but the water.

He yanked me tighter against him, bending his head to capture my lips with his as he held me still. I melted into him despite myself, desire mounting alongside my terror as I opened my mouth to his and our tongues met in a fierce tangle of passion. I hated him at that moment, wanted nothing more than to punish him for using my fear against me. Even though there was no way for him to know about the accident or the fact that I was terrified of water, my rage drove me higher and higher.

His hand slipped between our bodies, shoving my dress out of his way so he could slide it inside my white lace underwear and touch me. "Not here," I gasped into his mouth, but I couldn't stop him. Trapped between him and the water at my back, there was no escape from the onslaught of sensation he built inside of me. He worked in tandem with the adrenaline coursing through my veins, working my clit with his thumb as he pressed a finger inside and stroked that spot within me that made my legs twitch around him. "Rafe," I warned. His wicked touch distracted me from the worst of my fear, the harshness of my breath shifting from terror to desire while he finished me.

He yanked my head closer, swallowing the cry of my orgasm with the pressure of his lips on mine as I convulsed around him in my strongest orgasm yet. When I finally crumbled down from the white hot high, I slapped his chest in reprimand and pinched him until he stepped back and slid me down carefully.

"You asshole! I could have died!" I looked back over my shoulder, glaring at the offending water as I resisted the urge to cry. Even my fear hadn't prevented me from coming undone with his touch. It had driven me higher and higher.

He grabbed my face in his hands, rubbing his thumbs

under my eyes as he stared at me as if he could will me to understand one simple truth.

"*Never.*"

My heart pounded. The aggression in his stare as he watched me took me off guard, and I softened in his grip.

There was something dancing in his eyes, and I didn't think I'd ever understand it as he held me still and leaned in and captured my lips with his. The brand of his touch echoed through me, lighting me on fire despite the heat of desire only a moment before.

When he pulled away and took my hand to guide me down the street, I realized something particularly strange that hadn't been true when he'd sat me on the ledge.

There wasn't another person in sight.

My steps were wobbly as he guided me toward a little restaurant with outdoor dining roped off in the middle of the street. The sun had set fully while we had our moment overlooking the ocean, and stars lit the sky, and the shops kept the outdoor lights to a minimum to help reduce light pollution.

Never in my life had I seen so many stars or a moon so bright before coming to Ibiza.

He spoke in Spanish to the hostess at the restaurant, and she guided us to a table at the edge of the roped-off section. Moving to pull out my chair for me, he pushed me in as soon as my butt hit the chair. Tucking me up to the table while the hostess hurried off, he took his own seat across from me. Our server was with us as soon as he did, pouring ice water into glasses and setting them on the table while I reached over and snatched up my own to suck back greedy gulps. I'd been thirsty even before Rafe tormented me, so after he'd finished with me, I felt like a desert.

Rafe rattled off a list in Spanish without even glancing at the menu, shocking me as he ordered for me. It seemed presumptuous when he'd met me the night before, but I also didn't feel like dealing with the complications of choosing my meal with him. Knowing he'd be continuing to pay for everything we did together shouldn't have bothered me in the slightest, considering he could *clearly* afford it and I couldn't.

But the independent woman in me revolted against the idea, even if I knew it was probably a silly thing to worry about. I'd have felt compelled to order the least expensive thing on the menu out of obligation.

If I could even read it.

The server hurried off, leaving us in the small crowd of people dining outdoors. I rubbed a hand over my shoulder, wincing when the skin felt tight beneath my touch. It didn't look pink, not with the tone of my skin, but there was no questioning the symptoms of a sunburn.

"Does it hurt?" Rafe asked, studying the motion.

"Not too bad," I said. "Just a minor burn. Chicago isn't exactly known for its sunshine," I said shyly, realizing it was the first time I'd told him where I was from. I wasn't sure the decision had been a smart one, but there was comfort because it was a big city.

Isa was a common enough name.

He didn't comment, choosing instead to raise his water to his lips and take a sip. The server returned with a bottle of wine, pouring it carefully into two glasses for us. I smiled up at him, even if I wasn't sure I should drink. I didn't seem to be able to keep my head on my shoulders with Rafe when

I was sober. If I got drunk, I'd probably let him fuck me on the table.

For the first time since I'd met him, there was tension in our silence. Things left unsaid after he'd pushed me outside my comfort zone and taken control of me in ways I wasn't sure I should like.

I couldn't say I hadn't enjoyed it, but it shouldn't have happened. It was reckless, dangerous. Not to mention that someone could have seen us. What would my mother have done if she'd somehow seen me?

I shuddered.

"I need you to know something, Isa," he said, reaching across the table and taking my hand in his. "I won't ever let anything harm you."

"Accidents happen," I sighed. "I'd just rather not take unnecessary risks like that again. Please."

He squeezed my hand. "Living is not an *unnecessary* risk, Princesa. When you're with me, you're perfectly safe and you never need to worry about a thing."

"You aren't God, Rafael," I laughed, the smooth sound of his full name rolling off my tongue even though I'd never used it before. "You can't make promises like that, when you have no way of guaranteeing you can keep them. I'd much rather you promise me nothing rather than have you lie to me."

He chuckled, the sound fading into the darkness as the hairs on my arms raised in apprehension. "I am most definitely not God," he said. "But I will never make you a promise I don't intend to keep. Anything that wants to hurt you would have to go through me first, and trust me when I say that is extremely unlikely to happen."

"Okaay," I said, drawing out the last sound as the server brought us a platter with some type of Crostini. "That doesn't protect me from falling off a cliff, and there's just no need to push those limits."

He studied me, holding up a piece of the bread for me to take the first bite. His propensity for feeding me seemed odd, but I couldn't deny that it felt like an intimacy most men didn't afford to their casual flings. It helped me feel like I mattered to him in ways I hadn't expected.

Similar to the ways he mattered to me, even though he shouldn't.

The burst of acidic flavor hit my tongue as soon as I chewed. "Fear is how we know we're alive. I want to bring you to life, Princesa," he said, watching me carefully as I swallowed. His gaze on me felt knowing as I considered my response, eventually settling on the only thing I could give him if I expected the same in return.

Honesty.

"Then what do I do if I'm afraid of you?"

He stilled suddenly, setting the bread on the tray and wiping his hand on the napkin carefully. Something was so measured about the movements, like he worked to control his reaction and keep me from seeing something in it. "Why would you be afraid of me, Princesa? When have I given you reason to think I would harm you?"

"I didn't mean afraid of you physically," I admitted, furrowing my brow as the tight lines of his body relaxed suddenly. "I just meant—" I paused, not having expected having to explain my feelings. I had wanted nothing along those lines, and I should have kept my damn mouth shut. "We both know what this is. After my vacation, I'll go home and never see you again. You seem determined to make that as difficult for me as possible," I said with a quiet laugh. My relief that I'd found a way around my feelings was short-lived as his jaw clenched and his nostrils flared. Anger touched every line on his face, morphing him from trouble to terrifying before he smoothed out the lines and smiled.

"Is it so bad to want you to think about me after your vacation is over?" he said smoothly, picking up his bread and taking a bite carefully. His face was flawless, beautiful once again, and I had to wonder if I'd imagined a phantom where there was none.

It wouldn't have been the first time.

"No, of course not. I'd just like to go back to my life without being unable to function without you."

"Well, then I think we simply want very different things from this relationship, Princesa. I very much want you to need me, as much as I've quickly come to need you."

His face remained casual despite the odd words, and when the server brought more food, he delved into the plates to feed me bits from each of them and explained what it was he'd gotten for me to try. Even though they were delicious, exhaustion settled over me.

It had been a long couple of days, and Rafe's odd words rang in my head.

I couldn't decide why they felt like a promise.

The ocean breeze was heaven on my burned skin, blowing through the daybed by the pool like a cool gift sent from the spirits. I drifted in and out of consciousness while I read with Rafael at my side doing some work on his phone.

He'd determined a quiet day was in order while I recovered from the exertion of the day before, making me feel pathetic. I'd given in when I fell back asleep in bed after he made love to me after breakfast, and hadn't woken up until noon. My jobs back home didn't require so much walking and weren't nearly as exciting.

I had a feeling the new and regular orgasms weren't doing much to dissuade me from sleeping either.

I opened my eyes, looking up to find Rafe staring down at me. His face was relaxed as he studied mine. "How long have you been watching me?" I asked with a hoarse giggle. He grabbed the water bottle off the edge of the bed, tipping it so that water poured into my mouth slowly.

"A while," he said vaguely. "I like watching you."

"That is either very sweet or slightly creepy. I can't decide which." He ducked down and nipped my bottom lip. Kissing me, he groaned into my lips as he shifted his weight to hover over me as his lips moved against mine with a smile.

"It's probably a bit of both," he admitted, his chuckle a deep rumble as his chest shook against mine. The ring of his cell phone on the day bed broke the moment, shattering the intimacy between us as I held my breath. He glanced at the phone, sighing in frustration before he picked it up and looked at me while he answered. *"Espera un minuto,"* he barked into the phone, turning his eyes to me as he stood. "I have to take this, Princesa," he said, leaning down to kiss me firmly one last time before he walked to the edge of the pool where the steps led to the beach below. He leaned on the railing, watching me until his face hardened at whatever the person on the other end of the call said and he turned his cold gaze toward the ocean.

Grabbing my own phone off the bed, I pulled up Chloe's number and called her, needing advice on how to handle a man who kept secrets so efficiently that I couldn't even guess what they were. "Yo ho," she sang on the other end, the sounds of the city echoing in the background as I heard Hugo's voice yelling at someone playfully.

"Do you think he's married?" I asked, not even bothering to say hello. Without a clue for how long his phone call would take, I watched him pace back and forth on the walkway, barking orders at the person he spoke with.

There was a pause, and I wondered briefly if Chloe knew something I didn't. "What would make you think that?" she asked finally. "I didn't see a ring or a tan line the other night."

"No, there's no tan line," I agreed. I'd checked multiple times during our time together, wondering why I couldn't get rid of the nagging sense that something was just *wrong*. "He always takes his phone calls in private. Isn't that strange? It's not like I speak much Spanish so I couldn't understand what he said if he sat right next to me. The walking away just seems...excessive," I said.

"Let it go," she said. "Even if he were married, that's not on you. If you knew he was married and slept with him anyway? Sure, then you'd be partially at fault, but if he's going around and seducing women without disclosing that, then the blame falls on him entirely," she said. I started to interject when she cut me off to finish. "But, I don't think he's married. Married men who want to cheat don't pick one woman to spend their week with, they sleep with as many as they can in the limited time frame they have. At least, that's what I would think they do."

"So why the distance for phone calls?" I asked, picking at the fraying edges of the nail polish on my fingers. I shouldn't have done it since I hadn't brought any, and to be with Rafael I'd need to not have chipped nails.

"Maybe he just takes his business seriously. Men don't get to be as rich as he is without being professional. It's probably just a habit. You said he's in sales and investments, right? That sounds like it could be confidential."

"I hope you're right," I agreed. I'd never forgive him for deceiving me if he had someone waiting for him, but I'd also never forgive myself. I hadn't outright asked, and now I was terrified to.

How did I ask a question when I didn't want the answer?

13

RAFAEL

The call took much longer than I wanted it to, but I never stopped watching Isa. She might not communicate verbally as well as I suspected most women would have in her situation, but her body never bothered to try to hide anything from me.

Her body was an open book, and I'd use that to my advantage until she let me inside her head.

The moment my phone rang, she'd gone from joking about me being creepy to tense and insecure. While I loved that she was jealous over potential threats to her claim on me, she needed to understand that no woman would ever tempt me away from her.

I just didn't know how to tell her that without scaring her off. She wasn't ready for words like forever.

When I returned to our daybed, she was busily texting the photos she'd taken of the citadel the day before to her mother. She made no move to hide her phone from me or keep secrets, and the thought pleased me more than it should have when I couldn't be as open with her.

Probably ever, if blood and death threats made her squeamish.

The only part of the photos that didn't sit well with me was the way she specifically avoided sending any pictures of the two of us together. We'd taken a couple in the citadel, her beaming face next to mine as she curled into me comfortably.

"Why didn't you send her any of us?" I asked, settling in next to her and nodding toward her phone.

She laughed in response, the sound sarcastic in a way I didn't like coming from her. "She very specifically told me *not* to get into trouble," she said, touching a finger to my bare chest and looking up at me with a secret smile.

"To be fair, you didn't get into trouble. Trouble got into you." She gasped, slapping my chest playfully at the dirty innuendo. Taking the phone out of her hand, I dropped it onto the daybed and hauled her up into my arms with a broad smile on my face.

As much as I wanted Isa to tell her family about me, I had more pressing matters to tend to. Since it was probably better they didn't know about me until I was certain Isa would make the right choice, her family would wait.

She wrapped her legs around me with a laugh, my hands touching the naked flesh of her thighs where her bikini bottoms grazed the edges of her perfect ass. She went still in my arms when she realized where I was walking, neither her fight or flight instincts taking over as her breathing went rapid.

My first foot touched the water, submerging while I pretended not to notice Isa's rising panic. She couldn't live on an island and not be comfortable swimming. I'd push her as much as I needed to, until we unraveled the bulk of the fear that had kept her away from the water since she'd nearly drowned as a child.

The moment the water touched her feet, she clung to me tighter and tried to inch herself up my body. I forced my face into a mask of confusion, tilting my head at her thoughtfully as I stepped further toward the deep end. "Are you afraid of the water?" I asked her.

She sighed, nodding her head and burying her face in my neck as the water covered her from the waist down. "Mhm," she hummed into me.

"I'm sorry, Princesa," I said, rubbing my thumbs over her skin to soothe her. "You never said." I turned toward the stairs, hoping that the stubborn side I knew was inside her would come to the surface.

"It's okay. Just don't let me go. Please," she said with a little whimper. I felt an unreasonable amount of pride, that she was brave enough to confront her fears at all, but also that she trusted me enough to let me help her through it.

"I won't let you drown," I reassured her anyway, moving through the water slowly until it kissed the back of her shoulders. She sucked back a ragged breath, working to control her breathing. I didn't go any deeper, sensing she'd reached the limit of her tolerance for the day. In all my reading about severe phobias stemming from childhood trauma, I knew logically it would take time. She wouldn't suddenly not have a fear of water after one swim in a pool.

But I'd gladly take the baby steps she took with me, when she'd never even tried with anyone else. I moved to the loungers on a ledge at the edge of the pool. Lifting her up onto one of them, I deposited her in a lounger and admired her body as she forced herself to lie back, and the water moved over her skin. That emerald green bikini would be the death of me as she put her arms at her sides and forced herself to hold perfectly still. Pulling myself up onto the lounger next to her, I enjoyed the way the sun felt on my skin, even as I knew we'd only have a few moments to enjoy it before Isa should get into the shade.

It would take time for her skin to adjust to the strength of the Mediterranean sun, even with all the sunblock in the world.

"Have you always been afraid of the water?" I asked, watching as she forced herself to turn her head toward me, while she considered her words carefully.

"No. I—" she paused, sighing as my hand took hers in mine and she breathed a little easier. "I fell into the Chicago River when I was little. We were on the Riverwalk one day, and it just happened so fast," she said. "Odina and I both ended up in the river."

"Odina?" I asked, watching as she realized I didn't know who that was. I was sure it was hard to imagine having someone who was so a part of your identity, a mirror of yourself, and having someone not know she existed.

"My twin sister," she said. "We aren't close. We're totally opposite, even if we look the same."

"There are two of you?" I asked, chuckling because I knew it was impossible. Even if I hadn't seen for myself, there could never have been someone as flawless as Isa.

She shrugged. "Physically yes. Although she's the fun sister. She's so adventurous and unafraid. Sometimes I wish I could take just a little of that from her and give her some of my caution. Balance us out, you know? It's like she got all the extremes on one end of the spectrum and I got the other."

"Polar opposites," I said, nodding my head because I understood and very much agreed with the assessment.

"Anyway, I've never been comfortable with the water

since then. I wasn't breathing by the time they pulled us out." I only just managed to keep myself from asking how her mother could have allowed such a thing to happen. To let *both* your daughters fall into the river was unthinkable.

Insulting her family would do me no good in trying to earn her trust and her love. If she thought I would be an issue with her family, Isa would turn her back on me before I could blink. For now, they were her world. My judgements would have to wait until her perspective on life changed.

Until all that mattered to her was me.

Isa swung her sandals in her free hand as we walked back from the tapas bar on the beach, staring up at the starry sky above us. Her face was more relaxed than I'd ever seen it. Thoughtful in a peaceful way, rather than the concentration I'd grown used to seeing take over her expression.

When she turned those shining eyes my way, I reached over to capture her face with my free hand and lean down to kiss her. The way she smiled into my mouth filled me with hope that my plans for her hadn't been a waste of time and energy. I'd do it all over again, if it meant she could look at me with stars in her eyes and love on her face.

And I knew without a doubt that it was the blooming of love that danced behind her expression when she dropped her guard in these moments. It could be nothing else, even if it was rooted in lies.

Better to do what was necessary and then ask for forgiveness, than to ask permission and never have this time with her.

She glanced back at the tapas bar behind us wistfully,

her face twisting into a secret smile as her cheeks flushed. "What is it, *mi princesa*?"

She turned back to me with a shy glance, focusing her attention back on the beach and putting one foot in front of the other. "I just wanted to remember how it looked. That's all." I grinned down at her, promising internally to make the effort to take her back as frequently as possible.

El Infierno wasn't far from Ibiza.

The city lights illuminated Ibiza Town to our right as we walked back toward the hotel. Out in the distance over the water, the figure of *Es Vedra* loomed. "I'll take you to watch the sunset tomorrow night. Nothing compares to watching it with *Es Vedra* in the background."

She hummed softly, making me want a reminder of what the vibrations felt like with her pretty mouth wrapped around my cock. I resolved to find out, given that she'd proven to be a very willing student the first time. Approaching the steps that would take us to the hotel, I turned to tell her about the island being magnetic when I noticed a figure looming at the top of the steps.

Feeling the sudden tension in my body as the smile slipped off my face, Isa turned to face me and looked up to the man in question with confusion on her face. "Do you know him?" she whispered. Pavel's dark eyes shifted to her at my side, his face impassive as he studied her and giving nothing away. His gaze dropped from her face, gliding over her body and tilting his head to the side to scrutinize her scar.

The Kuznetsovs always did like their toys scarred and broken.

Just the knowledge that he'd laid eyes on my woman threatened my patience. Knowing the things he did to women drove me over the edge. I pulled the key card from my pocket, pressing it into Isa's hand while she looked between us and tried to fit the pieces together. Nothing in Isa's life had prepared her for the world I had thrust her into. She could never even begin to guess at the origins of the man watching her, as his face tilted in sudden interest when I tended to her rather than dealing with him first.

He would need to be handled. Quickly.

"Go up to the room. Now," I ordered, keeping my voice quiet. "I mean it, Isa."

"But—"

"Now," I stressed quietly. She swallowed, nodding her head and curling her fingers around the key card. I couldn't afford to kiss her or show her any affection to soothe the discomfort tearing her apart. Not when Pavel had already seen too much.

Having Isa out in public would always come with inherent risks. People knowing she existed was dangerous for her at best.

Deadly at its worst.

She turned on her heel, taking that first step slowly and then hurrying her pace as she gave Pavel a wide distance and made her way toward the entry to the main hotel. I moved up the steps carefully, watching until Isa faded from view within the main lobby. One of my men disguised as staff turned toward me from the pool area, raising a hand to show he'd seen her and would make sure she made her way upstairs as he followed her inside.

I gave it a few seconds to ensure she was tucked away safely, and then I turned my attention to Pavel. Whatever he saw in my regard must have finally resonated the danger of his situation as he backed away a step. "Rafael," he said with a chuckle. "You're a tricky man to get in touch with."

The attempt at humor fell flat, as my body slowly

followed the angle of my head and I spun to give him the full effect of my presence. Although I stood without the formality of my suit to encase me in black, Pavel would never be able to stand on his own against me. Even if I did look less intimidating than him; he in his full suit and me in a t-shirt and shorts.

I reached across the space between us. Taking his throat in my hand until his Adam's apple bobbed against my grip and he gagged, I bent him backward until he had no choice but to lean on the railing by the stairs for support. "Rafael," he gasped, the sound ragged and forced as I restricted his breathing.

"You've got some fucking nerve coming here," I said quietly, glancing at the suddenly empty pool area as my remaining men cleared it of hotel patrons.

"You didn't give me a choice."

Another gag came at the increased grip of my fingers on the side of his neck. "When I tell you to fucking wait, you goddamn wait until I'm ready for a meeting. I do not give the first fuck what it is you need, because I don't operate on your schedule. Take your fucking ass back to Siberia where it belongs."

He shrugged off my hand finally as I relaxed my grip, standing to his full height as he glared at me with contempt. "You didn't give me a choice but to come myself. Sending my man back with a missing finger was harsh, even for the infamous *El Diablo*."

"Nothing you have to say to me cannot wait a week, Pavel," I growled.

He paused, and I watched his decision to be *very* stupid cross over his face as he considered his options. "She's pretty," he rumbled, reaching up a hand to touch his sore throat. "I would hate to see her sad when I slit her friend's throat and hang her from your balcony. To waste such beauty on sadness would be a crime, no?"

I gave precisely zero shits about Chloe. A few days prior, I wouldn't have cared. In fact, if things with Isa went sour, her friend's death would be convenient for me. Since Isa had chosen not to tell her family about me, there would be no one to give my name in connection to her disappearance. There'd be no authorities for me to deal with.

They wouldn't have been much in the way of an obstacle, considering they were all in my pocket anyway. But I went through my life trying to be inconvenienced as little as possible.

It irritated me that I cared for Isa enough to not want to see her face when she realized her friend was dead. Particularly because she would learn the truth of Hugo's deception soon enough. That alone would crush her, with how close they'd grown.

"What do you fucking want, Pavel?" I growled my final warning. "As you well know, I have a woman waiting for me. I would much rather be in her company than looking at your ugly face."

He sneered in my direction, transforming the look into a smile as he tried to fall back on his fake humor that he believed mended broken alliances. But nothing could ever make up for what he'd done here, after involving Isa.

If his death hadn't already been guaranteed, it would be after tonight.

"I want to meet tomorrow. Bellandi's war on human trafficking is affecting my bottom line. I will not stand for it, Rafael."

I smirked at him, wondering how the man had survived for so long being so ignorant, but I rattled off an address instead. I wanted to deny him the meeting based on principle, but I very much looked forward to seeing his shock when he realized the truth.

Matteo Bellandi may have led the charge in the fight against trafficking in Chicago, branching out to other cities through his alliances, but his interests didn't extend as far as Russia. He had no desire to control the way the original families conducted their business in Europe.

That endeavor was mine alone.

14

ISA

I paced back and forth in the hotel room with all the glass doors closed. Something about that man had struck me as wrong, crawling along my skin like unseen insects. I didn't want to breathe the same air as him. It set me on edge enough that I found myself continually glancing toward the closet where my suitcase sat on the floor in complete contrast to Rafe's meticulous order.

He'd told me to unpack my things earlier in the day, but I couldn't bring myself to do it.

I barely knew him, and the hotel room was in his name. I needed to be able to make a quick getaway if things turned sour.

The stranger on the steps might have been the catalyst for that escape. I couldn't explain why, if asked. Rafe was allowed to have conversations with other people, but the way he'd sent me up to the room terrified me.

I glanced at my phone on the coffee table, overcome with the sudden desire to know more information about the man I was sleeping with. I hadn't thought I wanted to know, not when knowing less about him made it easier to walk away. But I took the fact that I couldn't force myself to zip my suitcase and walk out as a sign that I'd passed that point.

Walking away from him would break something inside me, but I'd do it anyway.

Because that was the responsible thing to do. The smart choice was to go home to my quiet and safe life in Chicago. Taking risks and trusting the wrong people only got you one place in life.

Drowned in the Chicago River.

Swallowing back my anxiety, I lunged forward and snatched my phone off the table. Bringing up the web browser, I'd only typed the first three letters of his name into the search bar when the knock at the door made me jump and drop my phone to the coffee table with a thump. "Who is it?" I asked nervously.

"It's me," Rafe's deep voice said from the other side. I brushed a hand through my hair, moving to the door to pull it open. He stepped into the suite, invading my space instantly as the door closed behind him.

He moved into the living room area, pouring himself a shot of tequila from the bar while I gawked at him. Aside from the occasional glass of wine, I hadn't seen him drink.

He stepped closer to me once he slammed the glass back down on the counter, his breath smelling like the sharp bite of alcohol as it touched my cheek. He glanced down at the coffee table, furrowing his brow briefly before his eyes came back to mine. "Have you been looking into me?"

My breath caught in my throat as I looked down to my phone, the open browser sitting there with the undeniable start of his name already typed out. I snatched it up in my hands, closing the app and locking the screen quickly as my cheeks burned with embarrassment. Googling a man like

Rafael seemed so arbitrary, especially when I was having sex with him.

Grasping my chin, he tilted my head up to look at his eyes as he took the phone from my hands and tossed it onto the couch. Unease slithered up my spine as his eyes glittered with something dangerous. "You shouldn't do that, *mi princesa*," he murmured.

"Why not?" My voice cracked with the quiet words, barely a whisper in the air between us.

"Perhaps you'll find answers you're not ready for," he said, gliding his thumb up to stroke over my cheek as I swallowed.

I tugged away from his grip, wanting distance between us. The man who stared back at me wasn't the same man who'd shown me around Ibiza. "I think maybe I should go," I said.

His eyes darkened more, his jaw clenching subtly as he watched me. There was a warning in that gaze. A warning I didn't have the information I needed to make the right choice. "Is that what you want? To go?"

I glanced over at the door, eyeing it as I struggled with my sense of flight and the desire to stay.

I didn't want to go back to reality. I didn't want to go back to being the girl who didn't feel anything. Tears stung my eyes as I considered my options. "You're scaring me, Rafael."

"You don't need to be scared, Princesa. What happens out there," he said, gesturing to the windows, "has nothing to do with what happens between us. I don't want to hurt *you,*" he added, stressing the final word as he stepped closer to me in my indecision, "but that doesn't mean I'm a good man. What you may find could change everything, and sometimes ignorance is bliss."

I swallowed, looking up at him as his hands wrapped

around me and tugged me into his chest. "I thought you worked in investments."

"All businesses have rivals, Isa. People determined to tear me down for their own benefit. For now, all you need to know is that my business is something entirely separate from our relationship. Everything else will fall into place when the time comes."

I swallowed, nodding with uncertainty. I knew, without a doubt, that I should be running for the hills and the door. But something warned me it would be a terrible mistake, and I couldn't force my legs to move to do it.

"Am I in danger? From him? You sent me up to the room in such a rush, I can't help but feel like something is very wrong."

"He's an overzealous business associate who lacks boundaries. I've agreed to meet with him tomorrow so he will stop bothering me and then we can resume our plans. So long as you intend to stay," he said. I nodded my assent, unable to find the words, but knowing that walking out would be a mistake.

"Good," he said, chasing away some of the shadows with a smile. His hand came up to grab the back of my neck in a firm hold, touching his forehead to mine as he walked me back toward the bar in the corner.

There was a single press of his lips against mine. His eyes watched me for a reaction while he sighed into my mouth and nipped my bottom lip erotically.

"Are you still afraid, *mi princesa*?" he asked, his fingers grasping the hem of my dress and lifting until the cool air struck the bottom of my stomach.

I admitted the truth with an honesty I didn't want to give. "Yes," I said on a gasp.

"And what does fear do?" he whispered, leaning his head

in to touch his lips to my throat and drag his teeth over the skin.

"It makes us feel alive." I echoed the words he'd given me when he pushed me past my limits. His hands dragged the dress all the way off my head forcefully, leaving me in nothing but a bra and panties while he was still fully dressed. He kissed me then, tangling his tongue with mine without further warning, and lifted me onto the bar in the same way he had the wall in Dalt Vila. Unhooking my bra and tearing it down my arms, his shirt brushed against my nipples as he spread my legs and stepped between them while he kissed me.

He only severed our connection when he moved a hand between our bodies, watching it glide down my stomach and inside my underwear to touch me with soft, teasing circles on my clit.

"I wanted to fuck you," he said, throwing me back to the feeling of his hands on me in public. To the forbidden desire and not knowing how far he might have taken it. "Right then and there. Did you know that, *mi princesa*?"

I gasped his name, tossing my head back when he pushed a finger inside me carefully. Twisting and turning ever so slightly, he watched my reaction to see if I was still sore. When I didn't protest, he added another while he worked my clit. "People could have seen."

"What would they see, Isa?"

"Us. Me," I whispered, my lips brushing against his as his face hardened into a cruel brutality. I didn't want to like it, didn't want to get off on the violence lurking in his skin, but my body clenched tighter around him. Pulling him closer, as if I could slip him inside my very soul and welcome his darkness into me.

"They'd see your face twist with pleasure while I fucked

my pretty little pussy. They would see me fucking what's *mine,*" he growled, covering my mouth with his. The moment his tongue swept inside, connecting us as it started to feel like we were meant to be, he swept his thumb over my clit in one furious motion and I shattered around him in trembles.

I tore my mouth away from his to cry out with the force of it, my lungs heaving with the power of the orgasm as it washed over me.

It was dirty. It was wrong. Coming with his claim on my body fresh in my mind, and yet the undeniable truth of how much I wanted that crashed over me. He pulled me off the bar and lifted me into his arms as he kissed me, keeping all my senses derailed by the force of his possession.

Shoving a few of the glass panels to the side with the furious swipe of a hand, he led me to the dining table that was open to the night air and set me to my feet beside it. He yanked my panties down my legs, his movements frenzied as he twisted me around to face the table and pushed me forward until I caught myself against the surface with both hands.

He thrust inside me, forcing through my wetness with a furious strike that set my nerve endings on fire. "Rafael!" I gasped, the pinch of pain accompanying the way he pushed in with firm and steady strokes until he reached the end of me. With his hands on either side of my ass, he held me still as he pulled back and thrust forward once more.

"You look so perfect taking my cock, *mi princesa. This* is where you fucking belong." The angle was so different from the other times he'd fucked me, striking against another spot entirely and eliciting a different kind of pleasure.

I felt him everywhere as he moved, gliding in and out of me slowly while he gave me time to acclimate to the feeling.

Then he wrapped my hair around his hand, guiding me to arch backwards to him while I struggled to grip the edges of the table. His other arm wrapped around the front of my body, cupping a breast in his hand and pinching my nipple lightly. "Fuck," I groaned when his hips slapped against my ass, feeling him press against the deepest part of me with every thrust and loving that brief moment of pain before his retreat stimulated me back to pleasure.

He chuckled against my neck as he released my hair, gliding the hand at my breast up to wrap around my throat as he slapped the other down on my ass. I yelped, heat blooming in the wake of his strike. "This fucking ass," he groaned. "One day soon, you'll take me balls deep here, too." The words were a promise. Spoken without a doubt that he believed them.

I shook my head against his grip, wincing when his hand pressed firmer at my throat and my head went light from the slight loss of air. "You'll take whatever I give you, *mi princesa*, and then you'll beg me for more." He pinned me in position, spanking the other side of my ass while he fucked me in furious strokes. His cock swelled inside me as his own climax approached, his groans sounding at my ears as he built higher and higher. "Touch yourself," he ordered, and despite my hesitation I slid a hand between my legs to touch myself tentatively.

Every drive of him inside me shifted me forward, my fingers slipping from my clit to touch the place where we connected. He groaned, releasing my throat to cover my hand with his so that together we gripped his shaft where it entered me. "Oh my god," I whimpered, hanging my head when the heel of his palm nudged my clit with each thrust.

"You were made for me, and I won't let you go, Isa," he said, his words driven by the heat of the moment. I groaned out my second orgasm, collapsing in his arms as he roared out his own release. Heat flooded me as he twitched inside me, pulling our hands away from between my legs to shove deeper.

He stayed inside as I caught my breath, supporting my weight so I didn't collapse face first onto the table. Touching a kiss to my spine, he pulled back. A trickle of fluid followed him, dripping to my thighs as I felt his gaze on me.

After stilling suddenly, I spun around to look at him and his length bobbing free from his canvas shorts. His mouth tightened as I turned my eyes down to my body and to the wetness between my legs. "Oh fuck," I whispered, pressing a hand to my mouth as my panic rose.

Grabbing my underwear from the floor, I turned and hurried toward the bathroom to clean myself up. "Princesa," he murmured, following after me as I closed the door in his face.

How could I have been so fucking stupid? That was the real danger of Rafael, making me forget everything that should have been my priority. Nothing existed but the feel of his hands on me. Until the moment we finished and I realized he'd never put on a condom.

I cleaned as thoroughly as I could, wincing at the light soreness from how rough he'd been as I removed all traces of his cum from my body. Tugging my underwear up my legs, I washed my hands and strode through the suite to get my dress from the living room.

I needed Plan B. Urgently.

"Isa," Rafe said, grabbing my arm and pulling me to his body while I struggled to slip my shoes on by the door. He'd covered himself up, his face written in stone as I made my way to escape the suite.

Even if only for long enough to get medicine, I needed to go. I shoved at his chest. "I need to go to the pharmacy."

"Princesa, it's the middle of the night. The pharmacy is closed." My weight sagged in his grip as I stared out at the night sky. We'd eaten dinner late, and after all the drama, he was probably right. It *was* the middle of the night. "The morning will be soon enough," he said, cupping my cheek as dejection settled over me.

The sooner it was taken, the more effective it would be, but without a pharmacy to go to, my options were limited. "First thing in the morning," I sighed.

He nodded, but something in his gaze felt almost...disappointed. It didn't make sense, and I brushed it off as the emotional reaction of a woman who had everything to lose. I couldn't have a baby; not then. Maybe not ever.

I would have made a terrible mother.

Instead, I focused on the other reason I had to be concerned about our mistake. "Do I need to worry about—" I paused. "You know."

His eyes darkened. "What, Isa?"

"Diseases. Infections. You know there's no risk from me, but you—"

"Ah," he chuckled darkly. "Fortunately, it has been a long time since I was with anyone before you. You don't need to worry about anything like that."

I nodded, letting him guide me toward the bedroom. He stripped off my clothes, helping me settle in the bed before he took off his own clothes and climbed in beside me. "Why are you so calm? What happens if—"

He shrugged, considering his words. "I am older than you," he said, his voice melancholy as if he was speaking more to himself than to me. Reminding himself of why my reaction might be more extreme than his. "I am ready for children. I understand what we have is new, but it wouldn't be an unwelcome turn of events."

His admission hit me square in the chest, as I let my eyes drift closed with exhaustion.

How could he say such a thing, when I wouldn't even find out if I was pregnant until I was already home in Chicago?

15

RAFAEL

She'd swallowed the pill as quickly as the pharmacist handed it to her. Her desperation to not bear my child did nothing for my mood, knowing I would need to drop her off with Chloe and Hugo only moments later.

I shouldn't have faulted her for not wanting a child at eighteen. I wouldn't have wanted anything to do with one even a year prior.

But Isa had changed everything for me. All I wanted was for the same to be true for her. For her to need me so desperately that she'd do anything to have a future with me.

She should have wanted to use a pregnancy to trap me as many other women might have tried over the years. The kind of wealth I possessed would change her life forever. I wouldn't have minded that in the slightest, coming from her.

She was quiet as she climbed back into the passenger seat of the McLaren, her body stiff and uncomfortable. Like she didn't dare to touch anything as I closed her door carefully once she was tucked safely inside. To say she'd been overwhelmed by my choice of car was an understatement. Maybe I would have been smarter to choose something less flashy.

I lowered my body into the driver's side. "Chloe and Hugo know you're coming?" I asked, glancing over at her to break the silence. She nodded, confirming what I already knew. I'd laid out the rules for Hugo myself in my text to him earlier that morning. The McLaren started with the distinctive purr of luxury, and I pulled out of my parking space to take her through the streets of Ibiza Town. It was far better to explore the city on foot, but my aim was to spend the least amount of time possible away from Isa. "I'm sorry that I had to delay our plans for the day."

Even if she would appreciate the delay, knowing that the alternative would have been her friend hanging at the end of a rope and bleeding all over the terrace where I planned to fuck her at least once.

Maybe I'd save that for the rooftop.

"It's fine. You couldn't have known that you'd meet a random girl to derail your business for the week," she said, twisting the hem of her dress in her hands. I wondered if the supposed side effects of the drug had hit her yet, or if she was still wrapped up in her own worry over an unwanted pregnancy.

For a moment, I'd considered arranging for a placebo instead of the real pill. Something similar had worked for Matteo Bellandi. But when I chose to get Isa pregnant, I'd do it with her knowing what I'd done. There wouldn't be any cloak and daggers regarding our child's conception.

I'd tell her it was time, and that would be the end of it. The nightmare inside of me actually looked forward to her shocked expression and the fight I'd face in convincing her she couldn't change it.

"Still. This business wasn't meant to be dealt with while I was here."

"From the way you speak of Ibiza, I always thought it was home to you. Where are you from if not here?" she asked, glancing out the window. "You have such fondness for the island."

"Ibiza is the closest thing to a home city I have, but I don't spend a great deal of time here anymore," I admitted. "I live on a nearby island, but it's much more isolated. My in-person business dealings always happen here out of necessity because the island is..." I paused, trying to think of a word that wouldn't convey just how isolated the island was.

Nothing said wealth like a private island, and nothing was quite as inescapable for Isa.

"More remote?" she asked.

"Yes. It's less urban. There are no hotels or places to stay on the island. Only the people who live there. But because I don't come to Ibiza as often anymore, business associates who want my time can be voracious. I apologize it has interrupted our time together," I said again, pulling up to the boutique hotel that I'd booked for Isa and her friends. It had killed me to put her in a three-star facility even for a few hours, but Alejandro insisted it was far more believable lodging for a program. Even if the program in and of itself was a charitable operation.

It would continue after Isa came home with me. Well, so long as it wasn't defunded due to her disappearance.

That would be most unfortunate.

With no valet parking, I pulled into one of the front parking spots and hurried out to help Isa from the car. She wound her way through the hotel, looking far more at ease with the lack of luxury than she ever did in the suite. I had to convince myself that was something that would remedy with time as she adjusted to being a very wealthy woman.

When she was my wife, she'd want for nothing.

She guided me into the elevator, turning to me to lean up and press a kiss to my cheek. "You don't need to worry about leaving me with my friends while you deal with your business. I'm capable of being without you for a few hours." She laughed, and the sound grated on my nerves.

I needed her to want to spend all her waking moments with me. Even if it wasn't practical to actually happen, she needed to want it as much as I did.

When the elevator emerged on her floor, she stepped out with a flounce and took my hand in hers to pull me behind her. Their room was at the back of the hotel, as far from the foot traffic of the elevator as I'd been able to manage. She knocked on the door despite having her own key to the room she was meant to share with Chloe.

Her friend swung open the door, all blond haired and blue eyed as she smiled at Isa excitedly. Isa stepped into the room, hugging her friend without ever releasing my hand, and taking me with her. Hugo stood from his seat, his posture going from relaxed to on edge the moment our eyes connected. "This is Rafe," Isa said, as she pulled back from Chloe's clinging embrace. "Rafe, these are my friends. Chloe and Hugo," she said, letting go of my hand to step into Hugo's chest for a hug. He wrapped his arms around her, enclosing her in an embrace that clearly felt uncomfortable to him with me watching with a clenched jaw.

"It's nice to meet you both," I said through clenched teeth.

I wanted nobody to ever lay a hand on my princesa, but that didn't mean I could make that happen. Not until she knew the truth of my identity, anyway.

Hugo rested his chin on her head, then pulled back to stare down at her as I might have expected if the friendship had been genuine. The expression on his face left little doubt that, no matter how it had begun, he did care for Isa much like Joaquin. "You good?" he asked as she smiled up at him.

She nodded, biting her lip. Given the way girls spoke to one another, I knew Hugo would know about the pregnancy scare by the time I returned from dealing with Pavel. "I should go, Princesa," I said carefully. She turned to me as I approached, tilting her head up to accept my kiss. "Call me if you need anything or if you aren't feeling well," I said vaguely, trying to convey the message that if her side effects became too much, I would step in to help her through them.

Or call a doctor to help her with the discomfort.

She sighed against me. "Okay, Rafael," she said, clinging to my suit. It was the only physical sign she gave of her unhappiness with my leaving her, and I took it for what it was. Isa wasn't a verbal communicator, and she probably never would be.

But her body told me no lies, only ever showing me the truth of her feelings for me.

"I'll be back as soon as I can," I told her, running my nose up the side of hers.

"You promise?" she asked, and the weakness to her voice almost compelled me to stay. It was as if she went through every moment of every day waiting for me to discover that she wasn't worth my time.

"I promise," I murmured, kissing her one last time before I spun on my heel and left her to Hugo's protection, to talk through her feelings with her friends. I could only hope Chloe would encourage her alongside Hugo, not serve as a deterrent to prevent her from giving herself over to her emotional connection to me.

I would hate to have to get rid of her blond friend if she got in my way.

The address where I'd chosen to meet with Pavel wasn't one of my finer moments. In the moments following the agreement to meet with him, I'd almost instantly regretted the choice. But it was one of my more frequented sites to do business in Ibiza.

My business associates tended to be distracted by the strippers who twirled on the pole. The finest women in Ibiza served me well, allowing me to negotiate deals that were more favorable to me than they might have been otherwise.

I owned the city, and I would never be forced to operate in the shadows as many others had to do within theirs.

My men were already inside the club when I arrived, guarding the women who danced on stage despite the limited audience. Far too early in the day for the club to be open officially, the girls working during these hours of the day were among my more trusted. The women who knew the score, could keep their mouths shut, and knew the types of men who walked into the club for my meetings wouldn't be gentle.

But I'd pay them well for volunteering for the hazard of the job.

My lead bouncer threw open the front doors as I strolled up to them, shifting my pace to an easy saunter the moment all eyes in the room fell on me. I moved through the room without sparing a glance for the men I knew would be in position should the meeting turn particularly sour, and I knew this one would. Pavel remained in his chair, glaring at the girl dancing on the stage as if he didn't sense my entrance. His fury only grew when she turned her eyes to me, smiling as she wound her body around the pole.

I ignored her, sitting at the table with Pavel with my back to her. All my girls knew the score. They weren't there for my entertainment.

"You're late," Pavel said, stubbing out his cigar into the ashtray on the table.

My response came easy, "You're lucky I'm here at all."

"I never thought I would see the day when the almighty Rafael Ibarra was caught in the trap between a woman's thighs," he scoffed. "Just because you have a pretty face does not mean she's capable of loving such a monster."

"You're so concerned with the woman. I should think you have far more important issues to address with your time, Pavel. Let me assure you, the time I'll allow you to waste is very limited." I tapped my fingers on the table as I leaned in.

He sighed his frustration at my unwillingness to make small talk before diving into the subject he'd been so desperate to discuss. "This universal alliance. I will acquiesce to most of Bellandi's terms, but I cannot agree to the terms of trafficking. He must know this is how most of my money is made. Russian women are the standard of perfection," he argued. "I could find you one to keep. She'd be much less bothersome than this American of yours."

My fingers itched for my gun as I sneered at him in warning. "I am uncertain what makes you think Bellandi concerns himself with Europe, but I promise you, this is not Bellandi's crusade."

"Yours?" Pavel asked, sitting back in his chair. He scoffed.

"Your time with those soft-hearted Americans has weakened you. If only your father could see you now, boy."

"He can't, because I tied him to a post while he screamed and set the platform beneath him on fire. Your friendship with my father ended with his death. It will not gain you favor with me," I said, inspecting my nails. "To be frank, I'm confused by your concern over the terms of the contract. You were not invited."

His face paled for a moment before turning red in his anger. "You intend to establish an alliance of this magnitude without Russia?" he scoffed in laughter. "Good luck."

"No. I intend to establish this alliance without *you*. Once you're out of the picture, the person I help rise to power in your absence will be someone who is agreeable to my terms."

He moved quickly, drawing his weapon and pointing it at me as his men moved to follow. "You think to threaten me?" he asked.

I stood from my chair, flipping the table to its side with a quick sweep as I stepped into his space. His gun touched my chest, the room waiting as they held their breath. His men pointed guns at my men, and mine returned the favor. But Pavel knew as well as I did that no one would walk out of the room alive once the first shot was fired.

Moving quickly, I grabbed the barrel of his gun with my left hand at the same time I thrust my right hand into the inside of his wrist. With the force of both hands, the gun turned on him as I pried it from his hands. He stood, raising both of his hands as his cowardice showed. It was easy to have a sense of false bravado when you had a gun in your hand.

The moment he opened his mouth to speak, I struck forward with an open palm. Catching the blow on the bottom of his chin, his head snapped back suddenly. He fell to the floor, as close to dead weight as he could get without actually being dead, as he blacked out and hit the ground with a thump.

His men hesitated, not wanting to sacrifice their lives if Pavel was already gone. Leaning over him, I slapped him across the face until he woke up. "I don't need to kill you today to know you're a dead man, Pavel," I growled, straightening to my full height. I brought my foot down on his kneecap sharply, his scream of pain as it crushed beneath my shoe soothing the edges of my anger and the frustration that I couldn't kill him then and there. Going back to Isa with a bullet hole after the inevitable shootout would be difficult to explain. I turned my back on him and made my way for the door.

He'd signed his warrant in blood the day he threatened Isa.

All that was left was to slowly carry out the sentence.

16

ISA

My body felt so heavy that it ached, but I'd be damned if I admitted it and called Rafe to take me back to the suite. I didn't even want to tell Chloe and Hugo about our carelessness, but with every step it got worse and worse until I just wanted to curl up in a ball and sleep for a year.

But Chloe wanted to go for a stroll through Ibiza Town. She chatted about all the parties they'd gone to while Hugo smiled, watching me thoughtfully. "So how is it?" Chloe asked finally. I'd waited for the question, knowing she wanted me to bring it up. But given the intensity of the night before and that morning, I didn't know what I could say.

"I feel like he's hiding something from me," I said, looking at her. "I'm probably just being paranoid."

"You're good at that," she agreed. "But either way, it's a fling, Isa. He doesn't have to spill his secrets and neither do you. Because in a few days you'll go home and he'll be nothing but a fun memory as you flounce on to the next guy."

"That's not me," I said with a sigh. "I don't think it's that simple."

"Isa, you aren't supposed to develop real feelings for him," Chloe groaned. "If you can't do that, then I think you should end it now." Hugo snorted at my side, sputtering on the swallow of water as he pulled the bottle away from his lips.

"Wrong tube," he grunted, smacking his chest lightly. We walked a few paces as I considered Chloe's words. She was right, I knew. My feelings for Rafe grew every day, even with the drama we'd had.

If I kept going with him, I wouldn't be able to help falling in love with him. "I don't think I can," I admitted, working to convince myself that the inability to walk away was because of my feelings.

Not because of the danger I saw in his eyes when I talked about leaving.

"There need to be some boundaries, at least," Chloe said with a sigh. "Force yourself to talk about going home. Talk about your family. Remind both of you that you'll be ending things soon."

"I don't think that's necessary," Hugo interjected. "You saw the way he looked at her. I think he's interested in Isa enough that he knows when she's due to go home. Have you tried talking to him about how you feel?"

Chloe scoffed, echoing my instinctive reaction. Emotions and feelings and the conversations about them: not my thing. "Yeah okay," she said.

"That's what normal people do in relationships, Isa," Hugo sighed. "When they feel insecure, they talk about it. When they feel like things are moving too quickly, they talk about it so they know they aren't alone."

"That's too much emotional involvement for a fling," Chloe argued.

"Maybe it's not a fling," Hugo disagreed as the pair of them stopped in the middle of the walkway. "It might have started that way, but you can't predict love. If Isa really has feelings for this guy, she owes it to herself to explore them. She should give it a chance."

"I know you did not just advise her to drop her plans for her future so she could stay and have a fling with some guy she just met. I'm *so* sure it has nothing to do with you living in Ibiza and wanting your friend to be close by!" Chloe shrieked, and I watched the conversation devolve into one of their fighting matches. Each one wanted the best for me in their own way, but neither knew the full scope of what might be at stake either.

"I have watched Isa go through the last year of her life without *ever* being so much as interested in a guy. Then this guy comes along, and she immediately reacts to him. All I'm saying is that it deserves to be explored. She doesn't have to know that she's staying in Ibiza right this second, but she should give it until the end of her vacation and not cut it short because she's scared. Living a life afraid of everything that makes her feel is no life at all," Hugo said.

Chloe opened her mouth, her anger rising to a new level as she narrowed her eyes at Hugo. "There's a...small chance I might be pregnant," I said, cutting off whatever Chloe had been about to say in response to that.

"You what?!" she shrieked.

"Would you keep it down," I hissed, taking her arm and guiding her over to the side of the road. "I took the morning after pill. It's probably fine."

"I can't believe you of all people would forget about

something like that," she spat back, staring at me with a slack jaw as if I'd lost who I was.

Sometimes it felt like I had.

"He makes everything else go away," I whispered, watching as she rolled her eyes.

"It's called being horny, Isa. We all go through that, but that's no reason not to be responsible."

"That's not what I mean," I argued. "Even when we're not having sex. He just—he makes me feel like I'm right where I'm supposed to be. He gives me all his attention, and it's unnerving and flattering all at once. He listens when I speak, and he hears the things I don't even say."

"Jesus fucking Christ." Chloe hung her head, rubbing a hand over her face. "You're in love with him."

I didn't respond, mulling over the words even if I wasn't ready to say them. They didn't feel untrue, as much as I wanted to be able to deny them. The truth in them hovered in the air between us as she gaped at me. "Isa?" Hugo asked, prodding me to respond. "Are you?"

"I've only known him for a few days," I evaded.

"Tell him how you feel, Isa," Hugo stressed, wrapping an arm around my shoulders. "For both of your sakes, just tell him how you feel."

"I guess at least if you're pregnant, you know he has the money to make sure you and the baby are taken care of," Chloe said, her voice soft despite the harshness of the words. "If you had to fuck up epically, this was a good time to do it. I'm amazed he let it happen though. A man with as much money as he must have has to be used to watching his back. How freaked out was he?" she asked.

"He wasn't," I said, furrowing my brow as I looked over at her. "He was perfectly calm. Just said he was older than me and he knows he wants kids, so it was only natural for him to not be as bothered as I was."

Hugo stilled at my side, looking down at me affectionately as he kissed the top of my head. "Well, I've never met a guy who didn't panic with a pregnancy scare unless he wanted a baby with *that* girl. It seems to me you aren't the only one who has some feelings to confess."

I nodded thoughtfully, pausing to start the process of walking back to their hotel to rest when I turned and ran face first into a man's body.

The familiar heat of Rafe's hands branded my skin through my sundress, comforting me until I looked up into his tense face and searched for signs that he might have overheard our conversation. He gave nothing away, bending to kiss me with that odd distance in his eyes while he nodded a greeting to my friends.

"How are you feeling, Princesa?" he asked, his face softening when his eyes returned to mine and he cupped my cheek.

"Tired," I admitted.

He nodded thoughtfully, pursing his lips as he looked to Chloe and Hugo. "Let's get you back to the suite then." His hand at my waist steadied me as he walked me toward a parking area and away from my friends.

It wasn't until I was already safely tucked into the McLaren that I realized he hadn't spoken a word to them, or even given me the opportunity to say goodbye.

♙♙♙♙♙

I mulled over his odd actions while we hung out on the rooftop terrace for the rest of the day, letting

Rafe feed me while I enjoyed the salty sea breeze on my skin. Maybe it was a cultural thing, being so possessive that he took me away from my friends with hardly anything but a glare.

I felt much better by the time late afternoon came, only slightly fighting his insistence that I would enjoy the sunset much better on his boat than I could from land.

My phone chimed with a text as Rafe steered the boat toward the tall island, keeping his distance from the island itself as he found the right position he was looking for.

I'm worried about you.

I sighed, wondering if there was merit to Chloe's message. The unfortunate truth was that I couldn't help but worry about me, too. I felt like I'd plunged into the deep end before learning how to swim. Rafe turned off the boat, joining me in the center of the lounging cushioned area at the back so that we both faced the sunset.

He pulled out a picnic basket and a chilled bottle of champagne. Moving to the edge of the boat, he tossed a towel over the top of the bottle and opened it so he caught the cork and tossed it back into the boat as champagne leaked into the sea. "You're going to get the fish drunk," I scolded.

He turned a light smile my way, shaking his head as if he couldn't be bothered with caring about the fucking fish. He poured me a glass as I sat up on the mat, accepting it with pursed lips. "I'm not sure I should drink."

"I spoke with my personal physician. You're okay to drink after taking Plan B," he said to reassure me. I nodded, taking a small sip of the slightly sour liquid as bubbles danced on my palette. Sitting down next to me, he took a sip of his own champagne and set it to the side to feed me a chocolate-covered strawberry. I took a bite of it, greatly preferring it to the champagne.

"You're awfully quiet," he observed, inching into my space until he nearly touched me as I lay back on the cushion to stare at the sky while we waited for sunset. "What's wrong?"

"Nothing's wrong," I said. "I'm just thinking, really."

"Ominous," he chuckled, laying back beside me. "What has *mi princesa* so occupied?"

Turning onto my side to face him, I bit the corner of my mouth as I thought over how to bring up my concerns. The need to know where he stood with our relationship was real, so that I could manage my own feelings and expectations. I didn't want to have expectations at all, and I shouldn't have.

But I certainly knew that I wanted him enough to question the life I'd planned for myself.

"Just thinking about how tiny my room at home will feel after this. How much I'll hate Chicago winters after feeling this sun. Sometimes I think coming here was a mistake," I murmured, watching his body still at my words. "Not one that I regret, but just because it's shown me how boring my life is. Hopefully college will change that."

The sun slowly crept its way toward the horizon, turning the sky pink in its wake as we watched in silence. His lack of response grated on me, showing me exactly where his head was at. Why would he care about my life back home?

He'd be out of my life.

"You shouldn't live a life you're bored with, Princesa," Rafe said finally, reaching over to cup my cheek after leaving me hanging without a response. Leaning in to kiss me, he reminded me of what it was to not be bored. "Boredom is for the dead, and you are very much alive." Reaching over to take my hips in his hands, he pinned me to the cushion and moved his body over mine. Trailing kisses from my lips to my neck, he reminded me of what it was to feel as if I could do anything and be anyone, as the sky burst into vibrant pinks with the sun fading over the horizon.

My life would be that much harder to bear when I went home. Starved for his touch. Starved for excitement.

Just empty.

17

RAFAEL

My princesa was drunk. After I'd made love to her beneath the setting sun, we'd returned to our picnic and she'd drunk three glasses of champagne. I could have stopped her, but something in me wanted to see her lose control in that way. Our romantic picnic had been derailed by her stress over a potential, though unlikely, pregnancy and her odd insertion of what waited for her at home.

I couldn't help my anger that she'd been on a boat in the middle of the Mediterranean with me, ready to watch the sunset, and been thinking about her life back home.

She wobbled as I helped her from the McLaren, unsteady even in her flip flops due to the tiredness that was in every line of her body. With a sigh, I reached down and scooped her into my arms. She giggled as I strolled through the doors to the hotel, taking her into the elevator as she curled closer to me. Her face snuggled into my neck, breathing me deeply into her lungs as I thought over my predicament.

With only six days left on our countdown, I'd never

expected to still have her discuss going home like it was a certainty. As soon as the elevator deposited us on the top floor, I carried Isa into the suite and deposited her on our bed. She sighed contentedly as I stripped off her shoes and sat her up to pull the dress over her head. She flopped back down the moment I released her, struggling to get under the blankets as I fought to pull her panties down her legs.

"I want to sleep forever," she murmured when I finally got her bra off and tucked her beneath the blankets.

I chuckled, leaning forward to kiss her lips and linger by her mouth. "But if you slept forever, I would have to follow you." My lips brushed against hers with the words, watching as her eyes filled with tears that she shoved down before they could ever truly form.

"If I slept forever, I'd never have to leave," she said finally, turning to her side and closing her eyes. The words felt like an admission, echoing in the silent room as she quickly fell asleep. I knew she hadn't meant to tell me that, given how at odds it was to her mention of college only hours before.

"You never have to leave regardless, *mi princesa*," I murmured, leaning in to touch my lips to her temple before I made my way to the balcony and looked out over the darkened water.

Her drunken and half-aware words felt like more truth than she gave me when she was awake and sober, a confirmation of everything her body told me. Isa wanted to stay, and she wanted to be with me.

The question would be if she let herself, and with only six days left to convince her that our future was worth walking away from her past, I just hoped I hadn't wasted this time on a fruitless endeavor.

She'd be coming home with me one way or another. If I

had to force her, I'd wish I'd done it the hard way in the process. She'd need time to adapt once we moved home.

Particularly if she wasn't allowed to leave.

***

I sat on the balcony, drinking my *cortado* while I waited for Isa to wake up. Her hair was a tangled mess around her head, her face flush from being pressed into the pillow as she slept through the night.

I didn't want to wake her too soon when she undoubtedly needed the rest, but my plans for the day also wouldn't permit me to allow her to sleep much longer.

We had a long drive ahead of us.

I moved into the bedroom, sitting on the edge of the bed and touching her shoulder lightly. "Wake up, Princesa," I murmured softly, earning a low groan as she mumbled something beneath her breath. "What?" I asked.

"Go away," she repeated. "Sleep."

I laughed as she raised a tired arm to swat me away, the force not even enough to dislodge my hand from her shoulder as she rolled onto her back and covered her eyes with an arm. "Isa," I said, chuckling beneath my breath. "I have plans for the day. You have to wake up."

"Like fuck I do," she groaned, closing her eyes as she proceeded to ignore me. I laughed quietly, enjoying this more feisty version of my woman that I knew hid beneath all the layers of responsibility and fear. Her rhythmic breathing filled the air as she drifted back to sleep, defying my order to wake up in a way that only she would dare.

I hoped she still dared to do such things once she knew the truth of who I was.

I tugged the blanket back, revealing her naked body to

the cool air of the room, and even still she didn't wake. With her right leg cocked to the side, she gave me a view of her entire body from head to toe. I only regretted that I couldn't see both her pussy and her ass at the same time.

Crawling onto the foot of the bed, I inserted myself between her slightly parted legs. My shorts rubbed against her thighs as I pushed them wider, making room for my knees as I leaned my weight over hers. She let out a little snore, lost to a surprising depth of sleep as I positioned myself to wake her up in the best way possible.

Leaning forward, I pressed the flat of my tongue to the soft tip of her nipple and bathed it in warmth. Her brow pinched as she felt it, but she still didn't wake up when I drew the hardening bud into my mouth and sucked lightly. Doing the same to her other breast, I watched her face as her lips parted and she let out a little gasp of pleasure in her sleep.

Who did she dream of when she closed her eyes?

If it was someone else, I'd find out eventually. He wouldn't survive for long.

Trailing my lips down and over her stomach as she gyrated her hips beneath me in her sleep, I kept waiting for the moment her eyes opened. Watching. Waiting for the second when I would see her eyes and know if she'd known it was me all along.

I shoved her knees high as I lowered myself to put my face at her perfect little pussy, leaning in to lick her from her entrance to her clit in a smooth glide. The unique taste of her exploded over my senses, drawing a groan from my throat as I watched her face and spread her folds wide for my assault. She ground her hips up toward my face, seeking more in the dreamland that she refused to leave.

I'd been determined to make her come before taking her,

but the dark and perverse part of me wanted to already be inside her when she snapped back to reality. I circled her clit with my tongue, sliding a finger inside her wet heat and working her until I was sure she was wet enough for what would come.

I grabbed a condom from the drawer, shoving my shorts off awkwardly and working it down my length with a grimace. While I wanted nothing more than to have nothing between us, I wouldn't do it knowing Isa would want to take another morning after pill to deal with the potential aftermath. I couldn't make her love me if she constantly felt sick because of my actions, but as soon as we were back on *El Infierno*, morning after pills would become an impossibility.

She clenched down on my fingers, burying a hand in my hair and pulling me tighter into her pussy. Chuckling against her clit, I withdrew my finger and slipped my hips between her legs. Watching her face as I slid inside her, she parted her lips on a ragged sigh and flung her eyes open to stare up at me. Her gaze was heated, her focus knowing even though she'd only just woken up.

"Rafe," she whispered, pulling me closer. There was no disappointment in her grip as her nails dug into my shoulders and I moved inside her. I thrust harder as she wrapped her legs around me to the best of her ability. She clung to me as I took her, making it easier for me as I rolled onto my back and kept us connected through the shift. She stared down at me in shock, her lips forming a shy pout at the change in position as I guided her to sit up.

"I want to watch you," I murmured, gripping her hips with both my hands as I guided her to move on me. She rolled them backward slowly as I watched her breasts bounce and sway with the steady motion. She took me back inside her, moaning when I pressed against her G-spot with the extreme angle.

Taking her hands in mine, I guided them to touch her breasts. She glanced down at them and bit her lip shyly, cupping them in her hands while I watched her ride my cock and play with her tits for me.

Isa would do anything I asked her to do. She would take anything I gave.

Because she was mine.

Reaching down to her clit, I stroked her while she rode me. Letting her do the work as she sought out her orgasm and used me to get it. Her face morphed with pleasure, her eyes closing slowly as she spiraled. "Eyes on me," I growled in warning. She flung them open, holding my gaze as she flushed. I rewarded her listening with a pinch to her clit, sending her shattering over the edge as she desperately tried to hold my gaze.

She collapsed on top of me in a heap, lifting her hips and doing her best to keep riding me through the climax that dominated her being. I laughed into her hair, pulling her off me and sliding her to her stomach on the bed. Shoving the pillows out of her face, I laid my body over the back of hers and slid my cock between her legs until I sunk deep inside her once more.

I covered her weight with mine lightly, lifting her arms up over her head and pinning her wrists together to hold her still as she lifted her tight little ass up to help me get deeper. "I think you like my cock," I grunted, pounding deep enough to make her cry out. "Don't you, Princesa?"

"Fuck," she whimpered, the response all but a direct confirmation. If I'd been less of a bastard, it might have been enough for me. But I was, and it wasn't.

"Tell me how much you love it when I fuck you," I

grunted, holding her still as I slid a hand beneath her stomach to help her support the weight that I pounded into the bed with every thrust of my dick inside her.

"I love it," she whispered.

"You think you'll ever find somebody else who can give you this?" I asked, as my somewhat irrational jealousy took over all reason.

"No," she whimpered. "No one but you," she confirmed.

I nodded, touching my lips to her shoulder gently before sinking my teeth into her flesh. The intensity of my bite turned bruising, determined to mark her as mine for all to see as she cried out beneath me. The edge of pain made her come again, her pussy clenching down on me as she writhed in my grip. "Only me, *mi princesa*," I growled, fucking her furiously until my own climax tore me apart.

I kissed the mark I'd left with my teeth as I came down from the high of my orgasm, partially expecting her to condemn me for the brutality. But there was nothing but warmth and the afterglow of sex as I climbed off her and guided her to the shower so we could get ready for the day.

"There's no one for you but me," I whispered as she stood beneath the rainforest shower. She turned green eyes my way, smiling slightly as I willed her to understand one simple truth. I didn't just mean today or tomorrow.

I meant forever.

Isa walked at my side as we made our way down to the marina. Her steps were cautious as she stepped onto the wood. I hoped that by the end of the day, her paralyzing fear of water would be a thing of the past.

If she trusted me.

I stepped into the same speedboat from the night before, reaching out a hand to help her step into it gingerly. She wobbled into her seat, breathing out a heavy sigh as her ass touched the surface and she undoubtedly felt more stable. "Where are we going?" she asked, narrowing her eyes on mine.

"Telling you would ruin the surprise," I said, pushing off from the dock and taking my seat. I powered up the boat as she held on to whatever she could reach, easing away from the dock slowly in favor of making my way toward the mainland.

"I'm not such a fan of surprises," she said. I smiled at her briefly, turning my attention to navigating the few boats traveling close to shore as we left Ibiza behind us.

"You'd better get used to them," I told her, patting the seat next to me. She sighed, darting forward to change seats as if she didn't trust her balance. With her at my side, I rested my spare hand on her bare thigh as her floral sundress rode up her legs. She went quiet, the hint of a future making her freeze up as always.

If I didn't find a way to get her to open up, to force her to see me as a permanent staple in her life, I'd lose the connection we'd started to forge. I needed to find the key to Isa's responsibility to her family if I wanted to stand a chance in getting her to walk away from them.

"Tell me about your sister," I said. Isa drew in a deep breath, laughing on the tail end of it as she spoke louder than normal for me to hear her over the wind rushing beside us as I picked up speed.

"Odina has always been troubled," she said. "Rebellious. Carefree. The opposite of me. I couldn't really tell you much else about her to be honest. She hasn't talked to me except to yell at me for as long as I can remember."

"Why?" I asked. In all my watching, I'd never understood Odina's hatred for Isa. Hugo and Joaquin had never been able to find out the truth from either sister, but there was no doubt in my mind that there was something much more sinister working in the hatred between them.

"She blames me for something that happened when we were little. Our mother—" She paused, glancing at me from the side of her eye and pursing her lips. She considered her next words carefully, debating the decision to speak to me about it at all. Finally she bit her lip and released it to look away from me. "Our mother took my side."

"It must have been a pretty big argument to cause a rift for all these years," I observed. I didn't look at her, sensing her need to not have my eyes on her for the remainder of our conversation.

"You could say that, yeah." Leaning her head on my shoulder, she finally turned her green eyes up to me. "My grandmother says that there's something broken in her. I'm not so sure that she's the broken one though."

"Well, I don't know your sister," I said. The lie rolled off my tongue easily, and I clung to the fact that I didn't *really* know Odina despite having met her once. "But you're far from broken, Princesa." Lying seemed like such a trivial offense for a man like me, but I wanted to be able to say that I'd always been honest with Isa.

I might omit the truth for her safety at times, but I would never lie to her just for the sake of it.

"You barely know me."

My fingers dug into the flesh of her thigh, gripping her harder than I wanted with the visceral reaction those words brought me. I wanted to tell her that I knew everything I possibly could. That I probably knew her better than anyone else in the world except herself.

"I think I know you better than you believe," I murmured teasingly. She scoffed, leaning back to let the sun fall on her face. I'd lathered her sunscreen on her before we left the hotel, but I made a note to reapply it for her as soon as we docked.

"It's nice to think so."

Looking over at how stunning she looked with the sunlight kissing her face, I wondered what she would look like lounging on my yacht when I finally brought her home. Even if my instincts roared for me to take her to *El Infierno* then and there, I rejected them in favor of continuing on as planned.

Isa would love me if she didn't already. I'd find a way.

18

ISA

Spain passed by in the windows as we made our way in the car that had been waiting for Rafael at the marina after docking his speedboat. It begged a very simple question. Something that made me realize just how little I knew of his life.

Was the McLaren his? If it was and he lived on another island, how did he get it to Ibiza?

I turned my head away from the window, studying the lines of his profile as he shifted gears and drove along the road. The corner of his mouth tipped up in an arrogant smirk. The same one I'd begun to get used to seeing when he noticed me watching him. It was a look that spoke to the fact that he knew just how handsome he was. That he knew he was irresistible to the female population. Every now and then the smirk took on a dark moment as he turned his eyes to mine, a hunter watching his prey and knowing he had it trapped exactly where he wanted it.

I hoped that part was unique to me, at least. I knew the arrogant smirk was likely shared with the women in his past. But the heat in his eyes felt unique, like he genuinely wanted me in the same way I wanted him.

Irreversibly. Uncontrollably.

Desperately.

I smiled, shaking my head despite the turbulent emotions running through me. He made me feel like I would combust inside my own body. Like he brought out a part of me that I'd never thought would see the light of day. I wanted to hate it, but I didn't.

He made me feel more like myself than I could ever remember being, and that scared the shit out of me.

"Tell me about your family," I said, turning my body in my seat as much as I could with my seatbelt fastened, so that I could get a better view of him.

"There isn't much to tell," he grunted. "My mother died when I was young. My father passed a few years ago," he said. "Neither had any family that they were particularly close to, with the exception of my father's brother. He lives further north with his sons. He and my father never got along, so much so that they moved to opposite corners of Spain to avoid one another. I spent some time with them when I was a child, but we're all typically too busy to spend any time together now."

He pulled off the main road and made his way along a smaller street as he slowed down. He nodded to a man we passed who stepped into the middle of the road after we'd gone. "Does anybody live with you on the island?"

"A great many people live on the island with me. I've made my own sort of family. Sometimes the bonds we form for ourselves are stronger than the ones we're given at birth. I live alone in my house, but we're a very close community."

"I'm glad you have that. I can't imagine all my family

being gone," I sighed, wrinkling my nose when I realized it had probably been an insensitive thing to say. "I'm so sorry."

"Don't stress, Princesa," he chuckled. "I'm not one to be offended by such things." I breathed my relief, glancing to the ceiling. "You talked about your sister a bit. What about the rest of your family?"

"My mom and dad work a lot to be able to support us all. They don't have the highest paying jobs, but they're dedicated and they always made sure we had food on the table. They're strict. I think mostly because of Odina's tendency to rebel against every rule ever created. Then there's my grandmother. She's terrifying," I laughed. "She's my favorite person in the world. It terrifies me to think of her age and the fact that she won't live forever, you know?"

Tears stung my eyes as Rafe pulled the car into a parking spot at the front of the empty lot. I looked across the road, swallowing when my gaze landed on a natural pool with a waterfall near the back as the water curved around the corner of a rock face. They were empty. Not a single person was in sight despite the large parking lot, the only exception being a man who stood guard on the other side of the street with his back to the pond.

"Nobody can live forever, *mi princesa*. But she must have had joy in her life. Having you for her granddaughter," he said, reaching over to unbuckle my seatbelt when I didn't move. He chuckled and threw open his door, closing it behind him as he walked around the front of the car. His lips moved as he said something to the man on the other side of the street, but the blood roaring in my head prevented me from hearing a word of it.

When he pulled my door open, I didn't move to swing my legs out. Frozen to the seat as I glanced over at the hand he extended to guide me out of the car. "You can't be serious," I hissed, turning my head to glare at him.

"Come on, Princesa," he reached in, taking my hand in his grip and tugging me from the car so firmly that I stumbled.

"No!" I growled at him, tugging my hand back from his grip. "I'm not getting in that water, Rafael," I warned. I glared up at him, furious that he'd driven me all this way for something he had to know I wouldn't tolerate. "I can't believe you brought me here."

Shaking my head, I grabbed the handle on the car, determined to wait in there until he had his fun or gave up on his stupid idea. A lifetime of fear wouldn't just be overcome because he felt like going for a swim.

A pool was one thing. They had edges and people to help if something went wrong.

They weren't questionable in depth, but a defined depth for safety. Never again would I step foot in a natural body of water.

Rafe sighed, closing the small distance between us quicker than should have been possible and taking my wrist in his grip. His thumb stroked over the joint gently despite the suddenness with which he'd grabbed me. "I'll be with you the entire time."

"That doesn't mean I can just jump into a fucking lake with you! Are you kidding me right now?" I pulled back, feeling like the day had served as a convenient reminder of everything I needed to remember.

He didn't know me, and I didn't know him.

"Take me back to Ibiza, please."

He quirked a brow, that intense gaze of his turning unsettling as he stared down at me. "No," he said, his lip twisting with the words. My pulse quickened, sensing that small hint of something that lurked beneath the surface. With a glance at the man standing next to the walkway to go up and around the falls, I looked back to Rafe with a flare of my nostrils and purse of my lips.

I huffed in disbelief as I shook my head and fought back the surge of emotions within me. I'd been so fucking stupid to think he understood that my fear came from a place of trauma. From something not so easily overcome. Leaning into his space, I laid down the challenge I knew probably wasn't my smartest move.

But something in the cruel set of his eyes made me want to defy him.

Something in the excited parting of his lips told me he wanted that too.

"Fuck this," I snarled, turning on my heel and yanking my wrist out of his grip. Hiking my purse up on my shoulder, I strode down the road we'd entered in on and made for the main street. Once I had enough distance and found a safe place to settle, I'd call Hugo to come and get me.

But I'd be damned if I would get in that water with him.

"You don't want to walk away from me, Princesa," Rafe murmured at my back. The words crawled up my spine, insidious and menacing enough to halt me in my tracks and turned back to glare at him.

I swallowed my nerves, pushing down the budding fear that he brought with his carefully crafted words. Rafe could be terrifying when he wanted to be.

I just wasn't sure if the frightening face was the mask, or if it was what really waited beneath the charming demeanor he gave me in all the other moments.

"And why is that?" I asked, pressing my lips together and

turning back around to hide the slight tremble in them. He was the kind of man my grandmother warned me about with her stories. The temptation and lure of evil spirits. as they resided in people who looked just like us.

But evil couldn't look like beauty carved in stone, could it? Even if it did explain why I burned when he touched me.

He stepped closer, until I felt the heat of his body at my back. His hand reached around me to grab my face and tilt it, so that I stared him in the eye with one of mine. "Because I'll chase you," he murmured, leaning down to touch his lips to my cheek in a slow brush of heat against my skin. His mouth slid up until his nose touched my hair, breathing me in deeply. He hummed just above my ear. "I think the real question is, what will I do when I catch you?"

I swallowed down the saliva in my mouth, clenching my eyes shut as I tried to think of an appropriate response to words like that.

What did one say, when the man she was falling head over heels in love with showed signs of being a monster?

"That isn't funny, Rafe," I whispered, stumbling over my own feet as he turned my body to face him. His hand gripped my hair harshly, tipping my head back until I met his unyielding gaze.

"Am I laughing, Princesa?" I shook my head slightly, wincing when his grip didn't relent. "I promise you, I am far scarier than whatever you think lurks in the fucking water."

He released me as suddenly as he'd grabbed me, taking a few steps away before he paused and looked back at where I stood, rooted to my spot and staring at him in horror. I looked to the road, watching as the man who stood guard puffed up his chest and stood a little taller.

It felt like I'd walked into a trap, and still didn't understand even the basics of what it would mean for me.

A cage without walls. A pressing force on my chest.

"Don't do it," Rafael warned me, drawing my attention back to him. He held out a hand, waiting for me to take it. It was a test, I realized, as he forced me to make a decision then and there. "I like it when you tell me *no*," he murmured, making my breath hitch in my lungs as he tilted his head to the side and studied me. "I think I'll like it when you fight me too, and so will you," he growled.

I swallowed, wishing I could deny the perverse part of me that craved everything he talked about. I *wanted* him to chase me.

I wanted him to catch me, and I wanted him to show me everything that I dreamt of in my most forbidden desires. But it couldn't happen. I could never give voice to that part of me, not if I wanted to have a chance of suppressing it when I went back home. So I stepped forward, watching his eyes soften with disappointment as I placed my hand in his.

My fear of water was nothing compared to my fear of my own body. If I had to choose to face one of them, it would be the water any day.

"Don't let anyone make you feel ashamed of the things you want, *mi princesa*," Rafe murmured as he guided me over to the walkway to go around the back of the falls. The sound of rushing water from the falls nearly made me hyperventilate, so much stronger than the memory of the river sounds that were in my head.

"Nobody is making me feel ashamed of anything," I said in response, watching as the stairs spread out in front of me behind the rock face as we made our way up to the top. The pools curved around the back and through a narrow passage in the rocks, before opening up into a larger pool with two smaller waterfalls pouring into it. The sound was less deafening, less intense, as Rafe guided me down the steps to stand on the pathway beside the pool.

Large, flat rocks curved into the water as Rafe guided me toward them. He dropped the towels on one of them, pulling his shirt off over his head while I stood frozen and staring at the water. I couldn't bear to get any closer to it, but needed to know how deep it could get.

The blooming flowers and trees around the waterfall were stunning as I slid to my butt on the towel, curling my knees to my chest and hugging them as I tried to breathe. Rafe dropped to the rock next to me, grabbing sunscreen out of a nearby basket.

Everything with Rafe was planned and meticulous. I wondered how someone like me fit into those particular behaviors when I usually did things my own way.

Stripping my dress off over my head, he squirted sunscreen into his hands and applied it to my shoulders in a gentle, soothing massage that was so at odds with the dominating man he'd shown me only moments before that I let out a breathless chuckle. His hands worked wonders on my skin, even as I tried to deny the way he made me feel.

His touch was a sin, dangerous to everything I thought I knew about myself.

Rafe stripped off his shoes and stood, lowering himself into the water as he stayed by the edge and waited for me to follow. I shook my head, furrowing my brow as I watched him.

"I don't want to," I said.

"That's exactly why you need to. You can't stay afraid of water forever. You have to face that fear," he said. He held up a hand, waiting for me to take his again.

I swallowed, sliding my flip flops off my feet and getting up onto my knees so that I could look into the water. I sat back on my butt, scooting myself closer to the edge cautiously as Rafael waited with an extended hand. Then he asked a question that should have been laughable considering the stunt he'd pulled and his vague threats.

"Do you trust me?"

I wished I could say the answer was no.

19

RAFAEL

She shouldn't trust me. Not when it came to her heart and her freedom, but in this I would never let her fall.

Still, I couldn't blame the hesitation to place her hand in mine as indecision warred on her face. "I won't let anything hurt you," I murmured softly, raising a brow and waiting for her to follow through on the command we both knew I'd issued. She'd be getting into the water with me, even if I had to force her.

Her fear of water might have worked to my advantage in keeping her isolated on the island, but I wouldn't risk her drowning in an escape attempt if it came down to it. Desperation made people do things that they would never have considered normally. If I stripped away Isa's free will, she might have walked into the ocean just to spite me.

Much like wandering around Southern Spain alone just to get away from me because she was pissed I'd brought her here.

"*You* want to hurt me," she whispered, her eyes darkening with a moment of understanding. "Is that what this is?

A way to hurt me without having to put in the effort of chasing me down?"

I sighed, reaching forward and grasping her around the hips. Tugging her into the water with me slowly, I enjoyed the feeling of her body wrapped around mine as she instinctively clung to me to protect her. She might pretend she didn't understand the nuances of the pain I wanted to cause, but her body told me no lies.

She understood the difference.

"I want to hurt you in ways you'll enjoy. Not with fears that grip you and torment you over a decade after your accident," I said, keeping one hand on the edge of the rocks so that I could support both our weights for the moment. "Besides, you're mine to hurt. Aren't you, *mi princesa*?" As much as I wanted her to cling to me, it would be a struggle for me to support both our weights as I swam. My feet didn't touch the bottom in the same way they had in the pool.

I'd known taking Isa here would be more of a challenge than if I'd pushed her in the pool at the hotel. But I knew she wouldn't want to reveal her fear in front of others, and clearing out the pool at a busy luxury hotel wouldn't change the fact that we'd have witnesses. The ocean was no place to learn how to swim, with its endless horizon looming as a threat. Even the calmest waters of Ibiza would be more intimidating.

These pools were deep, but they still had boundaries.

Prying one of her hands off my shoulder, I pushed through the urge to forget the purpose of the day when she whimpered. Her fingers scrabbled along the rock, looking for something to hold on to as I turned her in my arms so that she faced it. I pressed into her back, placing my hands next to hers on the rock and feeling her body tremble as she panted for breath.

"I can't," she whispered, shaking her head.

"Why, Isa?" Something lurked in those fears, something far deeper than what I imagined had to be normal for a drowning accident in her childhood. I reached a hand down her leg, my fingers gliding over the raised skin of the scar on her thigh. She jolted in my arms, moving as if to climb out of the water. But my body at her back prevented her from getting the leverage she needed to pull herself out.

I was a bastard. I was cruel. I was everything she should have avoided.

I couldn't walk away from what I'd started, even as I felt her unravel in my arms. Her fear was like a tangible poison, clouding the clear waters with darkness as she was lost to whatever trauma gripped her from her memories. "What happened in that river?" I asked, digging my fingers into the flesh of her thigh lightly to use that quick flash of pain to draw her back to the present.

She shuddered in my arms, shaking her head quickly. "I drowned."

"Then where did you get this scar?" There was nothing else in her history to indicate she'd had any other accidents. Not one hospital visit. Not a strange injury on a doctor's report.

Nothing.

She paused, her voice barely a whisper when she finally spoke part of the truth that tore her up inside. "My mother said it was barbed wire."

"You got caught up in barbed wire in the river?" I asked, trying to keep my voice light despite the agony tearing me up inside. To be five years old and be caught in the currents must have been terrifying enough as her lungs filled with water and set her insides on fire, but to survive all that while being caught in something that literally tore into her skin?

I exhaled, wondering why there'd been no record of the injury in the emergency report. I couldn't very well ask her, given that I shouldn't have ever seen the fucking thing. I made a mental note to have Matteo track down the people responsible, so that I could find the full truth of what Isa didn't say.

Her choice of words was unique. As if she herself didn't believe her mother.

"You don't think that's what it was," I observed, looking down to watch how still she kept her legs. Even for someone who didn't know how to swim, natural instinct in water was to move. To feel the fluidity of movements that we couldn't achieve on land.

Isa didn't move. She was as stiff as a log from her torso down, the only part of her that dared to move being what was out of the water.

"It was barbed wire," Isa corrected herself, clenching her eyes shut. "It couldn't have been anything else."

I knew better than most what it was to be haunted by spirits, by the tricks of shadows and light and what they could cause in our memories. Shadows had danced off the flames as my mother burned, looking like demons coming to raise hell on earth, to a child who watched his mother die a cruel death. They'd swallowed her whole until there'd been nothing left of the only woman I'd ever cared for.

Until Isa.

"What did you see in the water, Princesa?" I asked, waiting as the rest of her body went solid in my arms.

"I saw phantoms," she whispered. "Shadows in the water as they moved like nightmares. Coming for me. *Grabbing* my leg and trying to pull me under. I *know* they weren't real. They couldn't have been, but—"

"Nobody can tell you what you saw in the water.

Whether it was real or not, you saw it. You *felt* it in that moment. You've lived with it for all these years. Have you told anyone about them?" I asked, pressing closer to her to try to use my body to comfort her. Under no illusions that I knew the whole truth regarding the accident, I regretfully knew that pushing her to talk about the shadows was the limit for the day. I wouldn't learn the truth of Odina's hatred just yet, not with the way she shivered in my arms as she thought back to those phantoms.

Nightmares come to life, and yet she was comforted by a living embodiment of everything she feared in the water. I suspected my Isa also had a nightmare inside her, waiting to come out when I unlocked the part of her she so carefully controlled.

Containing her would be like holding a demon in my arms, and I looked forward to the fight.

"My grandmother says that water is sacred. That the veil between life and death is thinner in it. I was drowning, half dead already. She says what I saw was real, that I'm one of the few people to experience it before I die. They tried to take me, but they couldn't so they took Odina instead," she whispered, a tear dripping down her face as she cried for the sister she'd lost that day.

Whatever had caused it, Isa wore the guilt of it on her soul. Maybe that was why she'd suffered through years of abuse at her sister's hands before putting a stop to it.

"It sounds like your grandmother thinks it's a good thing," I murmured, inching my body away from hers so that she had to be on her own for a few moments.

"She thinks it shows how strong I am. That they couldn't claim me as theirs," she scoffed. "But they would have if my mother hadn't pulled me out of the water. Everything had gone dark already. There was nothing but blackness and the sound of flames roaring in my head."

"Flames?" I asked, stilling at her side suddenly as the memory of my mother's lips moving as she burned on the pyre echoed in my brain.

"They said it was just the sound of the current," she sighed. "That the woman screaming was my mother on the shore before she dove into the water."

Flames hovered at the edge of my vision as I said the words I didn't really want an answer to. I hadn't paid any attention to the date on the reports, hadn't bothered to care about the details beyond how it would influence my understanding of Isa. "When was the accident?"

"I was five," she responded.

"The day, Isa," I said, my voice sharper than I'd intended.

"June fourteenth," she said, her face turning more serious as she studied me curiously. My head roared with the connection, my mind working to convince me that coincidences happened sometimes. With anything else, it might have worked.

If it hadn't been the fourteenth anniversary of my mother's death.

20

ISA

His sudden stillness felt like an omen of disaster, but he brushed it off and turned a smile to me as if the moment had never happened. "My mother died in a fire on June fourteenth," he said, exhaling a ragged sigh as he propped an elbow up on the rock face and ran a thumb over my cheek to wipe away my tears.

"How is that possible?" I asked, my eyes widening as the implications of his words struck me in the chest. Three events on one day, in three separate years.

"Our connection goes back farther than you can imagine, Princesa," he murmured softly, touching his lips to my cheek briefly before he pushed off from the rock face and floated on his back. I eyed the water below him, suddenly longing to take that leap of faith.

But the shadows rippling in the clear waters did nothing to persuade me into pushing off the ledge. My hands clung to the rocks, needing the stability and the safety of knowing I could pull myself out of the water if something went wrong.

If something grabbed me and tried to pull me under.

The crystal clear waters showed straight through to the sandy bottom, despite the striking depth of the water. In spite of the shadows rippling, there was nothing in the water to grab hold of me. No barbed wire to get tangled up in and nothing to tear into my skin and rip the flesh apart as I struggled to get free.

Rafael noticed the deep breath I took as I spun to put my back to the ledge, my fingers still clinging to it desperately as my lungs heaved with the exertion of suppressing my panic. "I dare the spirits to try to take you from me," he said with a dark smile. "There is nothing that can keep me from you, Isa," he said, dropping from his back and moving his arms in the water as his legs kicked to keep him afloat.

I looked down at the water, at the solid bottom and the absence of a pit to lead me straight to the underworld.

And I let go.

Water rushed toward my face as I dropped into it, kicking my legs desperately to keep my head above water. A deep gasping breath escaped my lungs as I waited for the moment when something would grab me. For that second in time when my movement would attract the phantoms in the water.

Instead, Rafe moved into my space, taking my arms and sliding them beneath the water's surface to sway front to back and side to side slowly. There was nothing but him as the steady motion of his legs and arms sank into me and I absorbed his rhythm into my being the same as when we'd danced. My legs stopped kicking frantically, mimicking the slow but wide kicks of his until I felt like a mirror of his movements.

His hands slid down my arms until his fingers laced with mine.

Forged in fire. Forged in water.

Two opposites of the same coin, he moved our hands together and showed me how to float at the surface of the water as he held my eyes. "I'm the only phantom you need to worry about now, Princesa," he said, the words jarring loose a tendril of memory.

Of the phantom who'd tucked me into bed and the shadows that hovered around him.

Of the comfort I'd felt, despite the similarities between him and the beings who haunted my nightmares. Like I'd always belonged in the darkness, and my fear was all that stood in the way of me meeting that fate.

"If you can float, you can swim," he said, guiding me to my stomach. He slid his hands beneath me, supporting me through the motions as my panic rose and I hissed out a breath. The position should have been better, I hadn't had the ability to float on my stomach when I'd been caught in the barbed wire.

But something about having my stomach vulnerable to the creatures in the water somehow seemed worse. Only Rafe's hands on me prevented me from going underwater as common sense returned and I kicked my legs. I moved my arms through the water in the way I'd seen swimmers do in videos. My body slid forward, gliding through the water as Rafael's hands fell away and I nearly panicked. He swam at my side, encouraging me on until I huffed a small laugh of disbelief.

I still watched the water for shadows. I never went far from Rafe's side. But I swam on my own, comforted that the phantom at my side would protect me.

Because I was his to hurt, and nothing else would ever touch me.

Rafe stood on the balcony, leaning over the glass edge in a way that made me wonder how he didn't fear the fall should it collapse. But he wasn't afraid of anything, commanding the world around him as if he owned it. His phone was pressed to his ear as he dealt with something to do with his mysterious business.

I couldn't see his face, but the lines of his body were tight even from the back as I studied him. I turned away from the view, grabbing my phone off the coffee table in front of me and dialing Chloe's number. Having already spoken with my Grandmother earlier in the day, I'd had enough of the evasive lies I told my family. I didn't know how to bring Rafe up in conversation.

With the grandmother who would fear I may not come home if she could hear how much I loved him, or the parents who would be horrified to think of their baby girl living a life of sin, nothing good could come from telling them about the man who consumed me, until I had a grasp on what was happening between us.

"Hey," Chloe said with a laugh. The loud murmur of voices came through in the background, and I smiled as I imagined she and Hugo living it up in Ibiza. I was glad that, if nothing else, my inability to party on their level wasn't keeping them from doing exactly what they wanted.

"Hey," I said, speaking louder than I wanted. Rafe didn't so much as twitch on the other side of the closed glass, and it reassured me that he couldn't hear our conversation. "This is my daily phone call so that you know I am alive and not in a ditch somewhere," I teased.

She laughed on the other side, but the sound was more muted than I might have expected. "You seem off. Are you still struggling with your feelings?"

"Yes and no," I admitted. "He took me to some natural pools and waterfalls on the mainland yesterday. I think I'm just a little shaken up."

"Oh, honey. It's okay that you couldn't get in the water with him. If he didn't understand that then it's his issue and not yours," Chloe said, the voices in the background quieting as she separated herself from whatever they were doing.

"I got in the water," I whispered, my voice hitching as I said the words. Tears stung my eyes with the confession, unable to believe them even though I'd been there. "He taught me how to swim."

"Wait, what?" Chloe asked, her voice rising an octave. "After all the years I've tried to get you in the water, he comes along and a few days and you're magically cured of it? He must have a really good dick."

I laughed, despite how uncomfortable it made me feel for Chloe to talk about Rafe's cock. That part of him felt like it was mine, not something that any other woman needed to concern herself with.

Even my best friend.

"Well he didn't give me much choice," I said, needing someone to reassure me that what he'd done hadn't been in my head. That something had been innately wrong with his threats and the pressure he'd put on me to choose between a twisted chase and getting in the water.

Part of me wanted to brush it off, to assume I'd read too much into his words and the scenario because of my own twisted desires and the way they consumed me. But the other part of me couldn't help but hear his voice in my head, telling me he'd like it when I fought him.

"What do you mean?" Chloe asked.

"He surprised me. I didn't know we were going there or I never would have agreed to it. You know that, and apparently he did too," I sighed.

"So you felt obligated because you'd gone all that way? I'm sure he could have found something else for the two of you to do, Isa," Chloe said softly. "But for what it's worth, I'm glad he broke through and helped you with that."

"I tried to leave," I blurted suddenly, clenching my eyes closed as I said the words. "He wouldn't let me. He said he'd chase me, Chloe. I don't know if I'm just being weird, but he kind of scared me. Getting in the water was the less scary option and you know I don't say that easily." I twiddled with my fingers as silence hung between us.

"Do you think you're in danger?" she asked, her voice carefully measured as she crafted the words. Even with me reaching out to her for advice, I couldn't imagine it was an easy line to walk between being concerned and treading carefully because your best friend had feelings for a man she shouldn't.

"No. I don't think so. He didn't give me the impression he'd hurt me," I whispered, even if the words didn't feel entirely true.

He might have, but I would have liked it and that was a worse admission that I wasn't ready to make with my friend.

"So he just stopped you from leaving?" she asked. When I hummed my agreement, she continued on. "I'll see what Hugo knows about the name. He's been pretty quiet whenever he comes up, so I don't think he knows much. But I'll see what I can find out. You just be careful until then, okay?" she asked.

"Okay. Talk to you tomorrow," I murmured, ending the call and leaving my phone on the coffee table as I made my way to the bathroom. I started the shower, determined to scald my skin until nothing remained of the traces of darkness coating my skin.

I'd likely confused Rafe with my mixed signals. The best way to keep his darkness at bay was to control my own.

21

RAFAEL

Isa stepped out of the bedroom after her shower, towel drying her hair as she walked my way with her legs revealed by the shorts she wore around the suite. The cheap cotton didn't suit her skin, and the knowledge that she would soon be bathed in a luxury so unfamiliar to her that she'd never be able to go back settled over me.

The scar seemed more stark against her skin now that I knew the reason for it. As her skin turned richer from the increased sunshine, the paler, raised skin never changed.

She froze in place, her attention catching on me sitting in one of the chairs on the terrace. The chess board sat on the table between the chairs, and she squinted her eyes as she stared at it. Finishing drying her hair, she turned back into the bedroom to hang the towel in the bathroom before coming out more cautiously the second time.

"Have you ever played chess, *mi princesa*?" I asked, waving a hand to indicate she should sit in the chair opposite me. She shook her head as she lowered herself into it gracefully, crossing her legs as she leaned an elbow on her knee and looked at the board.

"I don't think I'd ever even seen a chessboard in person before coming here," she said, studying the pieces. She picked up a white pawn, turning the smooth marble in her hand as she ran delicate fingers over it.

The piece belonged in her hand.

"Chess can teach us a lot about life," I told her, taking the pawn and setting it back into its place on the board. "Every piece can move in a particular way," I said. I guided her through all the individual pieces and the ways they could move while she listened with rapt fascination.

Isa often downplayed just how intelligent she was, hiding behind her books and charitable work at the Menominee community center. She seemed to struggle with the difference between herself and Odina, never allowing herself to truly excel. Hugo said he'd seen her diminish her mind frequently, sometimes going so far as to forget about an assignment so she wouldn't have a perfect grade. He'd watched her circle the correct answer on a test and then change it when she was finished.

But within her lurked a mind I suspected would rival the smartest men in my organization. If only she existed in a life that encouraged her to own it, rather than act like it was something shameful.

"This is the Queen," I said, holding out the piece for her to wrap her fingers around. She took it, tilting her head as she studied it and ran her thumb over the crown at the top. "She's the most powerful piece."

"Not the King?" she asked, righting her head as she met my eyes.

"The game is over when the King is dead. But without a Queen, it never truly begins," I said softly, watching as she pursed her lips thoughtfully. "She can perform the most moves on the board. The Queen protects her King, no matter the cost."

She reached out a hand and grabbed the King, running her other thumb over the cross like she had the crown on the Queen. "This is probably the only game in existence where men gave a feminine symbol all the power," she said with a huff of laughter.

I grinned back at her, nodding my head. "You're probably right."

She placed the pieces back on the board. "The King controls the board, but the Queen is what gives him that power," she said, her voice dropping as she accepted the fact that she understood the basic premise.

"Exactly," I said. "Your move."

She widened her eyes at me, pursing her lips and looking down at the board. She moved a pawn, watching as I moved my own. The first pawn I moved had a tiny fissure on the top, a crack I only noticed when my palm brushed against it. I was too preoccupied with watching her to look down at the board, with observing her eyes as they flitted around the pieces and studied the game. She thought everything through, observed all the pieces as she bit her lip in concentration.

One day, she'd be a force to be reckoned with. Both on and off the board.

But today was not that day.

22

ISA

I pouted playfully as Rafe guided me up the steps to the private rooftop terrace we had to ourselves. I'd known about it, but never had the opportunity or need to utilize it. It was foolish to think that I'd ever be able to beat Rafe at chess given the limited time I had to try, but the competitive part of me that didn't often get the opportunity to rear its head wanted nothing more than to prove him wrong.

Even knowing chess was something that took people years to master.

Rafael pushed open the doors to the rooftop, bathing us in the dim lighting from the stars above. Music pulsed below us as people enjoyed the music by the pool. But none of the buildings around us were near as tall as our hotel, and it gave us the illusion of privacy. Even if people danced below us. Even if they swam in the pool or frolicked on the beach.

We were alone in our own little world as Rafe drew the cover back from the hot tub and turned on the jets. He stripped his shorts down his legs without preamble, stepping into the hot tub entirely naked and relaxing against the back of it as he closed his eyes. Opening them and glancing at me out of the corner, he crooked a finger for me to join him.

"Don't you ever get tired of being in the water?" I teased in reference to our expedition the day before and the way he'd traumatized me.

"The water is part of life on an island," he said, watching with darkening eyes as I shoved my shorts down my legs and tugged my shirt over my head. Making the walk toward the hot tub with his eyes on my body would have terrified me only a few days prior, but there wasn't a corner of my body he hadn't explored.

His tour of the Ibiza he loved involved a bunch of tours of his body, unsurprisingly. It wouldn't even surprise me if he thought he was the highlight of Ibiza.

He was mine.

I lifted a leg to step into the tub, gasping when Rafe's hands shot out from the water and he caught my calf in his grip. Leaning forward, he pressed a kiss to the scar on my thigh, trailing his lips down over the edge of my knee and down my calf. His eyes never left mine, the green and blue shock of his gaze staring up at me as he released me and let me take that first step into the hot tub.

Rafe's eyes on me felt like dancing with the devil, his touch like the greatest temptation toward sin.

I lowered myself into the hot tub in front of him, sighing as the scalding water surrounded me, and then leaned my back into his chest as he enveloped me in his arms. His mouth touched the top of my head, drawing in a deep sigh as the same contentment I felt washed over him. Nothing mattered when I was in his arms.

Not the way he'd scared me the day before. Not the fact that I'd have to say goodbye in four days.

It didn't matter that I'd go home to a life I no longer recognized and go about my business as if the glimpse of a life he'd shown me hadn't changed me forever.

There was only his touch. His heat at my back. His brand on my skin.

I laid my head back on his chest, closing my eyes with a contented sigh as I exhaled all the tension in my body and let everything else drift away. When I opened them, the stars and moon above stared down at me, reminding me of the invitation that had brought me to him.

I'd danced with the devil in the moonlight.

And I'd fallen in love with the man underneath the monster who hovered just beneath the surface.

Tears stung my eyes with the realization and the knowledge that I loved him in spite of knowing it was foolish. That it was beyond foolish and downright stupid. It would end in heartache for me, and a return to emptiness that I wasn't sure I could bear anymore.

"When I was little," Rafe murmured softly, "my mother used to sneak me outside at night to stare at the stars. I remember trying to count them." My body locked, afraid to move as he volunteered information about himself. I'd never felt like he would speak to me, like he was even remotely accessible in that way.

All his hints of something dark in his life and his history kept me from trying to pry too deep. He was right when he told me I might not be ready for the answers to those questions.

I'd never tried to Google him since he caught me and warned me away from it.

"That might be the sweetest thing I've ever heard," I said

finally when he didn't continue. Even if the admission had been small, the fact that he'd volunteered it of his own free will made my cheeks turn even warmer than they already were from the hot tub. It had been everything I wanted from him in that moment, and everything I shouldn't have gotten.

Knowing he cared enough to share even the smallest part of him would make it that much harder for me to walk away.

"I know it was pointless now, of course. Even if it had been possible to count the stars in the sky, what purpose would it serve?" he asked with a sigh. "But knowing that there isn't a purpose doesn't stop me from knowing you have nineteen freckles across the bridge of your nose and on your cheeks." My heart froze in my chest, furiously trying to count my freckles in my memory. In all my life, I'd never thought to put a number to the dots on my skin.

But he'd done it in days.

The significance of such a number stripped me of breath as his arms tightened around me. "I'll never stop wanting to know everything about you," he murmured, the words feeling like a promise despite the timer on our relationship.

"You counted my freckles," I whispered as my breath returned.

"You have one here," he said, reaching around to touch a spot on my chest that he couldn't see. "And here," he moved his hand down to the left of my belly button and just a little lower. Through the water, I stared at the exact spot when he dragged his hand away.

A freckle stared back at me, tiny and hardly noticeable.

"Everything, Isa," he murmured.

The words sounded like a threat as he maneuvered his way further inside my heart and showed me every mark on my skin, but I couldn't shake the feeling that for the first time in my life, someone saw *me*.

It couldn't have been normal for him to spend such effort on someone who would leave in four days, so that left me with one question. Did Rafe think we were something else?

Would he let me go home when the time came? Or would he drag me to the pits of Hell?

*M*usic pulsed through my veins as we walked through the dimly lit club. The soft purple and gold lighting with decorations through the bar space screamed of luxury. The music was more upscale than I'd expected of a nightclub in Ibiza.

I had no experience with going to nightclubs, but all the photos I'd seen before the trip made it seem like a massive party.

Excitement filled me at the prospect of seeing my friends, knowing that, while not everything was resolved between Rafe and me in terms of defining our relationship or the remote possibility of a pregnancy, at least I could put on a happy face for my friends and make them believe that everything was okay. I regretted telling Chloe about what Rafe had done at the waterfall and the way he'd made me feel.

Rafe wasn't perfect, but the fact that he'd counted my freckles went a long way toward convincing me he didn't mean to harm me. Maybe if I worked hard enough to convince them, I'd be able to shake off the last hints of fear of what Rafe might do when I tried to go home, that built with every day that passed. He couldn't possibly intend for me to walk away from my life for a man I hardly knew.

For a man who would threaten to chase me if I walked away from him.

There was something seriously wrong with me that I'd fallen in love with him in such a short time period, with everything working against us and the warning signs staring me in the face. I'd never been in love or even had the desire to fall in love before him, and yet he stormed into my heart as if there was never anything in his way. No matter what Rafe did or who he was when I wasn't looking, I couldn't shake the feeling that he would never hurt me.

That I was special to him in some way, and separate from whatever business consumed him and needed to be kept secret from me.

I knew when I went home, I'd finally work up the courage to Google his name. I'd probably learn more about him from the internet than I ever would from his own mouth.

Rafael led me to the terrace at the back of the club, finding my friends waiting for us outside. Hugo stood from his seat on one of the odd, round stools next to a table, making Chloe turn her attention to us. Her eyes widened briefly before she smiled, trailing her eyes down my body encased in the dress Rafe had supplied me with for the club. I didn't own anything remotely dressy, and somehow I doubted sundresses would be an appropriate attire for the evening.

Hugo looked so odd in his dress shirt and trousers, somehow older than the boy I'd spent over a year hanging out with. "This is such a nice club. Thank you for getting us in," Chloe said, turning her gaze to Rafe. He wore a suit, his jacket undone over his black dress shirt, making it so that he swam in a sea of onyx. From his dark hair, to the stubble on his face, to his clothes and shoes. The only color he offered was deep olive skin and bright mismatched eyes.

"It was no trouble at all. Owning a club does have its perks at times," Rafe returned, giving a tiny smile in response to Chloe's words. His arrogance seeped through as she pursed her lips to keep her shock from showing.

"You own this?" I asked, watching as Hugo took his seat and Rafael led me to the white sofa on the other side of the table with a hand at the small of my back. I sat down carefully, wishing he'd chosen a longer dress. The visibility of my scar set me on edge, something that I'd never really experienced aside from with Chloe or my family.

Even Hugo had never seen it, though I'd known that would change when we came to Ibiza. Wearing a bathing suit tended to do that.

Hugo's eyes narrowed in on the thin wrap of white flesh across my leg, tilting his head in thought as he turned an odd look in Rafe's direction with his brow raised in question. Rafe ignored him, settling as close to me as possible and wrapping an arm around me. "Yes," he confirmed.

"It's incredible," I said, glancing up at the starry sky above us. The music was softer outside, less of a mind-numbing vibration and closer to something soothing. People still danced between the rows of tables and on the long walkway through the back terrace, moving their bodies seductively and swaying to the smooth rhythm.

"Thank you," he murmured, taking the end of my hair in his grip and toying with it where it touched my waist. A server came over, taking our drink orders before she moved on and hurried back into the club. I imagined, being the owner, Rafe would expect to be served immediately.

"How does a man as young as you come to own the hottest club in Ibiza?" Chloe asked, narrowing her eyes suspiciously on Rafe. He withdrew slightly, and I watched as he smiled through whatever distaste he had for Chloe's question. But the stiffness of his body told me he didn't like her inquiry.

If Rafe would hunt me down if I left him, I had to wonder for a moment if I should worry for Chloe. She was tenacious when she wanted to know something, and she'd stop at nothing to get the answers if she felt something was wrong.

I couldn't imagine she hadn't already looked Rafe up, and I questioned why she hadn't told me what she found earlier in the day. But I still didn't want to know.

"Investments mostly," Rafe answered finally. "I have a very broad understanding of the markets and what will do well at any given time. It allows me to make lump sums of cash that I then reinvest into property investments frequently."

"Hmm," Chloe hummed, turning her eyes to mine. "That's not what Google says." Hugo elbowed her in the side, glaring at her as if he'd warned her ahead of time not to have this conversation. Hugo was far more aware of how I would feel if things went south unnecessarily because of Chloe's prying.

I guessed he just wasn't aware that she was probably close to accurate in whatever she hinted at.

"Google will say a lot of things about me, I'm sure," Rafe said. "Worse than high school gossip, and by the time Ibiza news gets on the internet it's much like a game of telephone. Exaggerated and dramatic for no reason other than seeking higher ratings." I hoped his words were true. That he'd stopped me from looking him up because he didn't want our relationship to be influenced by lies that were totally irrelevant to our relationship.

Our drinks were delivered in the moment of silence that followed, and I quickly grabbed my sangria off the table to take a sip of the fruity concoction. Chloe followed suit, though she twirled her straw around more thoughtfully.

"Come dance with me beneath the moonlight," Rafe said, running his nose over my jawline as he taunted me with words so similar to the ones that had brought us together in the first place. I nodded, setting down my glass, and accepted the hand he extended to help me stand up as I tugged the tight white and silver dress further down my thighs. He guided me around the edge of the table and to the small space where couples danced near us, raising a hand over my head to spin me into his arms so that he could wrap himself around my back as I laughed.

His hands slid down to my hips, guiding them to move with his as I tried to find that place where I was comfortable moving in such a way with him again. It was easier the second time around, with him knowing my body so intimately that he understood how to make me move. Once I'd found our rhythm together, he grabbed my arms in his hands and lifted them over my head to rest on his shoulder. His huge palms trailed down over the sensitive skin of my arms, caressing over the sides of my breasts and then coasting over my stomach delicately until they settled on my hips once again and encouraged me to roll them in a circle against him.

I was too short compared to his height for it to be as indecent as it might have otherwise, but the motion still reminded me of the way he'd encouraged me to move when I was on top of him and he was inside me.

Hugo and Chloe stepped up beside us. Chloe sighed as

she held hands with Hugo, moving to the beat despite the distance between them. Taking in my smiling face, she shook her head and smiled before losing herself to the beat of the music.

With her settled and entertained for the moment, I wound my body around until I faced Rafe and stared up at him as I touched my hands to his chest. He stared down at me as intensely as he had that first night we met, but a better awareness lurked within his gaze.

There wasn't a corner of my body he hadn't touched or explored, down to the number of freckles on my body. So, when I moved my hips in what I thought might be more seductive, I didn't pause to consider what he might think of me.

If I might look like an idiot. I'd never see any of the people at the club again, anyway.

Rafe smiled down at me indulgently, his body smooth and languid as he danced. He was often too serious, often caught in the trance of whatever darkness lurked inside him, but when he danced his body became soft and fluid. Taken by the music, he moved with me as if the end game was for me to be in his bed.

Even if that was already a given.

He glanced over my shoulder, his body going still so suddenly that I stumbled in my hurry to stop dancing and spin around. A man I'd never seen before held Rafael's eyes, his face so expressionless that it seemed unnatural. "Rafe?" I asked, turning back to stare at him as he took my hand in his grip and turned to Hugo.

"We have to go," he barked, pulling me away before I could even say goodbye to Hugo and Chloe. She looked around confused as Hugo tried to calm her down. We ducked through the club quickly, the sound of an engine revving outside as a car pulled up to the curb quickly as if it had been commanded.

I didn't recognize the person in the driver's seat as Rafe opened the passenger side back door and shoved me in. "Rafe!" I yelled when he made no move to get in with me.

"Take her back to the hotel," he ordered the other man, making me look between them in confusion. Rafe pressed his key card into my palm, closing the door quickly as I rolled down the window.

"What's going on?" I asked.

"This isn't chess," he said oddly. "In my world, the King always protects his Queen." I gaped up at him in shock, wincing when he tapped the roof of the car and the blacked-out window glided up between us. The driver hit the gas, peeling away from the curb quickly as I turned to watch out the back window as Rafe strode back into the club with his hands clenched into fists.

What in the actual fuck?

23

RAFAEL

Hugo and Chloe were gone by the time I shoved my way through the back doors of *Lotus*. I charged through the crowd as my eyes tracked around the room for the Russian bastard I'd seen in my club.

If Chloe had seen what was about to go down, I'd have to handle her. As it was, I made a mental note to tell Hugo to keep her from contacting Isa after tonight. I'd do my part to prevent them speaking to one another, and if Hugo did his, Isa would have no idea that she might have just seen her best friend for the last time.

At least if she didn't decide to stay, and thanks to fucking Pavel, everything was unraveling faster than I could control it. I'd kill him for that alone.

When my eyes landed on the Russian with the hand tattoos, shaved head, and conspicuously missing pinky, I snapped my attention to him fully and walked in his direction slowly. Giving him every opportunity to realize just how monumentally he'd fucked up by stepping foot in my club in the first place, after I'd clearly told him what would happen if I ever saw him again.

He smirked at me as I approached him, fear hovering just behind the false bravado, but whatever protection Pavel had promised him made him brave. Whatever had happened after he went crawling back to Pavel with a missing finger, he somehow thought I was the lesser evil than disobeying his boss.

A single jab to the throat disabused him of that notion, sending him reeling backwards as I grabbed him by the back of his shirt while he sputtered for breath. I carted him back inside the club and into the back rooms. One of my staff was kind enough to haul the basement door open, and I used the opportunity to throw him down the steps. I could barely hear the thump of his body as it hit each and every step over the pulsing music, and I almost wanted it to go away so that I could hear his screams more clearly later on.

But there were too many people around to hear him cry and the music would cover the sound. I owned the police, but I still didn't need the headache that would come with explaining why I'd exposed hundreds of patrons to the seedy underbelly of Ibiza.

I adjusted my suit jacket, glancing to the staff member and nodding for him to close the door behind me before I descended the steps. Darkness greeted me, welcoming me home with waiting arms as it surrounded my very being. The overhead light kicked on as I stepped down the final stairs, crackling to life with age and lack of use.

Years had passed since I'd needed to make use of this particular basement, not since I'd stopped doing my father's dirty work and taking fingers for unpaid debts had stopped being a common practice for me.

I had other people do that for me now, if the debt was large enough.

The Russian's body was sprawled out at the foot of the stairs, requiring me to step over him to start up the upgraded fireplace and turn to the table of dust covered supplies and blow them off so that I wouldn't have to go back to Isa covered in filth. I stripped off my suit jacket, folding it and draping it over a chair next to the table before I turned back to the man who writhed in pain and groaned on the floor.

"Who are you to Pavel?" I asked, without turning back to look at him. I knew exactly where he crawled along the floor.

I always knew where everyone was when they were around me, in tune to the energy in the air. The skill had been born out of necessity, trapped in a childhood where not knowing could mean a beating coming my way when I wasn't ready for it.

As the fire raged to life in the fireplace, courtesy of modern technology even if the room itself was dated, I ran my hand over the variety of fire pokers on my table. The brands on the end all varied, specifically forged for individual crimes. The one I desired was the largest of the bunch, and I touched the *Cuélebre* once before setting it into the coals of the fire to heat high enough that it would melt his skin.

"I'm one of his trusted men," the man coughed, watching as I turned my back on the table and leaned my hands against it. Studying him as he maneuvered himself to a sitting position, grimacing in pain with every movement he made.

"If that were true, he wouldn't have sent you here to die," I said. "He knew very well what I would do to you when I found you watching me again." His eyes went to the burning brand in the fire, and he swallowed back bile as reality set in. He wouldn't walk out of the basement alive. In fact, most of him wouldn't leave the basement at all.

Just his head.

He moved as quickly as his beaten body would allow, clambering for the steps while I grabbed one of the pokers off the table and used it to swipe his legs out from under him. His face bounced off the step as he fell, rolling down the stairs for the second time. When he landed with a heavy thud the second time, his eyelids fluttered but he didn't move.

A pity for me, since I liked to watch them struggle against the pain.

Slipping fireproof gloves onto my hands and taking the brand from the fire, I pressed it to his forehead quickly. His body jerked beneath me, his hands reaching up to grasp the metal of the poker as he tried to pull it away, and only managed to burn his flesh in the process. But the heat of the brand served to seal the metal to his skin, the heat melting his flesh until I pulled it away and stared at the *Cuélebre* of the Ibarra family crest.

When he finally went limp and stared up at me with glassy eyes as his breathing shallowed, I stripped off the gloves and dumped the brand back to the metal table to cool off. Rolling up my shirt sleeves, I took the surgical saw in hand with a sigh.

I wished I had Ryker's hatchet. Cutting through the cervical vertebrae with a saw took longer than I wanted to spend with the bastard.

He heaved out a sigh, fear filling his half closed eyes as I leaned over him and kept my body as far from the blood splatter as I could. He didn't struggle when the first cut severed his trachea and blood poured from the wound.

Even after he took his last agonizing breath, I kept sawing until the surgical saw struck the concrete floor.

I had a package to mail.

24

ISA

Chloe wouldn't answer her phone, and Hugo went silent after texting me to let me know he'd gotten himself and Chloe out of the club and safely away from whatever had gone down. Fear for Rafe was only overcome with my own fury. I was so fucking done with being ushered away when people he knew made themselves known. Was he ashamed of being with me? Was there a reason he shouldn't have been with me?

Or was I just really so far in over my head that I couldn't even begin to fathom the reality?

My fingers twitched on my phone, anxious to hear from my friends and not knowing if I should finally take the leap and find my own answers in a moment of desperation. Nothing could be worth the secrets between us.

People who loved one another didn't keep secrets, and the thought was a jarring reminder of a single truth that I'd somehow let myself forget and needed to be reminded of.

Rafael Ibarra didn't love me.

If he had, he would have said the words. He'd have told me the truth in a bid to get me to stay with him, but he'd never so much as asked me to extend my stay in Spain. He'd never hinted that it might be what he wanted. His passionate comments about me being his weren't enough.

In my heart, I'd wanted to believe they were some dramatic confession of his love for me. That they were the words of a man who didn't know how to express his heart, but Rafe wasn't a high school boy. He had no problems communicating what he wanted me to know.

I'd let myself fall in love with a man who would never return those feelings, and tears stung my eyes with the realization that some part of me had clung to the hope that he would reciprocate. That going our separate ways when it ended would somehow be easier knowing he loved me and thought of me when we were an ocean apart.

I'd still have gone home. I'd still have done what was expected of me, but I would have done it with a bittersweet smile when I remembered him at every turn. When the next man couldn't compare, I'd think of him and hope he was happy. I'd smile and remember that he'd shown me how to live, even just for a little while.

Knowing I'd been so stupid stripped all that away from me. I couldn't even blame him, since he'd made me no promises beyond our week together. Like always, my decision to trust the wrong person rested on my shoulders entirely.

Hopefully this time, it wouldn't hurt anyone else. I couldn't survive that guilt again.

His odd statement as he'd tucked me into the car and sent me away was the only piece that I somehow still clung to. Even as the jagged shards threatened to tear through my flesh, I held tight to the one remote possibility that men in his world protected their queen at all costs. My blood coated the fragments of hope as I thought back to all our time together, wondering if I was the Queen he would protect.

But he didn't call me his Queen, he called me *Princesa*.

So who was the Queen in his life?

The first tear tracked down my cheek, startling me into shock as I hurried to the balcony and threw open the glass doors. The warm night air hit my face as I leaned over the glass railing, looking down on the beach and where the slight waves lapped at the shoreline in the dark.

It felt like hours had passed since I'd returned to an empty suite, staring at the reminders of Rafe all over the room. Looking everywhere he'd touched me, everywhere he'd sat and smiled at me as I fell deeper in love with him every day. Tears dropped onto the railing steadily while I waited, frozen in place and unable to find the strength to move. I turned to look back at the bedroom door, considering my options and the bag I'd kept packed to make a quick escape if I needed to.

My phone rang in my hands, terrifying me so much that I jolted in place and dropped it to the floor with a heavy thump. Chloe's name flashed on the screen, the photo of us together at graduation staring up at me from the floor as I picked it up with trembling fingers. I swallowed and considered not answering, despite how much I wanted to know if she was okay.

Somehow, I knew in my gut that whatever she had to say would break me. That those shards would shred the last pieces of my soul that I clung to. Still, I took a deep breath and hit the button to accept her call.

"Isa," Chloe's harsh whisper said over the phone.

"It's me," I said, my voice quivering as I tried to hold it steady. "You okay?"

"Get out. God, Isa you have to fucking get out of there right now. Before he comes back."

"What?" I whispered, hating the fear that filled her voice. Fear for me. Fear that I felt down to my bones as I moved to the closet and shoved the last of my things into the bag. I tucked it back behind Rafe's suits so he wouldn't immediately see it when he came back.

Even with the warning filling my body with dread, the thought of never seeing him again tore me in two.

"He's a murderer, Isa," she whispered on the other end as a loud banging echoed in the background. "Get out. Go to the embassy. I'll meet you there as soon as I can."

My voice didn't convey the shock I felt. *Nothing* could come even close to hinting at the feeling slithering through my body. "Are you sure?" I asked.

"I wouldn't do this if I wasn't. Just get out," she growled. The line disconnected as I went back out to the balcony to grab my purse with my passport and wallet. I hurried forward on shaky legs, snatching it off the table where we'd played chess only the day before. It felt like a lifetime ago that I'd done something so simple with him.

I'd played chess...with a murderer?

My mind was a jumbled mess as I clutched the strap in the palm of my hand. I spun to go back inside through the door, stopping mid-step as my eyes landed on the face glaring at me and then at the purse in my hand.

He tilted his head, stripping his jacket off slowly as he closed the distance between us. I backed away a step, forcing a smile to my face as my butt connected with the railing at my back. I put my hand on top of the sleek glass half-wall, feeling the bite of it as my hand slid along the top and it dug into my skin. "You're back," I said, making a show of dropping my purse to the floor.

With my phone gripped in my hand, I watched his eyes fall to the purse at my feet. They trailed up over my bare legs, over my body encased in the camisole dress he'd put me in for the club. When they landed on my face, his mouth tensed as he clenched his jaw. Darkness like I'd never seen swirled in his gaze, taunting me. Daring me, as if he knew everything going through my head.

The man I loved was gone, replaced by a cold-blooded murderer as he transformed in front of my eyes. Nobody would look at this version of Rafael and question how he could kill someone.

"Were you going somewhere, Princesa?" he asked, the name feeling like a mockery of everything I'd thought was sweet in that cold, expressionless voice that was so unlike Rafe.

I shook my head, staring straight at him. I held up my phone, deciding to let my self-preservation take over. "I've just been trying to get in touch with Chloe and Hugo. They aren't answering the phone, so I'm worried about them." He took another step toward me, and I made myself stay casual as I dropped my other hand onto the glass railing and my phone lay balanced on the surface precariously within my grip.

He closed the distance between us, his body nearly against mine as he stared down at me with those haunting eyes. One of his hands raised, touching my cheek under the eye with the heterochromia in it. "You wouldn't lie to me, would you Isa?" he asked, his voice dropping lower as he touched his forehead to mine.

My heart pounded in my chest.

My breathing came ragged as I closed my eyes and tried to will myself to suddenly be a better liar. But I wasn't, so I did the one thing I'd gotten skilled at over the years. I deflected. I answered his question with a question of my own, easing the tiny margin of guilt I felt by not lying again. "What reason would I have to lie?" I whispered, opening my eyes to find his intent on mine. He touched a hand to my shoulder, sliding it down to caress the skin of my arm as he wrapped his fingers around my wrist. My hand twitched in response to the shiver that wracked my body, sending my phone teetering over the edge of the balcony.

I stared back at it in horror, watching as it disappeared into the darkness below. There was no chance it had survived the fall, and I'd officially lost all my contact with Chloe and Hugo in a moment.

"That's a shame," Rafe said, watching my face as I dragged my gaze back to his. He didn't say another word about the phone, sliding his fingers through mine as he guided me away from the balcony and toward the bedroom. I swallowed my fear as I eyed the closet with my belongings, remembering the words he'd spoken at the waterfall.

He'd follow me. He'd chase me if I walked away.

"You haven't asked what happened at the club," he observed, guiding me over to the bed where I sat on the edge cautiously. His fingers worked open the buttons on his shirt slowly, methodically undoing each and every one while my eyes narrowed in on the movement and the smooth expanse of skin he revealed.

"You told me not to ask questions if I'm not ready for the answer. This feels like an appropriate time to be cautious of what I ask," I said in response. He chuckled, pulling the shirt out of his pants as he slid the sleeves down his arms and tossed it to the side. His rippling muscles were at eye level with me, but for the first time, the overwhelming attraction between us was the last thing on my mind.

"That's probably wise. You look as if you've seen a nightmare," he said, toeing off his shoes and kicking them to the side as his hands went to his belt.

Not a ghost.

A nightmare come to life.

"I'm sure your friends are fine," he said, sliding his pants and boxer briefs down his legs so that he stood entirely naked in front of me. I bit down on the edges of my tongue, trying to decide what I could do to get away from the tension in the room.

How I could escape the fear that permeated every single pore.

"I'm sure you're right," I whispered. They weren't the ones trapped in a bedroom with a supposed murderer.

Rafael touched my face, his eyes knowing as he stroked a thumb over my cheek. "So beautiful, *mi princesa*," he murmured, his voice finally softening from the demonic echo of evil that had resounded through him since he walked into the room.

A chill crept up my spine as he slid his hand down my face and over the front of my throat. That darkness played in his eyes the moment his fingers touched the front, teasing with a light caress before he moved on to the straps of my dress and pushed them off my shoulders.

I sat frozen in place, unable to find the strength to move. Part of me knew the smartest choice I could make would be to pretend everything was fine. To pretend I didn't know any better and that he was still the man I'd thought I fell in love with.

But I couldn't move as his hands trailed over the skin of my chest and pushed the dress down to reveal my bra. He slid a hand inside to cup my breast, dragging the rough pad of his thumb over the raised nipple as I shuddered in response.

Desire filled me despite my fear, something darker and more forbidden taking over my body as he watched my reaction. "Is something wrong?"

I shook my head, knowing that I had to choose between two impossibilities. The fear of my own forbidden desires as they crashed over me and he took me when I didn't want to want him, or the possible consequences when he found out I knew what might be one of the secrets he'd kept from me. "I just don't like secrets," I told him. Trying to skirt my way around the real issue in an attempt to diffuse the situation, I brushed off my lack of response to his touch in a way that would make sense given the circumstances.

"Sometimes a relationship means protecting one another from the truths they aren't prepared to handle," he murmured, reaching around my back to unclasp my bra and guiding it down my arms.

"Relationship?" I asked stupidly.

His hands stilled on my body as his nostrils flared lightly. He licked his lips slowly, sinking his teeth into the plump flesh of the bottom one before he spoke. "What exactly do you think this is between us?" he asked, enunciating every word and wrapping his hand around the back of my neck. The pressure at the base of my head made me tilt my head up to look at him, my lungs heaving as he gripped the sides of my neck harshly.

"I'm not sure what to call it," I said, licking my dry lips as he used the hand at my neck to pull me to my feet. His free hand shoved the dress down my body, the slinky fabric pooling at my ankles as the air touched my skin. My body overheated with his proximity, the air feeling like he absorbed all the warmth into his skin.

Like a phantom from hell, come to drag me to the fires kicking and screaming.

He stared down my body, reaching his free hand inside my thong to slide through my lips in a teasing glide. When his gaze came back to mine, his lips twisted into a cruel smirk that felt different than all his rest. "My pussy seems to know *exactly* who it belongs to, *mi princesa*," he murmured, slipping a finger inside me.

Nothing could compare to the horror I felt when he slid through my flesh easily thanks to how wet I was.

This was a possible murderer. This was a man who'd threatened to chase me.

My heart raced with both fear and arousal as I stared at him, condemning me to the fate that had always lurked at the edges of my life. Darkness seeping in, taunting me and tempting me toward the red sea of flames.

He slid his hand free from me, depriving me of his touch as his hands came down on the front of my shoulders and he shoved me back onto the bed. My legs bent as I fell, my toes barely scraping the floor with the sudden change in position. He grasped my underwear in his hands, ripping them off.

Once they were off my ankles, he tossed them to the side and climbed up onto the bed. With his knees on either side of my hips, he pinned me down with the weight of his body and straddled me. Wrapping his hands around my waist, he shimmied us further up the bed until my feet were on the mattress. Staring down at me, he took my wrists in his grip and pinned them above my head as he leaned forward and touched his lips to mine.

The gentle kiss contrasted everything about the moment, the helplessness I felt with him looming over me and controlling my body so efficiently. "How should I show you that your pussy is right?" he asked, dragging the head of his cock through my folds. With my legs pressed together, the pressure of him as he nudged against my clit and then slid through me to bump against my entrance seemed even greater.

He pushed himself inside me in a single stroke, pressing through me in spite of the tightness he met as a result of the position. I gasped, staring up at him as he groaned and drew his hips back only to thrust harder into me. Whimpering, I pulled at his grip on my wrists. "Condom," I moaned, reminding him and staring up at him as indecision crossed through his eyes for a moment.

Temptation couldn't distract me from an unwanted pregnancy. If he was truly a murderer, if there was something as off as seemed likely, given the look in his eyes, the last thing I needed was to have his child.

I'd need to go home and never look back, not give him a reason to come after me seeking the child I hadn't meant to give him.

He ground his teeth, reaching into the nightstand and grabbing a condom as I breathed a sigh of relief. He withdrew from me and released my hands long enough to slide the condom onto his length. There was a brief moment where I could have fought, where I could have tried to get away.

But something kept me rooted to the spot.

Knowing it was my last time with the man I shouldn't love, I couldn't bear to walk away. Even as he drove back inside me with more ferocity than before, and drew a sharp whimper from my lips. Even as he clasped my wrists in his hands and pinned me once again, setting a furious pace as he fucked me with hard snaps of his hips that bottomed him out inside me.

"Rafael," I whispered, the name Rafe felt wrong with the

darkness swimming in his eyes. Rafe was the man I loved. Rafael was the phantom who lurked inside him.

Rafael was the monster I would walk out on while he slept.

He held my eyes as he took me, glaring down at me as if he could will me to tell him all my secrets. But the sins of the flesh were different from the sins of the mind, and as much as I hated his secrets, I would never tell him my own.

25

RAFAEL

She stared up at me with secrets in her eyes, an entire world away from where I wanted her to be. In the moment with me, enjoying my touch on her body. The distance and tension between us only served to enrage me further.

With every day that passed, it became more and more obvious that Isa would never voluntarily give herself to me.

I'd have to take her. I'd have to break her.

And then I'd rebuild her into the Queen she was meant to be.

I released her hands to reposition our bodies and shove her thighs apart, pounding deep inside her once more as she wound her legs around me. Clinging to me as I rode her like it would be the last time.

Something was wrong. I knew it in my bones, but as she screamed out her orgasm and shattered around me, nothing else mattered when she sent me spiraling with her.

I grunted, grinding my pelvis into her as she rode out the waves of her orgasm and I filled the condom with what should have been inside my princesa. When her breathing steadied, I pulled out of her and moved to the bathroom to grab a washcloth to clean her up. She didn't move in the time I was gone, her eyes drifting shut as if she needed to close out the world.

She blushed as I cleaned her but didn't speak, the sudden influx of silence between us feeling unnatural. My world wasn't complete without her smile and her voice in it, now that I finally had her with me.

I wanted to hate her for it, for making me so dependent on her happiness. Instead, we'd both hate me for stripping that away from her.

At least for a time.

I tucked her beneath the blankets, watching her as she fell asleep in the bed we'd shared nightly. Something had happened in the time since I'd packed her into the back of the car and sent her back here. Something had shifted between us, and I didn't think I could get us back to where we needed to be in time to salvage what remained of our relationship. My Isa would have questioned why I'd shipped her off.

She'd have rallied and fought against the potential of me doing something she wouldn't want to be a part of. The only explanation I could think of was her researching me in my absence. But with her phone shattered on the ground below the balcony, I couldn't find the information I needed.

Grabbing my phone out of my pants, I pulled up the messages that had come in the time since I'd been occupied with Isa. The glaring alert from Hugo in all capital letters drew my attention immediately.

ISA KNOWS.

The void inside of me widened as I turned my eyes back to her sleeping body and the innocence on her face. Pursing my lips, I moved to the balcony and pulled the glass closed behind me as I pressed the button to call Hugo back. "Tell me, Hugo. What exactly does Isa know?" I asked the moment he answered the phone.

There was a pause of silence, and then his response of what Chloe had told Isa in their brief conversation before he got through the door to stop it. "That's unfortunate," I said, spinning back to stare at Isa as she slept. It could have been worse, and perhaps she would brush off the rumor as simply that.

I wasn't optimistic enough to think that was the case.

"What do you want to do?" Hugo asked.

"Clear the streets," I said. "If she decides to try something stupid, I don't want any witnesses to what will come next."

He paused. "Why not just take her now?" he asked, and the question held merit. With everything crumbling around me, I could just slip a needle into her neck and she'd be on *El Infierno* before she woke up.

She'd never know a moment of fear, until it was too late to change.

"I need to know," I said, ending the call as I stepped back inside and crawled into bed with Isa. If she left me, she deserved to have to deal with the monster vibrating under my skin.

I'd warned her what would happen, and Isa would very quickly learn that when I made a promise?

I fucking kept it.

26

ISA

I sat up in bed slowly, in spite of the urgency in my veins to try to keep from waking Rafael. As the moonlight shone through the windows, I turned to look at his sleeping face over my shoulder. With his face relaxed and peaceful, I could almost forget the cold cruelty he'd shown me the night before. I could almost forget the empty look in his eyes as he came into the room, and the suspicion in his gaze when he'd suspected me of leaving.

But the ache between my legs from his rough possession served as the reminder I needed, compelling me to stand and move into the closet as quickly and quietly as I could. I pulled a casual dress out of my suitcase, tugging underwear up my legs and slipping sandals on my feet as I quietly shoved everything else back in.

Maybe it was better this way. With our romance cut short by me slipping away in the night, there would be no heartfelt goodbye. He wouldn't be subjected to my tears, because I needed to run away from a murderer.

I'd never have to wonder why he didn't ask me to stay and then berate myself for the foolish thought. I could just slip out and remain the mysterious woman who'd left him in the night. I scoffed as soon as I thought it, knowing that the only secretive thing about me wasn't a sexy secret, but one that had shattered everything I'd ever loved and destroyed my family.

Even if I'd been able to without fear of what he might do, I couldn't bear to say goodbye to him. I couldn't stand to face him when I walked out of the suite I'd called home for the best days of my life. I'd never expected to meet anyone when I came to Ibiza. I'd never thought that I would find a person who made me want to feel the things I'd been missing in my life.

Rafe had shown me passion. He'd taught me what it was to embrace who I was and be comfortable in my own skin. No matter what he'd done to drive me away, I didn't think I would change him for anything.

I didn't think I could erase him from my memory, even suspecting what he might have done.

Even if the idea of not waking up to him in the morning made my heart hurt.

I considered leaving my suitcase, worried about the noise it would make when I pulled it through the bedroom.

"Are you going somewhere, Princesa?" The deep rumble of his voice sent my pulse racing, echoing through the silence between us as I spun to stare at his flawless face in shock. The words were a direct reflection of what he'd said the night before, and I remembered my response as I swallowed. The fear I'd felt rose to the surface again, threatening to make me abandon my escape attempt altogether. Only the seriousness of Chloe's accusation kept me from coming up with some inane excuse.

I couldn't back away from the truth a second time.

His mismatched eyes bore down into mine, the deep

forest green of his right eye seeming so dark as his narrowed gaze dropped to the zipped suitcase at my feet. The light blue of his left eye turned positively glacial as he drew his stare back up to my face.

He invaded my space as he stepped closer, pressing his nude front against me without care. He'd never shown restraint or discomfort in his nudity, but the obviousness of me sneaking out in the middle of the night should have been reason enough for him to put on some pants.

Evidently not.

I swallowed, ignoring the firm press of his length against my belly in favor of returning his stare. One of his hands reached out to stroke my cheek with the back of his knuckle as his thumb stroked the skin under my eye. He raised a brow at me, waiting for my answer as I fumbled to find an excuse. I couldn't bring myself to lie outright, to create a fabricated story about my family.

If Chloe was somehow wrong, I would feel terrible for the deception. For giving voice to any of the fears I had about leaving my family behind with a lie.

"Chloe needs me." My voice left me in a ragged whisper as the almost-lie caught in my throat. All the intensity he leveled me with did nothing to soothe my frayed nerves or the terror pulsing through my veins. His singular fixation had always been jarring, but in the aftermath of the night before, all that I saw when I looked up at him was darkness.

The darkness in his soul. The darkness in mine.

"And you weren't going to say goodbye?" he asked, something odd in his tone as he tilted his head at me. His lips tightened as they pressed into a firm line, his nostrils flaring briefly before he wiped all traces of anger from his face and smiled at me. It wasn't unkind, exactly.

It stung like disappointment.

"I didn't," I paused, fighting back the tears that threatened, spurred on by the onslaught of emotions wreaking havoc on my body. The fear. The loss.

The grief over losing my first love.

"I didn't want to cry," I admitted, tilting my face down. "But I guess that's unavoidable now." I huffed out a brittle laugh, eyeing the empty smile on his face in suspicion.

God, what if Chloe was wrong?

He bit his bottom lip, turning to stare in the direction of the door on the other side of the suite briefly before he glanced back at me with tormented eyes. "I'll give you a ride. Come back when Chloe is in a better place," he suggested.

My breath caught in my lungs as he offered me the chance to get the answers I needed from Chloe without saying goodbye to him. But the splitting of my soul in two that I felt as I prepared to leave him told me everything I needed to know.

I'd never be able to say goodbye twice.

"Thank you for being so good to me, but I think," I paused, sucking back a fortifying breath. "I think it's time for me to go. There's only a few days before I go home."

"Or you could stay," he said.

I smiled, shaking my head. Even if he wasn't suspected to be a murderer, a man as wealthy as Rafe had no cares in the world. I couldn't put college on hold for a man I hardly, knew who would undoubtedly tire of me soon enough.

"I have to go home," I whispered, listening to the words as they echoed in the silence between us. It felt like a moment where my future was decided, like something snapped into place. As if we were always meant to find our way to this moment.

Leaning down, I snagged the handle of my suitcase. He stepped out of the closet, going to the balcony and grabbing my purse off the floor to hand it to me. Tugging on pants quickly, he watched me as I made my way to the door.

I drew in a deep breath as I prepared to make what felt like the biggest mistake of my life. Unlocking and pulling the door open, I accepted that it was the only choice I could make under the circumstances.

Even if it broke me.

Rafe caught my arm at the last possible moment, drawing me back into a kiss. His lips crashed against mine, his teeth bruising me as he devoured me brutally. The anger behind the contact faded quickly as I returned his passion, letting me coax him into a sweeter embrace that shocked me. I hadn't expected him to allow such a meaningful contact in our goodbye, as if he would truly miss me. But if this was my last kiss with Rafe, I wanted to look back on it and feel loved for even just a moment.

I wanted to remember everything he gave me, and I had a feeling I'd never be able to forget it.

When I pulled away, he let me step through the door. It stayed open as I made my way across the hall and tears ran in rivulets down my face and soaked the front of my dress.

He didn't stop me. He didn't chase me.

He didn't call out to me or do anything as I pushed the button on the elevator. He didn't even try.

27

RAFAEL

I stared out the open door, watching as she pressed the call button on the elevator. She turned to face me once she stepped inside, pressing the floor for the lobby.

She froze mid-motion, her hand hovering in the air as her teary eyes landed on mine. Seeing the cold fury on my face as I narrowed my gaze on her and twisted my mouth into a scowl, she swallowed visibly and paled. I watched as recognition slithered up her spine, her body convulsing as she tasted my rage in the air. She leapt into action as her lungs heaved, pushing the button to close the doors quickly as the sadness faded from her face to be replaced with absolute terror.

For the first time since *mi princesa* had met me, she stared in the face of the nightmare who had promised to hunt her down, and saw me for exactly what I was.

The elevator doors closed, cutting her from my view as I moved back into the suite and put on my suit. I grabbed my phone off the nightstand, bringing up Joaquin's number. He answered on the first ring, waiting for the signal from me as

I pulled on my suit jacket. I'd leave most of my belongings for my employees to deal with, sending them back to *El Infierno*.

I had more important matters to deal with.

"Follow her," I ordered.

He paused, then obeyed my command as was expected despite his own hesitation. "Yes, Boss." The line went dead, and I tucked my phone into my pocket. I grabbed some of the chess pieces off the board on the coffee table, tucking five of them into my suit pockets. Then I turned and strode for the door.

Isa had her five-minute head start.

I turned to face the room that felt filled with lies in the aftermath of her departure. It was where I'd thought Isa had fallen in love with me. Where I'd thought she'd see that what we had was enough to forgive my sins that had nothing to do with her, and accept that her future was by my side and not working to fix her family.

It was nothing but a lie, and I pressed the lobby button on the elevator as I turned my eyes away from what could have been. She'd had the chance to have a loving and doting husband.

She'd chosen the nightmare instead.

As the elevator descended, I counted out the number of days we should've had left. If it hadn't been for Chloe's interference, Isa would be waking up in my arms in a few hours. Instead, Isa would fear for her life, as the consequence of trying to take away what was mine. The elevator doors opened into the empty lobby as I strode through and walked out the front.

The streets were devoid of life. Not a single person walked along them, even at the busiest time of night in Ibiza. When El Diablo ordered them emptied, the streets fucking emptied. Isa might not be very familiar with Ibiza, but she knew enough to know it was unusual.

She knew enough to be afraid.

Gabriel pulled up at the curb, shoving open the passenger side door as I climbed into the SUV. He turned the vehicle in the direction of Hugo and Chloe's hotel, taking the back roads Isa would never have dared to take on her own. She'd stick to the safety of the main blocks, even in their abandoned state, when she realized that she couldn't grab a taxi.

When she remembered that she didn't have a cell phone to call anyone.

There was no one for her to turn to in the moment when she realized I would come for her. Nothing to stop me from chasing her into the night. From making her hurt the way she'd hurt me by leaving. "Leave the SUV, and go get my fucking car," I snapped as my own misery consumed me.

I jumped out of the car as Gabriel pulled into the lot at the hotel. My long strides marched in the direction of Isa, closing the distance between us while she headed unknowingly in my direction while she thought she ran from me and towards safety. But there was no safety for Isa.

Not anymore.

Reaching into the pocket of my suit as I ducked down the side alley where it would all end, I stroked a thumb over the black King from the chess set. Setting it in the middle of the roadway, I backed away and walked back to the main road.

With the Queen in hand, I went to hunt mine.

28
ISA

The streets of Ibiza were never empty. In the time I'd spent there, all I'd ever seen was the frenetic energy of the island. I hurried along the sidewalk as fast as I could and pulled my suitcase behind me in the eerie silence of the night. The look in Rafael's eyes when he'd stared at me in the elevator haunted me as I jumped at any sound.

A garbage can rattled around the corner, making me quicken my pace with a frightened squeak. My eyes connected with the green gaze of a cat as he made his way past in a hurry. Pausing to lean on my knees and catch my breath, I tried to shove down the paranoia suffocating me.

Having a heart attack before I made it to Chloe's hotel wouldn't do me much good. I had no clue how to get to the embassy and no phone to look up directions.

Rafael had been angry that I left him. He'd been hurt, and the glare I'd seen on his face had to be a consequence of that. Nothing more.

So why couldn't I convince myself that I didn't need to run?

I grabbed my suitcase by the handle again, picking up

the pace once more as I hurried down the road. Turning the corner to the street I thought I needed to take, I halted in my tracks at the sight of what sat in the middle of the road.

A single black pawn. The marble sparkled in the dim streetlights, practically glowing against the light stone of the street itself. Taking my hand off the suitcase and abandoning it on the side of the road, I stepped up to it and bent down to grasp it in my hand as what little noise there was bled away. My thumb ran over the marble as I stood, staring down at it and the tiny fissure on the top.

The same as the first pawn Rafe had moved in our game of chess.

His first move.

I dropped it as my heart stopped, watching it fall to the stone at my feet. My vision went white as I spun to look around. There was no one in sight.

No sign of Rafael, but I abandoned my suitcase. My feet couldn't move fast enough as I ran down the road. I charged through an intersection without checking for oncoming traffic, feeling eyes on me as I went. I couldn't hear anything outside my own panicked breathing as I ran.

Pain ripped through my knees as I kicked something and then fell over my own feet. My palms sliced open on the rough stone as I caught myself. Turning to look behind me as I stood to see what I'd tripped on, my eyes landed on the Knight where it lay on its side.

I scrambled to my feet and abandoned my purse in the middle of the road where it had fallen, my throat closing in on itself as tears streamed down my face from fear. I rounded another corner to get to Hugo's hotel. If I could just get there. If I could just make it to the safety of the hotel, everything would be okay.

It had to be.

Just a few more blocks separated me from safety when I found the Bishop on the road I should have turned down. I skidded to a halt in the middle of the street, the moisture of my own blood trickling down my legs while I stared at it. I backed away from the piece, turning down the opposite block and hoping it would lead me in the right direction.

It wasn't the path I thought I knew, but Rafael's tokens waited at every corner when I followed the main road. I sprinted, willing my legs to go faster as my flip flops slickened with the blood from my scraped knees.

There was no marble piece in the street when I turned the corner to circle back around. No sign of Rafe as I heaved a breath of relief. With the hotel almost in sight, I let myself hope. For just one fleeting moment, I let myself believe that I'd make it.

That I'd go home to my boring life where men didn't chase me through the streets of an abandoned Ibiza.

And then came the Queen in the road, shining in the center of streetlamps that led to the square where the hotel was. I screamed my fear and frustration into the night, turning down another side road in desperation.

It came to a dead end as I slowed, the black King staring back at me as if he had eyes of his own. As if he could see me and feel my fear along with me. My last free breath came in a broken sob, but I shoved down my desolation.

I whirled to run, stopping short when the movement brought me face to face with Rafael's cold eyes staring down at me. He stood with his hands in his pockets, his head subtly cocked to the side. Even in the dim light, I'd never mistake the handsome face that had stolen my breath.

Lost to the nightmare that stole him away.

I backed away a step, looking at the end of the alley over my shoulder before I swallowed and turned back to him. My heart beat out of control as my lungs struggled to get air past my panic.

"Checkmate, Princesa," he murmured, stepping toward me slowly as I raised my hands defensively.

"Rafael, what are you doing?" I asked, sobbing as one of his hands reached up to stroke my cheek with a mocking gentleness.

"It's time to go home," he said, his face twisting with a moment of regret.

A startled gasp broke free as something pinched my neck, my eyes tracking down to watch him withdraw a syringe from my flesh and toss it to the side. He wrapped me in his arms, holding me through my struggles as I beat his chest with furious hands and struggled to get away.

A car engine started up at the side of the alley as my vision turned fuzzy. My body went limp in his hold while he held my gaze. "Shhh," he whispered, his thumb making small circles on my spine. Everything felt heavy, but I fought to keep my eyes open. Fought to get away. "Go to sleep, Princesa. I've got you."

"Why?" I asked, my eyes barely open as he stared back down at me intently. Leaning down, he ran his nose up the side of mine as he scooped me into his arms and carried me in the direction of the fuzzy black SUV waiting at the corner.

"You shouldn't have left me," he said, as the sound of a car door opening hit my ears. I rolled my head to the side as the door for the back seat creaked open. Rafael climbed into the car, laying me in the seat so that my head rested on his lap. "It didn't have to be this way," he whispered softly. All I could make out in the darkness was the vague shape of his face and two shining eyes staring back at me.

A phantom from my memory.

My head lolled to the side as darkness crept in.

Then there was nothing.

*R*afael & Isa's story continues in Until Forever Ends. Coming March 25th!

>>Pre-order now.

*C*an't get enough of Rafe & Isa? Download the Exclusive Bonus of the start of the scene at the waterfall scene told from Rafael's point of view.

>>Download now.

*F*all in love with a Bellandi? You can find Matteo, Ryker, and Enzo's stories in Adelaide's Bellandi Crime Syndicate series.

>>Start with Bloodied Hands.

ALSO BY ADELAIDE FORREST

Bellandi World Syndicate Universe
Bellandi Crime Syndicate Series

Bloodied Hands

Forgivable Sins

Grieved Loss

Shielded Wrongs

Beauty in Lies Series

Until Tomorrow Comes

Until Forever Ends - Coming March 25th

Until Retribution Burns - Coming soon

Until Death Do Us Part - Coming soon

Insta-Love Novellas

The Men of Mount Awe Series

Deliver Me from Evil

Kings of Conquest - Cowritten with Lyric Cox

Claiming His Princess

Stealing His Princess

Printed in Great Britain
by Amazon